Knight of the Bleeding Heart

The Eglinton Knight series
Book 4

Margaux Thorne

Dragonblade Publishing, Inc. is an imprint of Kathryn Le Veque Novels, Inc.
P.O. Box 23
Moreno Valley, CA 92556
ceo@dragonbladepublishing.com

Produced in the United States of America

First Edition November 2023
Trade Paperback Edition

ARE YOU SIGNED UP FOR DRAGONBLADE'S BLOG?

You'll get the latest news and information on exclusive giveaways, exclusive excerpts, coming releases, sales, free books, cover reveals and more.

Check out our complete list of authors, too!

No spam, no junk. That's a promise!

Sign Up Here

www.dragonbladepublishing.com

Dearest Reader;

Thank you for your support of a small press. At Dragonblade Publishing, we strive to bring you the highest quality Historical Romance from some of the best authors in the business. Without your support, there is no 'us', so we sincerely hope you adore these stories and find some new favorite authors along the way.

Happy Reading!

CEO, Dragonblade Publishing

Additional Dragonblade books by Author Margaux Thorne

The Eglinton Knight Series
Knight of the Jaded Heart (Book 1)
Knight of the Broken Heart (Book 2)
Knight of the Wicked Heart (Book 3)
Knight of the Bleeding Heart (Book 4)

PROLOGUE

Boston, Massachusetts
July 4, 1839

N ATHANIEL LAWRENCE'S VOICE popped and crackled like the fireworks showering the night sky.

"That's the most insane story I've ever heard," he snapped at his assistant while his heels clipped down the corridor. Similar to his reputation in business, his long legs didn't hesitate or falter as they ate up the space to the library where a trio of formidable and well-paid lawyers waited for him. "It's clearly a scheme to con me out of money. Just throw the letter away."

"But sir," Mr. Hobart pleaded at his back, desperate to keep up with him while maintaining a dignified breath, "you're not letting me finish. If you would only let me continue reading you the letter, you might find it interesting—"

A firework *boomed* in the distance, and Nathaniel stopped and turned. Mr. Hobart skidded to a halt, the paper in his hand almost punching his employer square in the belly. Nathaniel ground his teeth, staring down at his newest employee, who had arrived with excellent recommendations, though none of which had mentioned his highly excitable and anxious demeanor.

"Mr. Hobart," Nathaniel said tersely. "I don't need you to read me the rest of the letter. I can read between the lines of what you've already told me." He crossed his arms and imitated a posh, nasally accent, turning his nose up in the air. "Mr. Lawrence ... the Duke of Fairy Land—"

"Wembley," Mr. Hobart cut in.

Nathaniel didn't bat an eye. "The Duke of Fairy Land has recently been made aware of a strong familial connection between himself and your late father, Mr. George Lawrence. We invite you to travel to England at your earliest convenience so we can discuss the happy and eventful news ... etc. Do you know what that really means?" Nathaniel cleared his throat, pulling back his wide shoulders as if he was readying for a grand soliloquy on the stage. "It means: the Duke of *I've Squandered My Fortune* Manor would like to con some uncouth, uncultured, gullible American into spending his hard-earned money on some run-down, pointless castle in the middle of nowhere."

"It's just outside London," Hobart replied meekly.

Nathaniel arched a brow. "And you are outside of your mind if you think I'm getting on a boat to see it." He sighed, wiping a hand over his tired face. The day was finally getting to him. It refused to end. "Mr. Hobart," he went on, retaining more of his composure. "I buried my father a few hours ago. I've shaken more hands today than I can even count. Now, I have a roomful of lawyers waiting to read me the will. My plan is to send them off quickly so I can finally go to sleep. Now ... I hired you because I needed someone to deal with mundane issues without needing to alert me of them. The letter you are clutching in your hand is an example of that. You've hounded me for the last two days about it, and you could have handled it yourself. So, if you'll excuse me?"

"But sir!" Mr. Hobart exclaimed as Nathaniel continued down the corridor toward the library.

Nathaniel threw a hand up over his shoulder. "No! Just deal with it! I have more pressing concerns at the moment!"

He entered the library and closed the door on another weak plea from his assistant. He didn't know what he was going to do with the man. Hobart was efficient as hell and had a brilliant head for numbers that rivaled his own, but most words quivered from his mouth like a flower in the middle of a windstorm. If Hobart was going to rise up the ranks of Lawrence Textiles, he would have to toughen up. This industry was no place for a man who constantly looked like he was always in need of the nearest chamber pot.

Nathaniel sailed into the room and took a seat, urging the lawyers to do the same. Samuel Tovis, Richard Elijah, and Mark Stanley of Tovis, Elijah, and Stanley stood shoulder to shoulder in front of the hearth, a trio as celebrated and feared as the Musketeers or even the Father, Son, and the Holy Ghost.

"If you'll allow me to be frank," Nathaniel said, annoyed at the weariness he heard in his voice. "It's been a rather long day, and, since this is a mere formality, I'd like to just cut to the important part if that's all right with you. Since my father had no other relatives besides me, I don't anticipate any surprises, and I'd hate to take up any more of your time." The expensive bastards charged by the hour, after all.

Mr. Tovis made a phlegmy sound in the back of his throat. The man was tall and reedy and had the pallid face of someone who preferred the indoors, but his voice was clear and strong as it flooded the room. "I think we can certainly try," the lawyer said, casting a glance to his partners, who held firm at his side. "As you know, our firm is the only one that your late father ever employed, and it has served him faithfully for close to thirty years. In that time, we drafted two wills for him. The first one was completed a decade ago, but that is not the one I have with me today. When Mr. Lawrence first noticed signs of his illness last year, he came to us to change the will. And that is the one I have now. My partners and I can attest to his sound mind and judgment at the time. He was not under duress or coerced in any way."

"Christ, Sam, I trust you. Just read the damn thing," Nathaniel drawled. He was already off to a rotten start if he wanted this to go fast.

Mr. Tovis's chest inflated, and he lobbed a glare at Nathaniel from behind his round spectacles. "Fine," he said stiffly. He held the single piece of paper out in front of him with both hands, as if the words written on it made it heavy and cumbersome.

As Mr. Tovis began to read the document, Nathaniel felt an instant blow to his chest at hearing his father's words. He'd assumed the will would sound formal, and yet he could practically see his father in the room, commanding and demanding as ever.

"I know it might seem villainous to you, but I hope you understand one day. I might not have been a great father, but I am certain I taught you two things in life: how to take a punch and how to pick yourself off the ground when one gets the better of you. This might seem like an awful sock to the jaw, but you will pick yourself up. You have to. Because any man who keeps his money after he dies isn't worth the box they throw him in," the lawyer read, emotion and nervousness spilling through his poise. Pushing his spectacles up his nose, Mr. Tovis met Nathaniel's unflinching gaze. "Then he included a list of charities to distribute his funds to, as well as an orphanage in London, which he says: *Made me the man that I am.*"

"His funds?" Nathaniel said, squinting at the lawyer. "You mean ... *all* of them?" He couldn't pull the exact number out of the air, but at his end, his father had accumulated hundreds of thousands of dollars. More than any man needed. Like him, apparently.

"I'm not finished," Mr. Tovis replied, the paper trembling in his hands. "And yes. *All* his funds."

"For Christ's sake ..." Nathaniel growled.

Mr. Tovis's speech was downright wobbly now. *"What's left goes to my son."* He lowered the will and looked at Nathaniel expectantly.

Nathaniel waited. "That's it?"

The lawyer wiped the sweat at his temples. "For the most part ... yes. Well, no, Mr. Lawrence ends it with: *Turn me over; I'm done on this side.*"

"For Christ's sake," Nathaniel repeated, falling back in the seat. "Is that supposed to be some kind of a joke?"

"I have to so say," Mr. Elijah said, leaning forward, picking up the slack from his partner, "I'm not sure. I've never known Mr. Lawrence to tell a joke before. I thought you would tell us … Perhaps it was a family joke?"

"It wasn't," Nathaniel said. He scratched his beard. He usually didn't keep a beard throughout the hot season. It was damned uncomfortable. Humidity in Boston was just as brutal as its snow in the winter. However, his father's illness had intercepted all his free time of late, and his scratchy beard had been the last thing on his mind.

"I'd forgotten that your father grew up in an orphanage in London," Mr. Elijah remarked when the air in the room continued to grow stale. "He was there for ten years?"

"Eleven," Nathaniel corrected him, staring down at his fingers. They were rough, lined with years of his never being content to sit still, but they would never compare to his father's. Nathaniel remembered holding those hands when he was a child, hanging on for dear life to keep up with the man's long gait. At six foot two, George Lawrence hadn't needed to walk fast to stay in front of everyone else, although he still did. He'd done everything fast and wouldn't slow down for anyone—not even his young son. Everyone around him just needed to learn to keep up. Nathaniel was still learning that lesson.

"But let me reiterate," Mr. Elijah said, his tone rising in optimism. "As it states in the will, Mr. Lawrence—Nathaniel—you still inherit Lawrence Textiles. Within time, you'll no doubt amass a fortune to rival his, and even build a house as grand as this one."

Nathaniel flinched. "What does that mean? What about this house? And the one in Newport and the horses and carriages and everything else?"

Mr. Elijah's expression reeked of apology. "All to be sold as soon as possible, with the money going—"

"Don't tell me," Nathaniel cut in dryly. "To go to charity."

"Indeed," the lawyer returned gravely.

The room fell silent, the sparks of the fireworks outside the only noises. Nathaniel continued to study his hands, though the skin on the nape of his neck tingled as he felt the lawyers staring at him, waiting for him to do something. Anything. Scream, shout, curse, rip the pages out of every damn book in the room. What his father had done was so out of character. The man hadn't been religious in the slightest, and Nathaniel couldn't recall one conversation they'd ever had about charity. Though, as to that, conversing wasn't his father's strong point, especially to his only child.

"So that's it, then?" Nathaniel said, standing.

"Sir, I'm so sorry, but one more thing," Mr. Tovis said, stopping him from retreating from the room. Nathaniel's fingers already had his necktie loose and the top button of his shirt undone around his neck. "Your father also stipulated that he wants you to present the money to the orphanage in person."

Nathaniel hung his head, stifling a curse. The day just kept getting better and better. "Go to London? Now? I think not. I've got a business to run."

He turned toward the door, but Mr. Tovis placed a hand on his forearm. "I'm afraid you have to. It was your father's last wish."

Nathaniel sighed. *Jesus Christ. Father is mighty demanding for a dead man.* That uncharitable thought immediately shamed him. But, then again, he wasn't feeling all that charitable at the moment.

"It might be good to get away," the lawyer continued. "Get some fresh air after all that's happened. I know it wasn't easy."

"Fresh air? In London?" Nathaniel snorted.

Mr. Tovis shrugged. "I hear it's next to an ocean." He chuckled.

"Yes, it's the same one we have here."

"Please," Mr. Tovis beseeched Nathaniel, gathering his things. "Just think about it. Lawrence Textiles runs like a well-oiled machine. It can stand for you to take time off."

Nathaniel scoffed. But could he?

Work was all that was keeping him afloat. It always was. A busy mind was the answer for everything. It got him through his father's long illness. On the other hand, his mind was racing now, and it wasn't solving anything.

He didn't know how long he sat in that room, mulling over his father's decision. Long enough for the fireworks to peter out in the sky and the fire to die in the hearth. It wasn't that Nathaniel was angry at his father. He couldn't care less about the money and could always make more. What kept him in that room, surrounded by darkness and books his father had never had the time to read, was why his father had kept all this to himself. Why hadn't he told Nathaniel? Why keep it a surprise? And if it was some sort of lesson, then why had his father thought Nathaniel had to learn it? Hadn't he been a good son? He didn't drink or chase women, nor was he content to sit on his father's achievements like so many of the men he went to school with. Was his father truly being altruistic, or had he seen something lacking in his only son?

Nathaniel heard a noise and swiveled to find his assistant blending into the corner, the same concerned and frazzled countenance from earlier marring his face despite the cloak of shadows. Mr. Hobart looked like he was desperately trying not to faint.

"Please don't bother me with that letter again. I am not related to a duke, nor do I care to be."

Mr. Hobart's eyes grew large, and he peered down at the paper in his hand as if he just remembered he was still holding it.

"Oh … ah … yes, sir … yes," he stammered, unsticking himself from the corner. His steps were slow and measured as he moved to stand in front of his employer. "Ah … right. But I truly think you might find this interesting."

It took everything for Nathaniel to lift his head. Everything felt so damn heavy. "I guarantee you I won't. I don't care who that duke is or what he wants or what he owns or how important he is. He is not my father's long-lost cousin—"

"Let me speak!" Mr. Hobart screamed. "I know it's been a trying day. I know what the lawyers just told you, and I know you told me to handle this. And I *did*. I *did* handle it. That's what I'm trying to tell you. I bought you a ticket to London. You are leaving next week. Because you absolutely, positively have to go."

Nathaniel stared at the assistant, a man who seemed to have grown five inches and a new, weightier pair of balls in seconds. But Nathaniel had a nice set of balls too. "I am not going anywhere," he said flatly.

Mr. Hobart calmly tossed the letter on Nathaniel's lap. "Oh, yes, you are. Because you are not just related to the Duke of Wembley—you are his heir." He shrugged, losing some of his steam. "You might have lost most of your inheritance today, but if it's any consolation, it seems you've gained a dukedom."

CHAPTER ONE

London, England
August 1, 1839

L ADY CHARLOTTE'S HEAD throbbed. Her father had been pacing for the better part of an hour, and his constant back-and-forth was making her dizzy—and irritated.

Finally, she snapped, "I don't know what you're so nervous about; you're not the one marrying him."

That got the reaction she was hoping for. Thomas Cordry, the Duke of Wembley, stopped in his well-worn tracks, granting his only child a flabbergasted look. The Marmoset monkey perched on his shoulder wore the same one on its tiny little face.

The duke fed the monkey a piece of apple while the lines bracketing his mouth deepened. "That's hardly the point, is it? He's *my* heir—"

"*Squawk! He's my heir! He's my heir!*" a blue and yellow macaw interrupted from the corner of the room where he perched regally on top of his cage—not inside it, as Charlotte would have preferred.

The duke lobbed an affectionate look at the loudmouthed parrot before continuing. "*He* is the one who will make certain the Cordry line lives on. And I'm not nervous," he added peevishly. "I'm anxious; there's a difference. And—might I remind you—I never said you had to marry him. It was just a thought, completely up to you, of course, and I will respect your decision either way."

Her father had said that before, and yet Charlotte still had a difficult time believing him. Not only was he a duke, but he was also a consummate meddler—letting others make decisions didn't come naturally to him. "It's not completely up to me, you know," she replied sourly. "He might not even want to marry me."

The duke's expression was comically histrionic, as if he'd just heard the sky was falling. "My dear, *everyone* wants to marry you. Mr. Nathaniel Lawrence will be no different. However, it wouldn't hurt for you to encourage him a bit. Men are simple creatures, darling. We need assistance whenever we can get it. Did I ever tell you about my first time in Vienna?" He chuckled whimsically as he stared off into nowhere. "If you think the French are depraved ... The women in Vienna wore their corsets so tight and low, they left nothing to the imagination. I swear to you, one woman's dress was so low I could see her entire—"

"Father, I don't need to hear any more about Vienna," Charlotte cut in sharply. As he opened his mouth to respond, she swiftly went on. "Nor do I need to hear about your escapades in Rome, Barcelona, or Amsterdam. I beg of you. I never need to hear about Amsterdam ever again. But honestly, it's as if you want me to dress like one of your women from Vienna in front of the American."

"Not at all," the duke replied gruffly. "That wouldn't be ... appropriate for you, my dear. I just want you to try, is all. Be as lovely as only you can be—and don't talk too much—although make a little conversation, be interested. You're always so elusive with all your suitors—"

"Because I don't *want* them to be my suitors. I like my life just fine the way it is. The last thing I want is another man thinking he can tell me what to do."

"In any case," her father replied, waving a hand in the air as if she hadn't said a thing, "it would behoove you to be more ...

engaging this time around. I hate to remind you, I really do, but you need to take into account that this American is most likely your only chance at becoming a duchess."

"I'm well aware, Father. So very well aware," Charlotte said, silently simmering. After all, how could she ever forget that her father had used the last of their funds to search for the American heir? Even if she didn't behave so *elusively* with all her suitors, a match was unlikely in the *ton* once everyone found out her dowry had been depleted. In their upper-class society, beauty—even Charlotte's otherworldly kind—didn't hold much currency; peers needed rich wives.

"Even so," she went on, clutching the book in her hand so tight her knuckles turned white. "I still wish you would at least try to petition the queen to amend the letters patent to include a special remainder for me to inherit the title. She's incredibly sweet, and I think she—more than anyone—would understand our plight. After all, if a male relative were available, she would not be queen.

"Bah!" her father said. *Squawk! Bah!* "The queen hates me. She'll never do it."

Charlotte steadied her rising impatience. "The queen doesn't hate you. I doubt she hates anyone. But did you have to be such a braggart the last time you spoke to her? You spent fifteen minutes boasting about how your menagerie was better than hers, and invited the entire party over to see it so they could confirm the matter."

The marmoset almost pitched off the duke's shrugging shoulder. Her father's ruddy cheeks looked like they were on fire. "Well ..." he started in a huff. "My menagerie *is* better."

Charlotte *humphed. It better be,* she thought. He'd spent enough money on it.

Sitting straight-backed in her squeaky Queen Anne chair, Charlotte pursed her lips as her father continued making his rounds of the drawing room, passing his pet monkey more apples. She was used to staying silent—keeping her inner thoughts to herself—but today she found it more difficult than ever.

Because today was about the American. And only the American.

Father and daughter waited in silence, a random *squawk!* and the grandfather clock's chimes providing the background noise for their intrepid wait. The American was late. They'd been notified that Mr. Nathaniel Lawrence's ship had docked three days ago in London, generously allowing a day for him to arrive at the residence. His letter had stipulated that he would make haste to join them as soon as possible. Perhaps he was lost? Americans weren't known to be the smartest people, and it wasn't like Wembley House was difficult to find—even for a textile merchant. The Georgian pile was one of the grandest estates in Hampstead Heath. Though … that was only if one didn't look too closely.

Charlotte slammed her book shut. "How much longer must I stay here?" she grumbled. She could be practicing her dances for the Eglinton Tournament's ball. The Basse Dance had been easy enough, but the Black Nag was still giving her trouble. As she was one of the Queen of Beauty's ladies-in-waiting, Charlotte's performance could not be any less than perfect.

Her father held a hand up in her direction. Again, the silly monkey echoed the action. "Patience, dear child. Patience. We must stay ready and vigilant. He will come, and then the future can begin."

"But what if he doesn't want any part in the future you have in mind?" Charlotte asked. "I hear Americans can be rather … odd."

"*Squawk! Americans are odd! Americans are odd!*"

The duke leveled his daughter with a perplexing frown. "There's odd and then there's insane. No one would dare cast aside what I am offering. Americans may not be the brightest peoples, but I daresay *our* American is a wealthy businessman. He'll be able to see the value. I am sure of it."

Charlotte heaved a deep breath, opening her book again. She wished that she shared her father's positivity. Alas, the only thing the two seemed to have in common was their appearance. Both were blessed with lithe, diminutive figures and rich blond hair that juxtaposed brilliantly with their pale alabaster skin. The duke had been considered a true beauty of his time, even though his features heavily favored the feminine. His overwhelming confidence and *joie de vivre* had mesmerized men and women alike.

Clearly, her father assumed that the American would be no match for his winning, persuasive personality. When all others had fallen under his magnetic spell, what was one more?

Footsteps sounded outside the drawing room. Father and daughter looked at one another and popped to their feet. But when their butler, James, arrived with no one following behind, Charlotte slumped back into her seat.

"A letter arrived for you, Your Grace," James announced, his tone noticeably apologetic. The whole household was holding its breath until the American arrived.

"Thank you, James," the duke replied, accepting the crisp letter from the shining silver plate. His glower was palpable as he tore it open and scanned the contents.

"Father?" Charlotte asked. "Is it from him? Is he apologizing for being late? That's the least he can do," she said, sotto voce.

The duke crumpled the letter up into a ball and tossed it back on James's platter. His scowl was so deep, Charlotte could barely make out his icy blue eyes. "No, no. It's not from Mr. Lawrence. It's just a note from Mr. Hemsworth, asking for yet another reference. The man acts like I have nothing better to do with my time than announce his talents for all and sundry!"

Charlotte paused, wondering at her father's harsh tone. Mr. Hemsworth may be a nuisance, but the investigator had done something no other person had done before—found the duke his heir. It had taken close to a year and all of Charlotte's dowry to accomplish the task, but the resilient man had found the missing link when everyone else had assured her father that there was no one to inherit the title. To her, Mr. Hemsworth was like a modern-day Merlin, casting a spell and conjuring a man out of thin air. She'd expected her father to kiss his middle-class feet for the rest of his life, not grouse over references.

"Perhaps one reference wouldn't take too much of your time," Charlotte said cautiously. "Surely he's earned it." She stood and walked over to her father, who was picking at his nails, with the marmoset curiously looking on.

"I don't have time for references," he groused. "I have a duke to create—and an American duke at that. I won't have him making a mockery of this house." He touched his temple with shaking fingers, wincing as his eyes closed. "Does anyone have any idea how much effort that is going to take? People look at me and my effortlessness and assume dukes are just born, but I assure you, child, they are made."

Charlotte smiled gently, cupping her father's cheeks in her palms. From his perch on the duke's shoulder, the monkey attempted to do the same.

Her father was utterly ridiculous, but he was all she had. It was difficult to stay annoyed at him when it was obvious that his confidence was all bluster. He was nervous—incredibly so. His breathing had grown quick and shallow, though Charlotte thought the tight corset he wore could also be encouraging that.

Fashion might have changed drastically between the centuries, but once a dandy, always a dandy. The Duke of Wembley never skimped on lace or theatrics. He let the younger men wear their bulky frock coats and loose trousers. The duke would never be so uninspired. With the help of the corset, puffed sleeves, and skintight breeches, he still sported the gallant inverted triangle physique, and had a terrific time accessorizing his ensembles with silk neckties and bright waistcoats. To the duke, clothing was life, and must be given the reverence it deserved.

"It will be fine, Father," Charlotte consoled him. She placed her hands over the duke's ridiculously large lapels, swiping away nonexistent dust. "If there's anyone in the *ton* who can make a man look like a duke, it's you. After you're done with him, the American will be witty, and chivalrous, and beautifully brilliant, just like—" Charlotte's gaze fell to the window, where a figure suddenly darted out into the manicured lawn. "What is that crazy person doing to that sheep?"

The duke twisted to look out the window. "That's the llama, dearest. Why is the silly man chasing the llama? It doesn't like being chased, does it?"

"Who does?"

"You don't think it's another of your crazed suitors, do you? Oh, Lord. He's probably trying to tie a love letter around its neck and direct it to you."

"Then it's best I put a stop to it right away," Charlotte returned, marching toward the door.

"Where are you going?" the duke called after her. "Don't go out there. Send James. That man could be mad! He has an unhealthy obsession with that poor llama."

Charlotte whistled, signaling for her dog, Jolly, to follow her. The fat pug had been sleeping deliciously on his pillow in the middle of a sunbeam but found his feet eventually.

She turned back to her father, feeling more tired than ever before. If obsession with animals made one mad, then her father was the craziest person she knew. Along with the duke, the monkey, the macaw, and—she was quite certain—the three-toed sloth hanging on the back of her father's chair (ripping its expensive upholstery to shreds) were all staring at her, waiting for her response.

"I'll be fine, Father," she said, exiting the room. "He'll be no harm to me. No one is madder than me right now."

IN A HURRY to shoo the man from the grounds before their visitor arrived, Charlotte was still tying her bonnet in place when she came upon the intruder. Fully awake now, Jolly skipped along, his little pug legs doing the most with what they could.

The intruder had stopped chasing the llama and was standing ten feet back from the animal, his hands up in a defensive position, as if trying to convince it that he meant no harm.

Charlotte adopted the same tactic toward the interloper, though Jolly wasn't nearly as discreet. His high-pitched barks startled the llama, causing it to skitter nervously. Charlotte kept her voice relaxed but impenetrably hard. "This is my land, and you have no right to be here. Please stop disturbing our animals—"

"Shh, be quiet," the intruder whispered, throwing out one rude finger at Charlotte. He refused to tear his focus off the llama.

Her mouth dropped open. "Do not shush me, sir!" she began, her words strained. "Again, this is my land, and you have no right to be here—"

"Shh!" he repeated, more insistently. "She's starting to like me, I can tell. She's going to let me touch her. Keep your pig quiet."

Charlotte's eyes widened toward her precious little dog. "Jolly is not a pig."

The man studied the dog from the corner of his eye, his confusion apparent. "Then what is it?"

"He's a dog!"

The intruder shrugged. "Its face is smushed and it has a curly tail ... That's a pig."

Charlotte scooped Jolly up in her arms, covering his soft ears with her hands. "He barks."

"I've noticed. So do pigs."

"And he's black!"

That pulled his attention. The man turned to her, punching fists onto his narrow wrists. Charlotte couldn't help but notice that this man also had a pronounced inverted-triangle torso, though it didn't look like he needed a corset or puffed shoulders to accomplish it.

She shook her head. What was she thinking? The man was a rude brute with a barbaric beard and wrinkled frock coat that looked like he'd slept in it for the past week. Marveling at his sea-glass-colored eyes was not sound judgment, nor was appreciating the sharp lines of his jaw. And Charlotte had perfect judgment.

"I've also seen black ones."

"Black what?" she asked, tearing her gaze from his full lips that were framed by the unruly beard.

"Pigs," he answered. He dipped his forehead toward Jolly. "You've got a pig there, miss. And a runt, at that. Better to just put it out of his misery before you get too attached."

Charlotte hugged Jolly closer. "Never! You are a horrid man! Is that what you're trying to do to my poor llama, put him out of his misery?"

The man rolled his eyes, turning back to the llama, who was halfway across the grounds now. "Damn," he said. "I was so close to touching it, but then you and your pig had to ruin everything."

Charlotte jutted out a hip. "That llama wanted nothing to do with you."

The man's figure tensed, and he cocked his head at her. A shiver went up Charlotte's spine. It was just a look, but it felt much too intimate, even dangerous. "Forgive me for not listening to you," he said, "but you clearly have no idea what you're talking about."

"About my own animal?" Charlotte smirked. "I'm quite sure I know more than you'll ever know. Now please leave—"

"I doubt that."

"And why is that?"

"Because," he said with a long drawl, "for starters, that's not a llama, it's an alpaca."

Charlotte frowned and squinted at the animal in the distance. She was no zoologist, but she knew a llama when she saw one. In any case, she had no idea what an alpaca was or what it looked like. "My father—the duke—bought that llama off a circus manager. People do not lie to my father."

The man lifted his shoulders carelessly, beginning a careful walk toward the animal once more. He looked utterly foolish. He was one of the tallest men she'd ever seen, and he was practically prancing on his tiptoes to get closer to the skittish beast. "Someone lied to your father, then, because that is an alpaca. How many do you have?"

"Two," Charlotte answered curtly. "And they are llamas."

Trailing behind him, she heard him sigh. "They're alpacas. Look how short she is. And notice her face. It's smushed in like your pig's. Llamas have snouts, like real dogs."

"Stop calling my dog a pig!"

"Wait." The man stopped in his tracks, twirling back around. "Did you say you have two? A boy and a girl?"

Charlotte held her chin higher. "Yes," she said sternly. She had no idea.

He studied her warily. "You have no idea, do you?"

Her confidence faltered. "Of course … I do."

"What are their names?"

Their names? How was she supposed to know that? And who named their llamas—or alpacas? It wasn't like they were useful like Jolly, who was an expert companion. For all she gathered, the shy animals loafed about eating through the cook's garden and sleeping most of the time.

The intruder raised a dark eyebrow. Charlotte couldn't decide what color his hair was. It was too dark to be brown and too light to be black. She had a feeling this would perplex her for a while. "Well?" he asked, rather impatiently.

Charlotte tossed up her hands. "George and Georgina," she said, lying on the spot. Not bad names for thinking under pressure.

The man's face scrunched up in disgust, as if she'd just eaten a small child in front of him. "That's ridiculous! After your late king, no less. Not very original."

"They're llamas. Does it matter?"

"No," he said. "They're alpacas."

Charlotte gave up. "Fine, they're alpacas—Wait a moment. Did you say 'your late king'?"

He nodded slowly, and it was like someone had thrown a bucket of ice-cold water over her. Charlotte froze, taking it all in. The slovenly clothes, the odd accent, the rude behavior, the barnyard beard, the fixation on ridiculous animals ... He couldn't possibly be ... Could he?

Her words wavered as they left her mouth. "Who are you? What are you doing here?"

In a flash, the man's smile widened to take up his whole face, and his white teeth gleamed against the sun. He whipped off his hat and performed a dismal bow that Charlotte would be offended with later, when her mind returned to working order. She was too stunned at the present time.

"I have an appointment with the duke," he said with a slight chuckle. "It's so odd saying that. Anyway ... I'm Nathaniel Lawrence."

CHAPTER TWO

HIS BOW WAS better the second time around. Even to Nathaniel's novice take on matters, the first one left something to be desired.

He blamed the girl. She'd ruffled him with her talk, confusing things like pugs and pigs and llamas and alpacas. Not to mention her unmistakable beauty. Nathaniel wasn't one to wax poetic, but there was no harm in calling a spade a spade. The duke's daughter was uncommonly lovely. Breathtakingly so.

Even when angry, which she clearly was now as Nathaniel and the duke offered each other pleasantries. Framed by this gold-plated room that made Nathaniel's father's mansion back in Boston look like a beggar's hole, the girl—Lady Charlotte—accosted him with a pinched expression and eyes that managed to balance disdain and skepticism to the perfect degree.

Nathaniel didn't understand her anger; *they* were the ones who'd contacted *him*, asking him to travel to London. Luckily for them, Nathaniel's irritation at the inconvenient request had ebbed.

Mr. Hobart had been correct—the time at sea had helped to marginally clear Nathaniel's head. Even so, he had no intentions of staying for an extended period, just long enough to take in the sights and deliver the money to the orphanage. He'd surprised himself by accepting the duke's invitation to come to his home.

Nathaniel still didn't believe a lick of the long-lost relative story. His curiosity had simply won out in the end. Meeting the duke was cheaper than a show, and Nathaniel had heard the gardens were nice.

The duke floated to his side and pounded him mightily on the back. The action did little to shift Nathaniel, who was almost two whole heads taller than the old, dainty aristocrat. "I heard Americans are hearty," the duke said, laughing. "You're as big as a tree, aren't you? Come in, come in, my boy. We don't stand on ceremony here. Take a seat."

Nathaniel smiled politely and began to move to a chair then halted dead in his tracks. He'd never seen a flamingo in person before, but there one stood—on one leg—in front of the giant, marble-carved fireplace.

He heard the duke chuckle. "Oh, don't mind Pinky. He tends to get cold and likes to warm himself by the fire. He'll move on soon enough."

As if on cue, the flamingo ruffled its feathers like it was overcome with a shiver. Nathaniel attempted to maintain his composure as the flamingo arched its long neck back and rubbed its head on its back feathers in a wiggly motion. Preening, he thought it was called.

Taking a seat, His Grace laughed at the animal's antics while playing with the lace cuffs at his wrists. Nathaniel was no slave to fashion, but even he knew the flamboyant cuffs were out of style. Still … if any of his friends back home would have described a duke, the Duke of Wembley wouldn't have been far off. From his bearing to his silks, he was colorful and eccentric, even up to his hair, which was shockingly white and long and pulled back at the nape of his neck with a shiny ribbon. The aristocrat appeared to be unapologetically himself in every way, and so vastly different from the businessmen Nathaniel regularly dealt with. They were always so somber, playing everything close to the vest. His father had been that way too.

"Would you like a drink?" the duke asked.

"Yes, thank you," Nathaniel replied, trying hard not to sneak a peek at the girl. Her unfriendly stare didn't unnerve him, though it *was* unnerving.

The duke's limpid eyes became even more animated. "Whiskey, gin, or bourbon? Yes, I hear Americans love bourbon!" He jumped from his seat, dashing the footman away from the drink cart with a wave of his ring-clad fingers. The duke had obviously prepared for this eventuality and had had the cart stocked with every liquor under the sun, although his "butlering" was decidedly below adequate. Nathaniel tensed as the duke fingered the bottles and fine crystal awkwardly, ready for something to fall from the man's delicate hands.

"Tea would be fine," Nathaniel announced, wringing a sigh of relief from Charlotte's lips. He glanced at her, but her hawklike gaze had moved on to her father's hands, which had now begun to tremble.

The duke looked down at his hands and clutched them together quickly in front of his chest. Then he barked at the footman to bring the tea, seemingly deflated that his barmaid skills were going to waste.

"I thought Americans didn't like tea," Charlotte said thoughtfully to no one in particular, diverting Nathaniel's attention from the duke. It was plain what she really meant (*Americans are uncultured swine*) and to whom she was speaking (*Nathaniel*).

"I'm sure some don't," Nathaniel said evenly, laughing so the silly chit didn't think she'd injured his pride. She hadn't even punctured a hole. "To tell you the truth, I don't particularly like it, but ..."

"But?" she prodded.

"It was the least of the evils."

"Evils?" the duke repeated. He lost his footing as he came back to his chair. He caught himself before falling on his face. "You mean"—his lips quivered, like he was petrified to say the obvious—"you don't drink alcohol?"

Nathaniel shook his head. "Not a drop. Never have."

The duke's face turned green, as if he was going to be sick. "You mean, for religious reasons?"

"No."

"For political ones, then?" the duke added hopefully.

"Not them, either."

"Then why on earth not?"

Nathaniel's chair groaned as he straightened and shrugged. "Just never had a taste for it, I suppose."

The duke scanned his fingernails, muttering, "I don't think you tried hard enough, but never mind that." He slapped his hands on his front thighs. "Enough small talk, don't you think? It's time we get to the heart of the matter of why I invited you here. I'm sure you have a lot of questions, and I'd like to get through it all today if we can."

Nathaniel released a chuckle. He weaved his fingers together and noticed that his palms had left a sweat stain on his trousers from his palms. Why was he nervous all of a sudden? It couldn't be the girl. She hadn't looked at him in four seconds. Her long blonde lashes were low anyway, so when she did grace him with a glance, he could barely make out the azure glint in her eyes. In fact, he hardly noticed the way her pouty lips parted infinitesimally at her father's actions, the way she sucked in a startled breath, or how the cords of her neck strained whenever her father spoke.

The duke reclined in his chair, treating it as his throne. He crossed one knee over the other, hooking his feet underneath. At that moment, the smallest monkey Nathaniel had ever seen sprinted across the room and launched onto the duke's shoulder. "Let me first apologize," he began, petting the animal's golden-orange fur. "You are probably confused by receiving the letter out of the blue. It must have come as quite a shock. It was to us as well. You see … these have been trying times. My wife and I, bless her soul, tried many years for an heir but were never successful." His voice became deeper. "She tried to the end, and, well … You understand."

"I think I do, yes," Nathaniel answered somberly, ignoring

the way the monkey also appeared horribly downcast at the discussion.

"A year ago, I had given up all hope and resigned myself to the fact that my title will end with me. But then a miracle happened."

"A miracle?"

"*Squawk! A miracle! A miracle!*"

Nathaniel swiveled his neck to see a giant bird in the corner. Why wasn't it in its cage? Was he at a zoo or a ducal estate? It was all terribly discombobulating, like he was balancing on a tightrope in the middle of a tornado.

The duke clapped his hands like a giddy child. "Yes, a miracle! You see, *I*, Thomas Cordry, am my title. It is *me*. And I can't bear the fact that it could get lost in history. My family has held it for over eight hundred years. So, I started a search. I poured everything into it, hiring the best investigators and heralds in the country. It's all I could think about. It consumed me. I barely slept, so obsessed was I with finding the missing piece in the puzzle of my life. Ask my lovely daughter; she'll tell you. Do you comprehend what I'm telling you?"

The hair on the back of Nathaniel's neck started to stand. He felt unwell, like a ghost had just walked through him. It was one thing to read this preposterous news in a letter, and another to hear it from a real duke's mouth. "I'm … afraid I don't."

The duke's chest ballooned. "You, dear boy! He found you. Well, he found your father, which led us to you."

"*Squawk! George is dead! George is dead! George is dead!*"

Where had that come from? Nathaniel had heard that parrots mimicked what was said around them, but the duke hadn't mentioned a George. The parrot couldn't be speaking about his father … could it? Had the duke trained the parrot to do it? Was his plan that elaborate?

Nathaniel bent over, leaning his elbows on his knees. It was rude; he understood that. His mother had raised him better, but sometimes things could not be helped. The duke—and his tumbling menagerie—had stunned the politeness out of him. "I don't see how ..." he stammered. He focused on the crimson carpet, trying to control the questions raging through his head. "My father was an orphan. He left England when he was eleven."

"Yes, he did," the duke said, standing in a rush, nearly upsetting the monkey. He marched over to a table and picked up a stack of papers before coming back in front of Nathaniel. One by one he placed the yellow-tinged parchments onto his lap. "He was found outside St. Lawrence's Orphanage in Hampstead on, presumably, the day of his birth in 1776. According to the note left behind by the midwife who'd delivered him, the baby's mother had died in childbirth and the father was my third cousin, once removed—William Cordry."

"*Squawk! George is dead! George is dead! George is dead!*"

Nathaniel was beginning to truly hate that bird. "If that's true, then why was the baby given to an orphanage? Why wasn't it given to the families?"

The duke returned a pitying look. "The mother's family didn't want it. She'd been thrown out for the ... indiscretion. And the father's family ... Well, let's just say this wasn't the first time they'd dealt with a situation like this."

"A situation ... like a bastard. You're saying my father was a bastard?" Nathaniel hastened a glance toward Charlotte. Her cheeks were flushed, and her hand was held to her lips. But she was no longer irritated. Oddly, she appeared concerned and regretful. For him? "I apologize, Lady Charlotte," he said.

"It's all right," she said softly, her lovely voice like a cool breeze. It was odd how it fit the situation and yet didn't at the same time.

Nathaniel frowned. "Please answer me," he told the duke.

"Ah, yes," the duke said, going back to his seat. "Everyone assumed that your father was a bastard. As I said, my cousin had a habit for making them. He also had a habit of convincing young ladies that they were getting married when actually he had one of his friends pretend to be a local priest."

Nathaniel scoffed. "Great relatives you have."

"You mean *we*," the duke said, putting too much emphasis on the word for Nathaniel's liking. "However, it seemed as though good old William had an awakening. Before his regiment sailed off to fight in the American War for Independence, he'd met your grandmother and married her in secret—with a true priest. I can only assume he told her to keep their union a secret until he returned, because she told no one—not even her family when they forced her to leave the home after they found out she was expecting. But my cousin never came back from America. He died in Virginia, I am told."

Nathaniel had never been to Virginia. And now he never wanted to go.

The duke paused. "My investigator found the wedding certificate in the old parish. It's real. I have to ask again, because your silence is rather startling, but … do you understand what I'm telling you?"

Nathaniel fingered the papers on his lap. He understood that they were filled with words and figures, dates and signatures, but they all smushed together in his mind. It took him a moment to realize his eyes were tearing up.

He should stop this at once. It had gone on long enough. Allowing the crazy duke to speak about his father seemed sacrilegious, disrespectful, but he couldn't find the words. It was like he was in the middle of a stream and the current was too strong. Nathaniel was getting carried away.

He passed a quick hand over his eyes, clearing away the would-be tears. "You're telling me that my father is legitimate. I'm afraid it's a little late for that. He never had an interest in what he left behind on this island, and I have even less of one."

"But I believe you might have one now, Nathaniel," the Duke said gently. "You are my heir. Did you hear that? My heir. Your legitimacy changes everything."

"*Squawk! George is dead! George is dead! George is dead!*"

"Not to me, it doesn't."

The duke smiled as if Nathaniel was a petulant child, one intent on being obstinate. He wasn't being obstinate; he was just being honest.

And he knew the duke wasn't being truthful. How could he be? This convoluted explanation sounded like it had jumped right out of a book. Like *Oliver Twist*. Yes. The duke had pulled the story straight from Charles Dickens. Nathaniel felt like a silly country bumpkin. He'd almost caught himself believing the tale. The papers were good. Whoever had forged them had done a decent job.

He scratched at his beard meditatively as he leveled the duke with a cold stare. Nathaniel blew out his next word like a whistle. "Thunderation."

The duke swelled with pride and bewilderment. "That's good, yes? One of your adorable Americanisms?"

Nathaniel jerked his head. "Not quite. I am such a fool," he said lightly. "I knew I shouldn't have come. I don't have time for this. I expected you to ask me for money right away, not beat around the bush with some ridiculous fairytale."

He shot up from his seat, pacing the floor. The duke sat restlessly behind him. "Fairytale?" Cordry asked. "Of course you should have come. Didn't you hear me? You are my heir. You're going to inherit all of this." The duke lifted his arms regally, showcasing the majesty of the room, with its rich, dark pink damask wall coverings and matching flamingo.

Nathaniel tapped his teeth together. It was a fine room to be sure, though it was hard not to notice the water stains in the corner of the ceiling, nor the loose threads hanging limply from just about every cushion and drape, or hear the way every chair cracked as it was used. Either the duke was a skinflint, or he was short on money. Nathaniel had a good feeling it was the latter.

He put up his hands. "You can stop with the game now. I'm onto you." He looked toward the window. "I should be leaving anyway. There's still some time in the day for me to get some work in. Thank you for allowing me to stay the night. I will not be an inconvenience and will be gone first thing in the morning." Nathaniel angled his body to the exit before he caught himself. He cocked his head at the duke. "Actually, speaking of work. You wouldn't consider selling me those alpacas, would you? I'll make it worth your while."

Flustered, the duke shook his head. "What? No, no, no, there will be none of that. You're going to be a duke. You don't have time to"—he scowled, as if thinking the word distasteful—"work. You have to move in with us, learn about the holdings and estates, not to mention the culture. You're too far behind, my boy. You simply have to catch up if the dukedom is going to succeed."

"Succeed?" Nathaniel asked. "Haven't dukes already succeeded? That's why they're dukes." This ruse was becoming too much, like they were piling a never-ending feast of rotten food in front of him and forcing him to eat.

"That's a bit of an oversimplification," the duke answered, putting his arm around Nathaniel's broad shoulders. He had to step on his tiptoes to do it. "It's like saying all Americans are ungrateful and can't be loyal. The truth, as always, is somewhere in the middle. No, Nate—can I call you Nate?—you see, the Cordry family has had a rough go of it in recent years. My father didn't help matters, I'll tell you that much. Unfortunately, I never had a head for numbers either. I am an artist—or rather, I love to buy art, as well as other things, like my animals. I see the beauty in the world, and unfortunately, men like me are doomed to suffer from a light wallet."

Nathaniel arched a brow, staring at the water spot. "You don't say?"

The duke closed his eyes dramatically and sighed. "More like a nonexistent wallet. Oh, we've kept things afloat, kept up appearances, but … Well, let's just say we've entered some lean years. But that's all in the past now that we've found you."

Nathaniel let out a mirthless laugh. Now they were getting somewhere. "Why?"

The duke slapped his hand on Nathaniel's chest. "I did my research, son. You're a wealthy man—one of the wealthiest in your part of the country, if my sources are correct. Whoever thought a little textile merchant could make so much? And now, with your father's inheritance, that means you can give all the love and attention that Wembley House and the other houses desperately need."

Nathaniel turned to Charlotte. "How many other houses are there?"

"Six," she answered quickly. "Terribly sorry."

He nodded before pulling away from the duke's tentacle-like clutches. "So, it's up to me, then," he said, his amusement making the duke frown. "To save everything … return it to its grandeur."

The duke nodded eagerly. "Yes! Now you're getting it. Aren't you grateful that I'm granting you this rare privilege? Who would have thought a simple American like you could grow up to be a duke? Wonders never cease. Don't you feel lucky?"

Nathaniel scoffed, rubbing his eyes. "Oh, I feel something, all right. Among other things."

"Like what?" the duke asked.

Nathaniel blew out a long gust of air, once again fixating on that water spot. "Ah, let's see. I'm feeling a bit overwhelmed—"

"Naturally," the duke cried with blazing patronization.

Nathaniel went on, "I feel a little inadequate."

The duke nodded indulgently. "Of course you would. I forgot to ask the investigators, but you do know how to read, correct? I never know what to expect from Americans. Did you attend university?"

"Harvard, yes," Nathaniel replied offhand. "And I guess … Well …" He lobbed a grimace at that damned flamingo, who was now shitting all over the carpet. "I feel incredibly sorry for you, because I don't have a dollar to my name."

CHAPTER THREE

THE GIRL BROKE into laughter, and it struck Nathaniel as one of the oddest sounds to come out of such a magnificent-looking creature: deep and hacking, not mellifluous in the slightest. Ever since he'd entered the room, he'd had to claw his eyes away from her so as not to make an uncultured swine out of himself. On second thought, he should have let himself gawk at the beauty; after the news he'd just dropped, he was quite certain he wouldn't be conversing with this insane family for very much longer.

The duke unglued his mouth and tried to form a sentence. "I ... I don't understand. What do you mean, a dollar?"

"Oh, so sorry, a dollar is my currency," Nathaniel explained flippantly. "Should I have said pound? Because I don't have any of those either—"

"Stop talking," Cordry barked with the tenor of a man who was used to his orders being obeyed. He rubbed at his eyes, and all four of his jeweled rings sparkled like the champagne bubbles that he would probably not be drinking tonight. Nathaniel guessed he would need something stiffer.

Cordry inflated his lungs, plastering a smile on his dejected face. "I was told your father was quite wealthy."

"He is. He was," Nathaniel replied, trying not to get too upset about using the past tense. *Time. Time.* Everyone said it would take time.

Cordry gestured for Nathaniel to go on, but when he didn't, the duke lifted an imperious chin and said, "And he lost the money somehow?"

"No, no. He kept it to the end," Nathaniel explained.

"So where is it? Clearly, you do not have it."

"I'm afraid not. He gave it all to charity."

Nathaniel didn't think it was possible, but by the looks of the sneer, the duke had found a word he hated more than *work*. "All of it?"

"Every last dollar—I mean pound." Which wasn't precisely true. Nathaniel had his savings, which some would consider more than adequate—however, he wasn't about to tell that to this swindler.

The girl snickered again, and Nathaniel not only heard it but felt it in his chest. He was aware of every smile, every rustle of her skirt; he even pinpointed the main ingredient in her soap: bergamot. Nathaniel was certain that he would know exactly where Charlotte Cordry was on this green earth for the rest of his life.

Quite simply, she moved him. And it wasn't just her beauty, although she was as close to exquisite as a person could be. Her long blonde hair was the color of ripe corn on a fair July day, with its various degrees of buttery hue. Her eyes were bluer than the water off the Nantucket Sound. But there was more. From the head-scratching laugh to the way her hands seemed to dance in front of her with the silky sway of a humpback whale breaching the surface. And the sharp keenness of her expression whenever her father said something regrettable. Yes, he noticed that the most. There was something about Lady Charlotte, and it was almost worth going along with this charade. But a man had his pride, and Nathaniel wouldn't spend it playing whatever asinine game this daft duke had in store for him just to spend a few more minutes in the presence of this otherworldly woman.

Cordry stumbled back, his face growing even paler than his

stark white hair. "But I … How can …?" An idea seemed to come to him. "But you still have the business, so you can make money and be just as wealthy as your father."

"Indeed," Nathaniel replied, "and that's why my plan takes me back to America as soon as possible. You say that you are your title—well, my business is me, and I will not be separated from it. I'm sorry, Duke, but you picked the wrong man to con. You might be able to blind others with your houses and your trinkets, but not me."

Nathaniel's words were like a bag of bricks, hitting the old man senseless. In his catatonic state, Cordry bumped into the side table, causing the Grecian vase centered on top to wobble precariously. At the same time, Nathaniel and Charlotte leaped to the rescue, throwing their hands around the neck of the pottery before it had a chance to smash to the floor.

Their eyes met above the vase as the air in the room vanished. The tips of Nathaniel's fingers overlapped Charlotte's, and it took a Herculean effort not to move them, not to caress her smooth, delicate nails.

Charlotte pulled away first. "Father, are you all right?"

The duke was clutching his chest, his breathing ragged and disjointed. He leaned on the table between them, placing both palms flat on the fine wood. The orange monkey climbed off his shoulder and onto the lip of the vase. "I'm fine, my dear. Perfectly fine," Cordry said, inhaling so deeply that his nose made a whistling sound. "It's just been a tiring day. Distressing information can be so vexing for the soul. Perhaps I should retire. Yes, I think that's the right idea. Maybe after a little sleep, I'll figure out what to do next."

"*Squawk! What to do next! What to do next!*"

Charlotte's countenance radiated concern, and for a moment, Nathaniel actually felt sorry for the duke—until his words sank in.

He blocked Cordry's path to the door. "What is there to do next? From everything you've just told me, I am the rightful heir. You have the paperwork to back it up. Whether my pockets are full or empty doesn't matter. Isn't that the truth? Or are you ready to tell me you've been lying this whole time?"

This was what Nathaniel had been waiting for. He'd sprung his trap and was ready to catch the beast. Now, all that was left was for Cordry to finally admit this had all been one big ploy to cheat the Lawrence family out of its money. Nathaniel might not be as cultured and well-to-do as these upper-class snobs, but he was not so bombarded with grief that he couldn't think straight—nor did he let animals shit on his carpet.

Nathaniel clenched his fists as he crossed his arms, waiting for the old man to come clean.

But the duke did not speak. Nor did his parrot.

"Move," Charlotte said firmly. One word. Effortless and commanding. Reeking of authority. Nathaniel couldn't explain why it made his heart race.

He stood his ground. "Not until he answers my question."

"Later," she snapped.

"No, now."

Charlotte placed her slender arm around her father's middle, ushering him around Nathaniel; however, the duke swayed her action. His pallor was getting grayer by the minute, and Nathaniel was confounded by the reduction of the man who, just moments before, had been a bustling light of energy.

"It's fine, my dear," he said, patting Charlotte's hand. "The boy has come all the way from Boston. The least I can do is waylay his doubt. I had no idea you New Englanders were so skeptical ..." Cordry lifted his long, aquiline nose, pulling back his shoulders until he was square with Nathaniel. "You are my heir whether you choose to believe it or not. I am a duke, not a swindler. And you're correct—it doesn't matter if you come to us poor or rich. You will inherit regardless. However, that doesn't mean I have to like it. I was quite willing to accept a rich American as my heir, but a poor one ... A poor one is like a broken, priceless vase." Suddenly, his hand shot out, shoving the Grecian vase to the floor, reducing it to pieces.

Cordry shook his head and let his daughter lead him out of the room. "No use to anybody."

LATER THAT NIGHT, Nathaniel nursed his bewilderment over a glass of milk in the kitchen.

That damn bird's annoying words still throbbed in his head. *Squawk! George is dead! George is dead!*

Those were the truest words spoken at that disastrous meeting.

Nathaniel simply had to make the best of it. He'd known he was walking into a trap. Why, then, did it still bother him so much? Because the duke's story seemed a little too plausible?

No. It didn't. Nathaniel couldn't look behind; he had to keep looking forward. First thing in the morning, he would go to St. Lawrence's Orphanage and start the proceedings to give away his father's money, and then he could get ready to leave this backward island that was so preoccupied with its past.

Once he was in Boston, he could begin rebuilding his fortune from the ground up. It wouldn't be difficult. His father had laid everything out for him, creating a textile business that performed as precisely as the new, well-oiled machines flooding the factory floors.

And yet that thought filled Nathaniel with a restlessness he couldn't shake. If America was the land of the free and the brave and the new, then why did it feel like he was returning to something unbearably old? Would a future collecting money born from his father's back be enough for him? What he needed was a challenge. What he needed was a spark.

A spark.

Nathaniel's mind filled with images of Charlotte's scowl after he'd refused to allow her father to pass by him. In a matter of seconds, the woman had morphed from the sweet and luscious to the cold and austere. She could freeze a burning man with a lash of her tongue. Nathaniel debated lighting himself on fire just to test his theory.

No, the best thing to do with Charlotte Cordry was to turn his back, forget her and England as if they were just some bad dream. But the harder Nathaniel tried, the more her vision stuck in his head. And by his third cup of milk, he was punch-drunk with regret.

Mostly he wanted to tell the girl that he was sorry. Sorry that he couldn't help. Sorry that believing in fairytales had never been his strong suit. As a young boy, he'd gone to bed with the music of percentages and bottom lines lulling him to sleep. If his father ever read him something, it was from the *New York Evening Post*, and those stories were dryer than the desert in *Arabian Nights*. He couldn't be more different than the father she clearly adored. The father who appreciated art and fine things and exotic animals. The father who collected so many precious artifacts that he could afford to break them idly.

Stupid man. He couldn't be easy to live with. Nathaniel could commiserate. As much as he'd loved his own father, he hadn't hesitated moving out of the mansion as soon as he came of age and could afford a place of his own.

A man needed his own space. Now that Nathaniel considered it, a woman probably did too.

CHARLOTTE'S FATHER NEVER did take that nap; nor did he go to sleep that night. And he made sure the entire house knew it.

It was close to midnight, and Charlotte could still hear the pounding steps reverberating from the duke's bedroom, along with the high-pitched whine of his violin. He said playing helped him think. Unfortunately, it didn't provide the same solace for the rest of the household. It couldn't be helped, Charlotte told herself as she tossed and turned in her bed, one pillow underneath her head and one pinned against her other ear. The duke was prone to tantrums. *All* dukes were prone to tantrums, her father had lamented once. Still … Charlotte couldn't help but think that his were worse than most.

The Duke of Wembley made a habit of shutting himself away when his melodramas took over. The servants whispered that they'd only begun after Charlotte's mother died in childbirth—along with the profligate spending. All men mourned in different ways, he'd also informed her a day after purchasing a Rembrandt—right out from under King George's nose. *Judge not lest ye be judged.*

Charlotte wondered how the American mourned. From Mr. Hemsworth, she'd learned that his mother had died a few years ago from "female troubles." Mr. Lawrence couldn't be more than thirty, and now both of his parents were gone. And his father sounded like an eccentric sort. Who gave away their entire fortune to charity? He must have been difficult to live with, she surmised.

Charlotte sat up. Not even the heavy curtains closed around her bed could keep out the noises. It didn't help that she allowed Jolly to sleep with her. Pugs might have the most adorable faces of any animal, but their poor nasal passages made for loud snoring.

Swiping aside her curtain, Charlotte scooted off the bed, just as her father was in the full swing of Beethoven's Sonata No. 9. She ventured to the window that looked out on the grounds behind the house. From here she could make out the Doric temple just past the pond, and the red-brick walls of the secret garden down the slope of the hill on the opposite side.

She would miss this place. Now that Mr. Lawrence told her father that he wanted nothing to do with the dukedom, petitioning the queen about amending the title was the only option. If only she could make her father see reason! The queen was their only hope. Charlotte was his heir—and she was a damn good one.

Her father had told Nathaniel that they were getting by. They were getting by because of Charlotte. She was the one who spoke to her father's secretary and estate manager every day. If it were up to the duke, they would have an elephant and a tiger right now instead of dinner on their plates every night. Thinking of the Wedgewood china, Charlotte lamented what she would have to sell next under her father's nose. Another vase? More silver?

Selling off their valuables had been something of a habit of late.

The dresses she'd commissioned for the Eglinton Tournament had cost a small fortune, but she needed to look the part. This was the social event of the year. Charlotte refused to go to Scotland looking anything less than magnificent among her peers. Her father owed her that.

Charlotte wasn't sure how she did it—smiled in front of her friends and fellow ladies as if she wasn't terrified about her future. On the surface, she was a prime catch of the Season, but only she and her father knew that her dowry was depleted. And she meant to keep it that way until she could find a solution for her father's mess.

Queen Victoria wasn't attending the tournament, but Charlotte was certain that the news and gossip would make its way back to her. If she could present herself well, be a shining light at the event, she was certain the queen would see what an asset she was to the *ton*. But the duke needed to be the one to petition to allow her to inherit. Charlotte couldn't do it. Therein lay the problem. If only women didn't have to rely on the men in their lives … what would the world be like then?

A light flickered in the distance, snatching Charlotte's attention. It was coming from the stable block. Just one light, barely noticeable, and dimmer than the stars up above. But there was no reason for anyone to be in the stables. Just as there had been no reason for a crazy man to chase across the grounds today in hopes of touching a llama—rather, an alpaca.

Charlotte grabbed her robe hanging from the nearby chair,

putting it on over her nightgown and tying it firmly in place. Jolly barely budged from the bed. At least someone wasn't bothered by the raucous violin. She headed for the door. No one had told Mr. Lawrence about the mini rhino. Although it had never bitten anyone at Wembley House, its past owner had made sure to mention that it had taken off a finger or two before. That was the only reason that Charlotte left for the stables. She had to tell herself that two more times before she believed it.

CHAPTER FOUR

LANTERN IN HAND, Charlotte padded lightly into the stable block following Nathaniel's light at the far end of the brick enclosure. She didn't worry about disturbing any horses. Even though the stables could house twenty comfortably, all of the thoroughbreds had been sold off. Her father's menagerie had only been too happy to fill up the space.

Charlotte passed the miniature rhino, the giant tortoise, and the anteater before she came upon the American. No surprise, Mr. Lawrence was perched at the edge of the alpaca's stall, simply watching the animal as it slept.

She saw him stiffen as she approached, though he didn't speak. "How did I know I would find you here?" she asked, breaking through the awkward silence.

Nathaniel frowned when the alpaca tremored at the sound of her voice. "It was a little too loud inside."

Charlotte couldn't help but smile. "You mean you don't like my father's violin playing?"

He tossed her a wry look. "I think I'd like it a little more if it wasn't done in the middle of the night."

Slowly, Nathaniel left his crouch and settled on the ground, his long legs hugged close to his chest. He looked like a common stable boy with his dusty trousers and linen shirt.

Charlotte pulled her robe tighter around her neck. At least

she was somewhat decent. Other than her father, she'd never seen a man without his waistcoat and necktie. He might as well be naked. Now, that was an odd thought.

Charlotte felt her face go red. "I don't mean to disturb you," she said. "I just thought I should warn you—"

"About the rhino?" Nathaniel cut in. "Yes, that was quite the surprise."

"Not only that. There are also rumors of an alligator in the pond—though I've never seen it—and the zebra. Oh, and the kangaroo. He's been known to kick."

Nathaniel rubbed his beard in a hypnotic movement. He squinted an eye up at her. "The zebra or the kangaroo?"

Charlotte cocked her head. "Both, actually. Though, between the two of them, I'd watch out for the zebra. He bites and spits too."

Nathaniel chuckled, turning back to the alpaca. Its breathing had reached a steady rhythm. The animal didn't love the fact that two humans were in her stall, but seemed to resign herself to the intrusion.

For all his bulk, Nathaniel had a calming presence. Even with his scruffy visage and even scruffier demeanor, a stillness pervaded him that had a rather settling effect. As they sat there, watching the alpaca, Charlotte's nervousness evaporated, and she found herself relaxing into the peaceful scene.

Nathaniel Lawrence was nothing like she'd imagined. Surrounded by animals her whole life, she understood that they were better judges of character than people. And from what the investigator had divulged, Nathaniel was a decent person. So decent, in fact, he was of the few owners that treated his factory employees like real people and not animals. Not only did he provide safe conditions for his workers, but he also provided housing near the factory as well as more leisure hours. However, she also heard that he—like his father before him—was a workhorse with no life to speak of outside of his factory walls. And he was in a hurry to get back to that life.

Which was why something continued to rankle Charlotte. Something didn't make sense.

She spoke just above a whisper. "I understand my father's obsession with his beasts, but not yours. What is it about this alpaca? Why did you offer to buy it?"

Nathaniel scooted an inch closer to the animal but immediately stilled when its head jerked. "I don't have an obsession with animals," he explained, retreating back to the stall wall. "Just alpacas. They're a gold mine. Haven't you heard about alpaca fur? It's softer than sheep's wool, and even rain resistant. Some of the fabrics I've seen with it look as decadent as silk." He sighed. "The only problem is that it's difficult to come by, since it has to be shipped from Peru and can be a challenge to weave. However, I've heard of a few men who've created machines that can do the job." He gave her a wry smile that made Charlotte's stomach turn viciously warm. "You didn't know you had a little golden goose here, did you?"

Charlotte laughed, admiring the unconventional animal. "My father certainly did not. He only bought the pair once he heard someone had gifted two to the new queen. He knows plenty about fashion, but nothing about how his fabrics are made."

Nathaniel's face softened. "Oh, that's all right. That's my job."

Charlotte tucked her nightgown underneath her and took a seat on the stone floor. "So, is that why you're here? Are you trying to cut off tufts of her fur when she's not looking? I'm afraid there isn't much. She was shorn at the beginning of the summer before it got too hot and uncomfortable for her."

Nathaniel perked up. "Did you keep the fur?"

"I doubt it. I'm not sure where it is." Charlotte shrugged. "We only have two of them. How much can you possibly make from two?"

His face turned somber, and he surveyed her critically. "Two can easily become three and three can easily become four. Before you know it, you've got yourself a thriving farm. You need to think like a businessman."

Charlotte frowned. "I'm a lady, not a businessman."

Nathaniel grinned. Under the shadows of the stables, he looked more devil than angel, and yet when he smiled, something seemed to open up, like a burst of sunlight through a wall of clouds. Charlotte couldn't resist smiling back.

His beard continued to be a source of constant interest. She hadn't noticed earlier, but its color was different than the dark hair on his head. It had more red in it, along with some flecks of gray. It reminded Charlotte of an oil painting, mingling its brush strokes together to create a startling image.

"And you never will be with that attitude."

Was that all it took? *Attitude?* What an American thing to think.

Charlotte studied the alpaca. The animal certainly didn't look pregnant, but Charlotte wasn't quite sure what to look for. Her belly was big, but not terribly swollen. Perhaps if the animal would let them feel her belly, they might have a better understanding, but that wasn't going to happen anytime soon.

"Is she pregnant now?" She paused, biting her lip. "Can you tell?"

Charlotte noticed the patch of skin above Nathaniel's beard grow pink. "Well … if I had your permission … I would bring the male next to her and see how she behaved."

"How is she supposed to behave—completely in love and smitten?" Charlotte was taken aback by the annoyance in her voice.

"On the contrary," Nathaniel said, rubbing the back of his neck. The sound of his hair scraping against his palm made a lightning bolt of electricity shoot up her spine. "Apparently, if the male comes near while she's already pregnant, the female will spit at him repeatedly until he leaves her alone. If she is not pregnant, then she will sit next to him placidly, inviting him to …" The tops of his ears matched his cheeks. Nathaniel's gaze fell to the floor. "Inviting him to mate."

Charlotte clicked her tongue. "Ah."

"Yes. Ah. This is probably not an appropriate conversation, is it?"

Charlotte could feel her own ears burning now. She threw back her shoulders, fighting for bravado. "For a lady? Probably not. But for a businesswoman? It would behoove me to learn how to create more of them."

"That was quick," Nathaniel said.

"You made a persuasive argument."

"I do that from time to time." Charlotte was taken aback by the gentleness in his voice. "You'd probably be the richest woman in England in no time. Have all the money to give this home the love and attention it needs, just as your father wants."

The words dropped from his lips like an anvil, catapulting the conversation into an awkward lull. They'd done so well steering clear of what had happened earlier. With it out in the open, it felt like the pair was back at square one—or worse, opponents in a battle they hadn't started nor seemed interested in finishing.

For some reason, Charlotte desperately wanted to take off her nightcap. She detested the fact that Nathaniel Lawrence was seeing her in it this way.

A rough sound came from his throat, and his eyes finally made their way back to her. "I should apologize," he said gruffly, as if he was unfamiliar with the task. Charlotte wanted to tell him that maybe he wasn't as different from a duke as he thought. "For how I treated your father earlier. I still think he's lying, but I was raised better than that. I shouldn't have goaded him. He's clearly on edge and not well."

Charlotte's throat tightened. No one ever mentioned her father's peculiarities. His friends just preferred to laugh at him behind his back. Could Nathaniel smell the alcohol on the duke's breath? Did he notice the stumbling footsteps? Her father hid it well, but Charlotte could always tell when he was in his cups—which was more often than not.

"No, you shouldn't have, but I understand why."

"You do?"

"Of course," she said quickly, nibbling on her lip. Charlotte inched closer and could smell him, that woodsy, spicy scent that lingered whenever he was near. It was refreshing, like walking barefoot over newly shorn grass. "He wasn't lying, by the way. You …" She hesitated. "If you leave, you should know that."

Nathaniel's voice turned deep, guttural. "Is that so?"

"It is. I saw the papers. They're real. All of this could be yours—*is yours*—if you want it."

Even probably me.

That thought sprang forth unbidden in her mind, startling Charlotte's nerve. She felt dizzy, and worried that Nathaniel could read the panic in her face. Quickly, she masked her expression, hoping that she appeared calm and complacent. "You could even have the alpacas!" she said, her voice much too loud, her laughter much too aggressive.

She needed to go back to her room; she was turning into a simpleton.

Nathaniel's chuckle was soft. "Well, it might just be worth it for the alpacas," he joked. Charlotte thought it sounded forced.

She tried to move her legs, but they wouldn't budge. She passed a glance at the alpaca, who appeared to be pretending to sleep. Its adorable little face looked more annoyed than restful, as if it were sickened by the ridiculously nervous behavior from the humans.

With a sigh, Charlotte pulled her robe tight around her neck and started to stand. "I think the violin has finally stopped. I should go. It's late—"

"Do you want to touch it?"

Charlotte flopped back onto the floor, her knees hitting the pavers with a *thump*. "Touch what?" she squawked.

Nathaniel raised his arm, holding his hand out to her. With wide, distrustful eyes, Charlotte gazed at it for far too long until it came to her in a rush. *The alpaca!* He was talking about the damned alpaca! What had she thought he meant? She didn't let herself answer that question.

"She seems pretty relaxed with us here," Nathaniel said, motioning to the animal. "Obviously, since you sheared her at the start of summer, her hair isn't that long, but I think it's enough to get a good idea. I tell you, experiencing it is worth it."

Charlotte continued to stare at his palm. Wide and full of crisscrossing lines, callused and tanned, this was no hand of a gentleman. But Charlotte couldn't lie to herself. She wanted to touch his hand more than the alpaca. Just this once.

Without thinking, Charlotte placed her hand in his, struck by the comforting warmth. It was all so ridiculous, her tiny hand in his, but a frisson of awareness electrified her at the small gesture. In a mere day, this bewildering man with his muted clothes and unrefined manner had imprinted himself on her, and she doubted that she would ever forget him or the way he made her feel at this moment.

Charlotte wanted to cry and then scurry back to the house. And then return and throw herself onto Nathaniel Lawrence for one passionate kiss before he left. Would he kiss her back?

Yes.

Of course he would kiss her back. If Charlotte knew anything with certainty, it was that men wanted her. Always. It was confusing, because she never wanted them. Until now.

After the kiss, Nathaniel would leave and be out of her system for good, and she would grow old and think back on this night with a worldly, indulgent chuckle.

"All right," Nathaniel said, his shoulders pumping wide under a shuddering breath. Was he as affected as she was by the touch? "Let's go slow. I don't want to scare you—I mean her."

Tentatively, he pulled Charlotte toward him so that they were kneeling side to side on the ground. With a gentle tug, he led her to the animal, whose eyes had now opened and was watching the proceedings with avid interest. Still … the alpaca didn't shy away.

The heat of Nathaniel's skin burned into her arms, and Charlotte grew panicky from her lack of dress. What would her father think? He was thinking of himself right now. Only himself. Charlotte would do the same.

Nathaniel switched her hand over to his left. With his right hand, he circled her middle, bringing her closer. Charlotte encouraged herself not to read into it. It was only a touch, but that touch was everything. Proprietary. Deferential. Soothing.

"A little bit more," he whispered in her ear. Charlotte nodded, her heart beating down the walls of her ribcage.

"I think she's going to let us do it," she whispered back as they reached out about a foot away from the animal's side.

"Just a little bit more," Nathaniel added.

His hand on her hip cushioned her into his side, causing her breast to press against his chest. Charlotte had never felt so alive before, her senses so heightened to another person. She could feel his breath move in his body, see the wave of his Adam's apple as he gulped, hear his heart quicken in unison with hers. It was like they were one, and the alpaca approved, knowing that they were all just animals on God's green earth.

They were there. Just inches away from satisfaction. And then, the alpaca's ears flickered and went back. Its neck shot up and it bounced to its feet, shooting out of the stall in the blink of an eye. In its haste, it bumped into Nathaniel, who lost his balance and pitched forward onto Charlotte. They landed with an undignified *plop* on the ground, Nathaniel's torso covering hers.

They burst into laughter at the same time. "I'm sorry! I'm sorry!" he said, though he made no attempt to move, and nor did Charlotte encourage it.

Her hands under his chest, she stretched her fingers so they held the balls of his shoulders, ready to push or pull, she wasn't sure what. With the light behind him, his face was dark. Charlotte became fixated on the shine of his teeth and how one of his front teeth was slightly bigger than the other.

"You're not who I expected you to be," he murmured as if pulling her thought out of thin air.

Charlotte smiled shyly. "I'm told women are hardly ever what they seem. Are you disappointed?"

Nathaniel angled his head. His eyes were so light, they reminded her of a mirror she could fall into if she wasn't careful. And she, most definitely, wasn't being careful now. "Do I look disappointed?" he asked.

No. He looked ready and willing, and all of a sudden Charlotte's conscience kicked in. "We should go inside, Nathaniel."

"Call me Nate."

"Don't you think we should go inside, Nate?"

He moved his hand to her neck, caressing her skin with the pad of his thumb. His head moved back and forth in the same lazy fashion. "I don't know, Charlotte. For the first time in a long time, I don't know what I should do."

Charlotte's smile twisted to the side. "That's kind of exciting, isn't it?"

He nodded, and a lock of hair fell onto his forehead. "Just as exciting as a lady being a businesswoman."

"Do you really think I can do it?"

"It's what I do. Your father may see the beauty in things, but I see the potential. I evaluate their strengths and weaknesses."

It was a novel concept. People only ever saw the potential in Charlotte's beauty. "What are my strengths?" she heard herself asking. Almost desperately.

Nathaniel shook his head. "It's better to ask about your weaknesses."

Charlotte frowned. She desperately didn't want to hear about those. "Why?"

"Because then you can learn."

Nathaniel's muscles shifted under her hands. "I'm not in the mood to learn anything right now."

Had she really just said that? Was she actually flirting in the middle of the night in an alpaca's stall?

Nathaniel's lips went wide. "I think there's a lot you want to learn right now."

"And you can teach me these things?"

In answer, Nathaniel lowered his head, and Charlotte sucked in a breath, readying herself for the touch that she'd really wanted all along. She closed her eyes and arched her body into his hard chest. His breath was warm and husky; his beard tickled her chin. She opened her mouth and—

A scream rang out. "Charlotte, I need you!"

Nathaniel jumped away faster than the alpaca, slamming against the far side of the stall.

She scrambled to her feet. Her cap was on the floor. When had her cap come off?

"Charlotte!" The voice boomed louder from the house.

"That's Father," she said, knowing it was obvious but needing to say something. She hastened to tie her cap under her chin, but her fingers were shaking too much.

Nathaniel started toward her, his hands outstretched. "Here, let me."

"No!" Charlotte left the stall before he could touch her. "Sorry, I mean. Thank you. I have it. I better go."

Nathaniel shoved his hands in his pockets. *Good.* They were safe there. "I'll go with you," he said.

Charlotte nodded dumbly, grabbing her lantern. She walked back to the house as if she had wings on her feet, making sure to be two steps ahead of him. The thought of looking at him seemed untenable. What had come over her? Why had she behaved so wantonly? So *wanting*-ly?

They were through the doors and up the stairs, almost on the second level, before Nathaniel acted. He clasped her upper arm, stopping Charlotte as they reached the landing. Forcing their bodies square, he searched for her eyes to meet his. His expression was remarkably pained. Maybe even regretful? She didn't have the time to ask, because the moment he said, "Charlotte," her father emerged from his room.

"Nathaniel!" the duke said, bounding down the corridor. "Stop mooning over my daughter and get in the drawing room. I've come up with an idea!"

CHAPTER FIVE

T HE DUKE STORMED down the hallway toward them carrying a candle, his nightgown and cap fluttering violently in his anxious wake.

He only addressed them again when he was on the stairs. "Come along. Come along," he barked excitedly. "We don't have all night, you two. Quickly. Quickly! Back to the drawing room!"

Nathaniel and Charlotte followed, though he noticed she was still doing everything in her power not to touch him. What had he planned to say to her before the duke interrupted? That he didn't usually seduce girls in the middle of the night in an alpaca's stall? That didn't exactly roll off the tongue. But Nathaniel didn't regret it. Would never regret it. Nor would he forget the sweet, soft way Charlotte had felt underneath him, all snug and warm, smelling like bergamot and anticipation.

Yes. Anticipation. Because she'd wanted him to kiss her—just as much as he'd wanted to. He'd seen it in the shine of her eyes, the tautness of her chin, the fullness of her lips as they'd canted toward his.

Nathaniel's rod was still hard just from thinking about it. With all his might, he tried to deflate his ardor before he reached the drawing room. It was bad enough that the duke had caught Nathaniel with his hands on his daughter—he didn't have to throw it in the older man's face with a giant cockstand.

The duke led them back to the formal room, where he placed his candle on the nearest table, encouraging Charlotte to light the candelabrum over the mantel. Thank the Lord for small mercies—a thick curtain had been placed around the macaw's cage, so the parrot was quiet, save for its melodic, chirpy little snores. The flamingo was also out of sight, no doubt because the hearth wasn't lit, and Nathaniel could only assume the tiny monkey wasn't hanging off the duke's shoulder because it was long past its bedtime.

"Good," Cordry said as the room was illuminated. He slapped his hands together, rubbing them quickly as if trying for warmth. "Now we can start."

It was difficult taking the man seriously in his sleeping attire, even though the duke's *was* rather exceptional. He sported a purple damask robe edged in vibrant emerald green. His cap, naturally, matched.

"Your Grace?" Nathaniel said cautiously, stepping in front of him, his voice and head lowered. He felt Charlotte creep in closer, like she didn't want to miss a word. "I want you to know—I need you to know that I didn't seek out your daughter tonight, nor did I spend much time alone in her company. I would never disrespect your hospitality like that. We were merely talking about—"

"Alpacas," Charlotte piped in.

Nathaniel threw her a grateful look. "Yes, alpacas and—"

The duke closed his eyes in irritation and flicked a careless hand in the air. "Enough. Enough," he replied. "There's no time for that tonight. You're certainly not the first man to try to coerce my daughter out in the middle of the night to profess his undying love. Half the *ton* has beaten you to it."

Nathaniel's spine lengthened. "Is that so?" he asked softly to no one in particular. "I'm afraid she didn't mention that during our alpaca conversation."

Charlotte covered her face with her hand. "He's exaggerating," she said, spying at him from between her fingers.

The duke scoffed. "Hardly. She has a bevy of admirers. It's quite something."

"It's hardly something. There have been some flowers and letters … a few sonnets," Charlotte explained, growing more awkward under Nathaniel's hard stare. "And some middle-of-the-night singing. It's nothing. Truly."

Nathaniel flexed his jaw so hard that he thought his teeth might break. Was Charlotte a flirt? Had Nathaniel been just another conquest? "It doesn't sound like nothing." He should have left it at that. Why he said the next words was beyond him. "And did you kiss everyone in your *bevy*?"

Charlotte jerked back. "What? Of course not!" Reclaiming her stance, she stared at him. "And may I remind you that I didn't kiss you either."

Was he a little jealous? Hell no. He was a lot jealous! "You were going to."

"I wasn't."

"You were."

"Was not!"

Nathaniel took a step toward her, but quickly stopped, placing his hands on his hips. "Don't you think I know when a woman is going to kiss me?"

Charlotte yanked at the ties of her robe, strangling her middle. "Clearly," she began, affecting an accent as snobbish as she could manage, "I wasn't aware of your abundant knowledge and experience."

Nathaniel threw back his head. "Oh, I have an abundance," he chortled. "Boatloads. Tons of knowledge on the subject." That was a lie. More like a dinghy of knowledge. And a skiff of experience.

Charlotte lifted her chin. Her face was deliciously cherry-colored, and her golden hair frazzled into a halo around her silly cap. "Well, I'm glad we got to the bottom of that."

"As am I."

The duke cradled his head in his hand. "Children, please, stop squabbling. I have an idea that will solve all our problems."

Nathaniel's glower never left Charlotte. "I don't have a problem," he returned.

The duke gave a pointed look to his daughter and answered, "I'm afraid you do, son."

Nathaniel rolled his eyes and broke away from the others, looping his fingers together and placing his hands on the top of his head. He needed to quit this house before he became as insane as the duke. His emotions were running wild, and it was all because he could still feel Charlotte's luscious breasts pressed up against his chest. Still smell the mint on her breath. Still feel the ravenous need that he was afraid would never go away.

He retreated to the window, leaning his head against the cold glass. Fogging it up, he said with an exasperated breath, "Go on, then. What is this plan?"

In the reflection, he saw the duke actually jump with glee before skipping to his daughter and hugging her tight shoulder.

"You are my heir," the duke began, gaining some composure. "Whether you want to believe me or not. However, as you've said before, you can reject the title and return to America, and never speak to us again. That's your right. However"—Nathaniel saw Charlotte tremble in her father's arms. Did she know what was coming?—"that would be a mistake. You want to build your father's business, don't you? No doubt you want to be your own man and become an even greater success. Just think what the connections of the *ton* could do for you. Aligning with me wouldn't just make you one of the richest men in Massachusetts anymore; you could be one of the richest men in *America*."

Nathaniel let the words sink in, not for his benefit, but for the duke's. Why wasn't he leaving the room? Why was he continuing to listen to this madness? It wasn't true! None of what he'd heard in the last twelve hours was remotely real!

Except for those short moments with Charlotte. What he'd felt with her was undeniably genuine. Even now, his breathing refused to slow. The pounding of his heart could not be restrained. His physical being had mutinied, and Nathaniel had no idea when it would come under his control again. All because a beautiful woman with a not-so-beautiful laugh had talked pretty to him.

No. It was more than that. It was so much more than her beauty.

That was why his feet stayed where they were. That was why Nathaniel allowed the duke's unlikely fantasy to take root in his mind. The old man was persuasive, yes, but Nathaniel's growing infatuation was even more so.

Nevertheless, if the duke's delusions were real, Nathaniel still had no interest in the title. He knew next to nothing about the British peerage system and loathed the thought of taking part in it. The balls and formal occasions that he had been forced to undertake in Boston had been bad enough. And yet … and *yet* … A ball with Lady Charlotte on his arm could be manageable. Tolerable. Heart-thumpingly bearable.

Not that the duke would ever offer his daughter. He was only offering a measly dukedom.

"I know how to build a business. I don't need this," Nathaniel said, though his words were limper than he'd expected.

The duke clearly picked up on the show of weakness, because his grin got wider.

"Oh, yes, of course, of course," he said. Charlotte's father reminded Nathaniel of a genie, begging its owner to wish for something he didn't need. "But it *is* something to think about, isn't it? And we could make it so that this new world opens to you, and you'd barely have to do a thing."

Nathaniel stayed silent as he faced the duke, his arms crossed.

The duke went on. "You wouldn't even have to stay here. Accept the title, become my heir apparent, and then go back to America the second you do what is asked of you and leave the running of the estate to us. You could have the best of the old and new worlds."

"But you'd expect me to send money." Nathaniel laughed

caustically. "Let's not forget that."

Charlotte's father chuckled, not trying to hide the truth of what Nathaniel said. "It would be in your best interest to send a little every now and then."

Nathaniel stepped away from the wall. "And why is that?" he asked. "What is the job you would have me do?"

The duke squeezed Charlotte before nudging her forward. Her expression ranged quickly from confusion to fury. "Give me a grandchild. If you don't want to believe in the title, that's fine. Just give me someone who will."

When Nathaniel didn't move, didn't bat one eyelash, the duke added, "And I'll throw in the llamas. You can take them back to America with you. How's that for a deal?"

NATHANIEL FINALLY BLINKED.

And that spurred Charlotte into action. She rounded on her father. "Have you completely lost your mind? *Llamas?* You're selling me for two llamas? I mean alpacas. They're alpacas, not llamas. You didn't even know that." She clutched her head in her hand, turning away from these men who were negotiating her fate as if she wasn't even in the room. "I can't believe this is happening to me."

"Well … they *are* two very nice llamas—or alpacas," she heard her father say. If he thought that would make her feel any better about the situation, then he was grossly mistaken.

Charlotte felt him on her heels, but she spurned his attempts to face her.

"What's wrong?" her father asked. "You were going to marry him anyway. That was the plan."

Nathaniel snorted. "I'd like to hear this plan."

Charlotte glared at him before turning to her father. "It wasn't the plan," she said testily, her composure completely gone.

"*You* said I had a choice in the matter. *You* said you would give me time to *think* about *maybe* considering the possibility that I *might* one day *entertain* the idea of marrying him."

"Be still, my beating heart," Nathaniel replied drolly. "Pray, don't go on; I think I might be tearing up."

"Oh, be quiet, you!"

Her father grabbed her by the shoulders, ducking his head so she would meet his eye. What Charlotte saw there made her heart go cold. She'd seen that manic look before and knew she was powerless against it. These intense moods ruled her father against all else, and swaying him was futile.

"Daughter, I don't know what you told yourself, but you always knew this was the plan. Have you even thought about what will happen to you when I'm gone? You're an intelligent girl. You must have. Without a dowry, you have nothing to live on. Despite your protestations, you know you have to marry, and he's the logical choice. You didn't think I was listening before, but I was! You said you didn't want a husband telling you what to do … Well, here he is! He just told you that he doesn't want to stay! You get the best of both worlds too! Can't you see that I'm doing this for you? You know how much you mean to me."

Dammit! Charlotte's eyes began to water. *Don't cry in front of these two!* The truth of his words filtered through. Her father was impossible, but that didn't mean he was wrong. Marrying the American was the only option if she wanted to keep Wembley House in her life. In the back of her mind, she'd always known that. However, the notion of a choice had always made the possibility seem manageable. Tolerable. Bearable—though *not* heart-thumpingly so.

"If you care so much for me, then petition the queen, ask for the title to be amended," Charlotte whispered plaintively. "You can do that. She'll get Parliament to change it in my favor."

The duke shook his head. "No, no. You know it's fruitless. I will not embarrass myself to that child monarch."

"Why is your pride more important than mine?"

"It is irrelevant. I have an heir! What am I supposed to do now, pretend he doesn't exist?"

"Yes!"

"No!" the duke said with the finality of hammering nails in a coffin. He took Charlotte's hands and made a great show of kissing them. "I wouldn't ask you to do this if there was a better option. In your heart, you know it."

Charlotte cast Nathaniel a look from the corner of her eye. His expression was harsh, and he looked just as flabbergasted as she was. But he also looked interested. Much more interested than he'd been earlier in the day and that scared her.

"I just…" Charlotte shuddered. "I thought we would have more time to get to know one another, and now you want a grandchild as soon as possible. It all feels so … cold."

Nathaniel jumped in. "You mean it feels English?"

"Oh, I assure you," the duke replied, his tone oddly conversational, "it's been a pleasant summer."

"I wasn't talking about the weather," Nathaniel replied.

Charlotte whipped her hands out of her father's grasp. She stormed over to Nathaniel. "Who are you?" she asked. "Where is the man who was so kind and sweet before? I don't understand how you can behave so abominably now after … after."

"After what?" he asked softly.

They stared at one another for an interminable moment. A small smile played on the man's face, and Charlotte was reminded of their time together, the time when she would have given anything for him to press those lips to hers. Nathaniel seemed like a different man now, a harder man, and yet her want for those lips was still perplexingly there.

His gaze intensified. "Perhaps that man you are referring to got spooked after realizing the girl he was pouring his heart out to has entertained half of the *ton*."

Pouring his heart out? So maudlin! Charlotte scoffed. "Again," she said, "I'm glad we got to the bottom of that."

"Again," Nathaniel replied stiffly, "so am I."

On second thought, she cared nothing about those lips. "Well, there you have it, Father," Charlotte said. She backed away. "You have your answer. You'll have to think up another plan, because this man clearly wants nothing to do with me. In his mind, I'm damaged goods, not fit for a wife. And I have to say, for the first time in my life, I'm actually overjoyed that someone has such a low opinion of me."

Nathaniel's words caught her just as she began her retreat. "Oh, now, I wouldn't say that."

Charlotte's hair fanned out like an umbrella as she twirled back to him. "*What* wouldn't you say?"

"Oh, I don't know …" Nathaniel kept a steady gait as he lined up opposite Charlotte's father. "I wouldn't say you're not fit for a wife. Quite the opposite, actually."

He studied her like a businessman, like she was an alpaca with a seven-inch-long coat just waiting to be sheared. "You come from good stock, come with good connections, and come with the requirement that I not pay much attention to you. A wife on the other side of the ocean is perfect for a man like me who prefers to spend the majority of his time in his office."

"Be still *my* beating heart," Charlotte commented snidely. She flopped into her squeaky old chair. Her legs could no longer be counted on. "I thought you didn't believe him, that the paperwork was false. A con to steal your money."

Nathaniel raised his brow. "I thought *you* told me he was telling the truth. Was that a lie? *Am* I being conned? It's in your best interest to be honest now. It would appear that your entire future rests on your answer."

Damn him for being right! The lie was on the tip of her tongue. This was her chance. Charlotte could tell him everything was one big falsehood and provide Nathaniel with enough doubt to drive him away for good. She would lose Wembley House, but she would retain her dignity.

But she couldn't. Because she'd seen the papers, and she believed her father. For all his faults, he wouldn't lie to her about this.

In the end, Charlotte held her tongue and prayed that she wouldn't regret it.

At her persistent reticence, her father grasped his chance. "So … so you'll stay," he stammered, and the glimmer of hope brought life and color back to his chalky face. "You'll marry my daughter and give me an heir to teach and train and continue my line?"

"And then you'll leave?" Charlotte's words cut to the quick.

Nathaniel nodded. "And then I'll leave."

The duke let out a whoop. Charlotte had never heard him make that noise in her life. "We'll have the wedding tomorrow. Oh, this is so exciting. I could have an heir by next summer. My legacy is saved. I am saved."

"Tomorrow?" Charlotte asked, her head spinning. "How is that possible?"

Her father cast his head down sheepishly. "I attained a special license from the archbishop. But don't worry, I swore him to secrecy on the matter."

Charlotte closed her eyes. "No, Father, that's not what I meant. I can't possibly be married this summer. I'm a lady-in-waiting, remember? For the tournament? All ladies-in-waiting are unmarried. They might not let me participate if I get married before the event."

The duke rolled his eyes. "It's nothing."

"It's not nothing!" Charlotte said. "I've been practicing for months. I've spent a fortune on dresses. Everyone I know is going to be there. All the connections you want Nathaniel to make are a part of it. It's not fair that I should have to forgo it just because of your desire for an heir!"

Charlotte labored for a breath. Both men were staring at her with wide eyes, but it couldn't be helped. Her entire life was thrown into an upheaval. They'd taken away her choice; they would not take away the tournament.

"What is this tournament?" Nathaniel asked.

"It's a medieval tournament," the duke answered, his sigh telling Nathaniel exactly what he thought about the new hindrance. "The Earl of Eglington is hosting it at his estate in Scotland in a month. Three days of jousting and balls and dinners. She's right," he lamented begrudgingly. "It is the event of the year. Maybe the decade."

Nathaniel shrugged as if they were speaking about a pointless musicale. "And she can't skip it?"

Charlotte was surprised her head stayed on her neck. "I told you I won't. I'm a lady-in-waiting."

"I have no idea what that is."

"That's where I come in," the duke said giddily. "I'll teach you everything you need to know to get by in the *ton*. Oh, I can't wait to get started. First thing in the morning. I'll teach you to be a gentleman, and we'll do so much shopping!"

Nathaniel's mouth drooped. He looked like he'd been asked to eat a bowlful of spiders. Oddly, that made Charlotte feel a little better.

"Fine," he snapped. "We'll get married after the event. You wanted time for us to get to know each other? There it is. And then I'll leave."

The duke shook his head like he was in the middle of a seizure. "No. No. No. No. That will not work. No. I want an heir by next summer. No waiting. Who knows what might happen in a month? I might fall off my horse and break my neck—"

"Father," Charlotte broke in. "You're an expert rider."

"I might eat something and have a reaction and keel over and drown in my soup."

"You've eaten the same things every day for sixty years!"

The duke coughed pathetically, patting his chest. "I might come down with something. Tuberculosis runs in our family."

"It runs in everyone's family," Nathaniel said dryly.

Charlotte glared at her father. "Enough. I know what you're doing, and I'm sorry but I'm putting my foot down. I will not marry before the tournament. There's nothing to be done."

"Unless ..." The duke's eyes glowed so bright that the hair on Charlotte's arms stood up. "Unless we do it in secret. Then, after the tournament, we can pretend that we had a small, intimate affair in our chapel. No fuss."

Charlotte eyed him dubiously. The man loved fuss. He lived for it. "A small, intimate affair for the Duke of Wembley's daughter? Who would believe that?"

He shrugged, nodding at Nathaniel. "Heir or not, you're marrying an American. Trust me, my friends will understand the need for no fuss. Terribly sorry," he added to Nathaniel.

"I understand completely," Nathaniel returned easily.

They all paused. The room became cloyingly silent. But there were no more words to say. All the cards had been laid on the table. After tonight, there would be no going back.

"So ..." the duke said, a heavy question in his hopeful voice. "We are in agreement, then? Secret marriage now, heir by next summer?"

Charlotte could feel Nathaniel's eyes on her. Was he looking for her approval? Why would he start now? She closed her eyes as the weight of the world crushed her shoulders.

Finally, Nathaniel nodded, slowly but achingly final.

"May I ask," Charlotte said. "Just this afternoon you were dead set against the idea. What changed your mind? Why now are you willing to go along with my father?" She laughed nervously. "It can't be just because I told you to believe him. It can't possibly be because of me."

Oh, but she wanted it to be. Here she was giving him a chance. One more chance to be the man he'd shown her in the stable. To say the right thing. To tell her what she needed to hear so that she could feel a modicum of assurance over everything they were set to do together.

"Perhaps I'm not as different from the duke as you thought. I see and appreciate beauty just as much as the next person," Nathaniel drawled in that honeyed accent of his, coming to stand in front of her. For a split second, Charlotte was certain of what was to come, and her inner self rejoiced. "And like I told you, I see potential."

Yes.

"Potential?" she said lightly. *In me? In us?*

"The alpacas," he said bluntly. "You know how much I want them."

Charlotte deflated. And for the only time, she actually saw the appeal of being an alpaca. She couldn't wait to get pregnant.

Hopefully, Nathaniel would stick around long enough for her to spit on him.

CHAPTER SIX

T HE FOLLOWING MORNING, Nathaniel lay prone on the library floor underneath a Windsor chair, his hands continually moving. It was the only way he could keep his mind from doing the same. He didn't want to think. Thinking was dangerous. He'd spent a miserable night turning the events of the previous day over and over in his head like a phantasmascope, and he'd gotten nothing but a lack of sleep.

Nathaniel would never describe himself as a reckless sort of man, nor an impulsive one, and he would bet none of his friends back home would either. And in the course of one day, he'd signed his life away like a man making a deal with the devil for the keys of the kingdom.

And the devil was known to lie. Even with Charlotte's assurances, Nathaniel still wasn't certain about being the heir. The wedding was set for that night, but he would do his due diligence first. And that meant a trip to St. Lawrence's Orphanage, where he could speak to the priests. Only then would he know if the duke's claim was genuine. Nathaniel wasn't raised with a great trust in religion, but he had to put his faith in the priests. With nothing to gain, he had to assume the priests would speak the truth on the matter.

The only problem was that Nathaniel wasn't sure what he would do if he found out the whole thing *was* a lie. Would he call off the wedding? It should be an easy, straightforward answer. It scared Nathaniel that it wasn't in the slightest. His father had always laughed at the idea of *not* looking a gift horse in the mouth. Especially if one hadn't earned it! Of *course* one should look! One must always appraise what they were given.

However, his father had never dealt with anyone like Lady Charlotte. Nathaniel wanted to do a lot of things with her mouth, and none of them involved looking inside it. And he knew a gift when he saw one. He'd be a fool not to take her and run. Title or no title.

"What in the holy blazes is going on in here?" the duke exclaimed.

Nathaniel was so wrapped up in his work—and rambling thoughts—that the outburst caught him by surprise. He launched off the floor and bashed his head into the underside of the chair.

"Goddammit!" he yelped, palming his forehead, searching for blood.

"My sentiment exactly," the duke said. His shoes came into Nathaniel's view as he stood next to the chair. The shoes were shockingly staid, black leather with a gold buckle. Nathaniel was almost disappointed. "What are you doing making all this noise? Noise shouldn't happen until the afternoon, and even then, it should be muted. My servants tell me you've been up for hours!"

Nathaniel had thought the first question would be about his being under the chair, but apparently, his early rising was of greater importance. He climbed out from underneath the Windsor, wiping his hand on a scrap of linen the servants had been polite enough to leave for him.

He glanced at the clock on the mantel. It was ten in the morning already. And the duke was just getting up? Nathaniel was a fan of some of the deadly sins, but sloth was not one of them.

"I like to wake early," he explained, attempting to right his appearance. He'd left his jacket on the back of the settee so it wouldn't get dirty on the floor, and made haste to put it back on. "There's always something to be done."

The duke cocked his head, his lips twitching as if he were wondering if what Nathaniel said was a joke or not. When he retreated into a frown, it was clear he'd found his answer. "There's always work to be done for the servants, dear boy. Not for the duke. A good duke takes his time in all things." He sighed deeply, flicking his white hair off his brow peevishly. "I wasn't going to start this until the afternoon, but I'm afraid the first of your ducal lessons must begin right away. And I haven't even had my chocolate yet."

"You mentioned these ducal lessons last night. I don't understand why you think I need them. I'm leaving, remember?" Nathaniel asked. "After I do my duty? Who cares if I know how to act correctly?"

The old gentleman cast a critical eye on Nathaniel as if sizing him up for battle. Nathaniel couldn't help but puff out his chest.

"I'll care. My daughter will care. And you're not leaving right away. You'll be in my house for the next month. There will be social gatherings and events. I will not have you embarrassing my daughter before the wedding is announced."

"You didn't seem to care much about your daughter's feelings last night when you sold her for two alpacas."

Nathaniel regretted the words the moment they came out of his mouth. A thunderous glower came over the duke, and Nathaniel tensed. The duke had every right to punch him in the face for such an insolent statement, and Nathaniel would take it, knowing he'd deserved it.

But it didn't come. Rather, the duke answered him in a chilly tone. "I care about her feelings. More than you will ever know."

Nathaniel swallowed hard and nodded. The air grew thick around them, and he looked away, embarrassed. He hadn't been admonished in a long time. He would have preferred the punch.

"Now, as I was saying," the duke continued, erasing the solemnity from his face. "Dukes do not wake early. The only time a duke should ever see the sun rise is when he's coming home after a long, sybaritic night. Do I make myself clear?"

"You are being very clear," Nathaniel replied drolly. "But something had to be done about the chairs. Their constant squeaks were putting my teeth on edge. Your servants were good enough to provide me with some hide glue, I strengthened all the joints in the drawing room, and now I'm on to the library. It's a temporary fix, but it'll do for now."

The duke shook his head sadly. "I have no idea what you just said." Quickly he put up a hand as Nathaniel opened his mouth. "And I have no wish to. I'll just pretend the last ten seconds never happened."

Nathaniel clenched his jaw, taking a seat on the settee. He had a feeling if he was going to get through this conversation, he'd need to be sitting. But even that was wrong.

"See. Right there. That's exactly what I'm talking about," the duke announced, marching toward him, pointing a ruby-ring-clad finger. "The way you just sat down. Nothing like a duke!"

"Because I'm not a duke!"

"But you will be!" he insisted. "Here. Get up. Get up. Do it again. With feeling this time!"

Nathaniel's gaze hopped all over the room. He had absolutely no idea what that meant. Still, he lifted from the settee and sat back down again, taking a painstaking five seconds to accomplish the task with intention.

The duke was not amused. "Please do not take offense to this—I'm just asking," he said, cupping his chin in his palm. "But *were* you born in a barn? It's an honest question, because your manner is positively bovine."

Nathaniel glared up at the rude man. "It's just sitting."

The duke clutched his chest. "My dear boy, *it* is never just anything. Everything a duke does is a show, a master class in how to be. It's an art form, really. Here, let me show you. Please, pay attention, I'd hate to have to do it again."

Sit? Nathaniel wondered. Wouldn't he be doing it all day? How tiring could it be? But ever the respectful student, he got up from his seat to watch the duke's performance.

The older gentleman clearly enjoyed being the center of attention and reminded Nathaniel of the peacocks he'd seen earlier idling around the grounds. The duke lined up in front of the settee and fluffed his jacket tails out grandly before … sitting.

His hopeful eyes landed on Nathaniel greedily. "Did you see?" he asked.

Thinking it best to stay quiet, Nathaniel nodded weakly.

The duke smiled. "Yes, I know you did. There's no flopping, no falling. It's a graceful movement. And when I lean back into the cushion—always a cushion—I do it like I'm reclining on my very own throne. And my legs. You must have noticed them. I let them flare out, stretching them like the entire space belongs to me, which it usually does. A duke never makes himself small. He is always the largest being in the room. Every movement has precision and intention, but it should be effortless and elegant, as if you have no care in the world. Now you try again."

Nathaniel cringed. He'd been afraid the duke was going to demand he try again. And without a doubt, he knew he would fail. It was plain he didn't understand, and he couldn't envisage a time when he would. Nothing Nathaniel did was effortless or elegant. Everything required hard work and muscle and sweat and perseverance. That was what his father had taught him. To now show work would be a lie.

"I'm afraid I really must be going—"

Before Nathaniel could finish his sentence, the duke's attention was snatched away. A dash of pale yellow fabric skimmed past the library door. "Ah, Charlotte, my dear," he called out. "There you are! Come in. Come in. I have need of you."

Charlotte was clearly not in the mood to placate him. With heavy bags under her eyes and a pinched expression, she sulked into the room. "I'm hungry," she grumbled, giving her father a hard look. "And tired."

The duke returned a pitying smile. "This won't take but a moment. I just need you to sit for Nathaniel. Show him how a duke would do it."

"But I'm not a duke, nor your heir," she replied flippantly.

"You are to be a duchess," her father assured her. "And you are exceptional, and he needs to see the difference between those to the manner born and those"—he pursed his lips at the jar of hide glue on the floor—"not."

A breathy sigh came out of Charlotte. Her obsession with having a choice was no doubt taking another beating this morning. In the end, she did as her father asked. She glided into the room, sailing past Nathaniel without a word of greeting. Moving—no, floating—to the settee, she lifted her skirts slightly and reclined back onto the cushion.

And for the first time since this preposterous conversation started, Nathaniel understood exactly what the duke meant. It was clear as day. There was sitting, and then there was *sitting*.

"Did you see *that*?" the duke asked, quite breathlessly, as if he too was under Charlotte's spell. "As graceful as a ballerina. Look at the line of her shoulders, the arch of her brow, the lift of her chin. Perfect. Absolutely perfect."

Nathaniel didn't give one goddamn about those things. All he could focus on was the cinch in her waist and how it fanned out deliciously into her succulent hips. He wanted to bite those hips, see if he could get them to move in a fashion that was decidedly not duchess-like. Would her skin taste as decadent as it looked? Would he kiss the goosebumps of her inner thighs and dream of cream?

"Nathaniel!" the duke barked. "Did you hear me? I asked if you saw the way she moved?"

Nathaniel gulped, searching for a polite answer. What he saw couldn't be expressed in polite words. "Uh ... yes ... yes," he stammered like the dunce he'd become. "She moves ... well."

Charlotte cackled—again, with that strange noise. Nathaniel could feel his ears turning pink.

"I really should be going," he said, performing a dismal bow before returning to the Windsor chair. He picked up the hide glue from the floor.

"You can't possibly be going anywhere," the duke said, sneering at the glue. "It's time for breakfast. We can continue our tutorial at the table."

"Thank you," Nathaniel replied, "but I already ate."

The duke shut his eyes, and Nathaniel was almost positive that the older gentleman said a curse under his breath. He obviously couldn't bear to look at Nathaniel and all his disappointments anymore, so the duke closed in on his daughter. "And what's your excuse?" he asked petulantly. "Since you are dressed to go out, I assume you have forsaken me this morning as well?"

Nathaniel hadn't noticed, but it was true. Charlotte wore a matching lightweight yellow shawl over her dress. Her hat was long and conical, accessorized with an array of multicolored feathers at its sides, and she held a frilly white lace parasol in her gloved hands. She reminded him of summer and the pure, heavenly feeling of lying in the grass as the sun dried you after a dip in the nearby lake. Did Charlotte know that feeling? And, if so, had she done it with her clothes on or off?

"I'm off to Madame Moreau's," she answered, tugging her gloves higher up her wrists. It was only then that Nathaniel noticed little frays sprouting up from some of the seams. She caught his stare, and her lips formed a tight line. "I have to go in for one more fitting for my dress for the Sinclair Ball. Since everyone else is doing the same, the madame asked if I could go early. I don't mind. I could do with some fresh air."

Something spurred Nathaniel to act. He stepped forward like he was at a ball and asking a woman to dance for the first time. "Might I join you, then? I couldn't ask for a better tour guide of the city. You can take me to St. Lawrence's Orphanage first if it's nearby—that way you can stay as long as you need at the dressmaker's shop."

Nathaniel had planned to ride, but the opportunity to spend time with Charlotte in a closed conveyance seemed utterly necessary. Expedient, even.

She did not agree.

Her mouth moved like she'd swallowed stinging nettle. "I don't think that will work," she started slowly. "I'm in a hurry—"

Nathaniel came closer. "Are you scared to be alone with me? Surely since we're to be married tonight, time in the carriage together won't hurt."

"Quite right. Quite right," the duke intoned. "You two should spend time together while I prepare for the wedding. Oh, dear Lord, there's so much to do. I need to talk to Cook, and we should definitely have some music, don't you think? Violins or flutes? I also love a good flute."

Nathaniel didn't have any idea what the duke was blabbering about. He could only see Charlotte, her pulse jumping at the side of her neck. Her chest expanded as her breathing quickened. Was he doing this to her? Did he affect her as palpably as he hoped? Their wedding night might be a success after all.

Yes. It was done. He'd answered his own question from earlier. There *would* be a wedding this evening, regardless of what the priests at the orphanage told him today. It was inevitable. He'd known it the moment they sat with the alpaca.

He took another step, and her eyes grew larger, as vivid and blue as the peacock's chest feathers. She brought a poised hand up to her face, covering her mouth and nose.

"Don't be afraid of me," he said softly, genuinely, allowing his teasing and confident veneer to fade away. "We can make this work to all of our benefits."

"Because of the potential you see?" she asked in a tone he couldn't read.

"Yes," he agreed readily. "That's right."

She snorted. "Not if you continue holding that." Charlotte sent a pointed look to the hide glue in his hand. "I'm not afraid, merely repulsed. For both our sakes, I hope it's from the glue."

CHAPTER SEVEN

"**A**RE YOU REALLY bringing the pig inside with us?"

Charlotte glared at Nathaniel as she exited the carriage outside the orphanage, cradling Jolly snugly in her arms. "I will not dignify that question with an answer," she said tartly.

Nathaniel released a dragging breath as she passed him, leading the way to the entrance. Despite her surly companion, Charlotte managed to appreciate the looming structure. St. Lawrence's had to be the nicest orphanage she'd ever seen. Sitting pleasantly on the corner, it was a large, handsome building made of bright red brick with projecting wings. Scaffolding surrounded the building, and men were busy working on the roof. It appeared a cupola turret was being added to the middle. It would look more like a palace when that feature was completed. Charlotte had been expecting something more like the factories she'd recently witnessed sprouting up in the city—square and perfunctory, austere in their simplicity. She was happy to be wrong.

As they made their way forward, Charlotte noticed the keystone above the entrance included a rich engraving of St. Lawrence, with the saint holding a Bible in one hand and a grate in the other.

She was just about to ask Nathaniel what the grate symbolized when he huffed dramatically and knocked on the door. "Do you really think it's appropriate?" he asked, nodding toward Jolly, whose darling tail curled up into the crook of her arms.

Charlotte was dumbfounded. He wouldn't let the matter go. She wondered if all Americans hated adorable dogs this much. "Jolly is incredibly civilized."

"At least put it on the ground so that the damn thing can actually act like a real dog. I doubt he even knows he is one," Nathaniel growled. "You treat him like a child."

"Oh! That reminds me," Charlotte replied. "I caught him relieving himself on your bed this morning after you'd left your room." She feigned sympathy. "Terribly sorry. He's quite territorial. I daresay, he knows he's a dog, after all. Besides," she went on, "I brought him with us because I thought the children might want to play with them. You know … I thought you would be an animal person, since you love alpacas so much."

Nathaniel rolled his eyes, turning toward the door. "I'm an animal person," he muttered. "I just prefer ones that serve a purpose. As of yet, I haven't found one animal in your household that does."

Charlotte smiled mischievously, stretching Jolly out in front of her. "Jolly does have a purpose," she said. She kissed his squashed nose and held him out to Nathaniel. "He brings me joy. Jolly told me that he thinks he could bring you joy as well … if you let him."

Nathaniel regarded the dog as if he had two heads and flippers for feet.

"Don't just stare at him," Charlotte admonished, bouncing Jolly in the air. "He wants you to kiss him."

"I'm not kissing the dog."

"But he'll love you forever if you do."

"I neither want nor care for the dog to love me forever."

Charlotte shrugged, and the animal's fat rolls bunched higher along his neck, making it seem as if he was wearing a Tudor ruff. "Just one kiss. I promise, it will change your life."

Nathaniel shook his head, though a smile begrudgingly formed on his face. "I think my life has changed enough in the past day. Jolly can wait."

Rustling noises from the other side of the door alerted the duo that someone was finally coming to welcome them. Nathaniel swiftly faced forward, fiddling with his necktie, making sure it was straight. For Charlotte, it was an opportunity too good to pass up. Just as the door began to open, she thrust Jolly into Nathaniel's face, where it issued a wet kiss to his lips.

"Ahh!" Nathaniel griped, jerking back. He swiped his hand over his mouth. "You are the most wicked—"

"Hello. Can I help you?" A young, pious-looking man stared at them expectantly, his hands clasped in front of him. He wore a simple black cassock with a black belt around his waist but kept his head bare, showcasing his flaming red hair that stuck out at all angles.

Before Nathaniel could compose himself, Charlotte spoke up, explaining who they were and the point of the visit. The priest's expression remained dour and rather daunting until she mentioned Nathaniel's father's donation. Then it was as if the heavens had opened, because the young man's face split wide with a toothy smile.

"Oh, yes!" he said, ushering them through the door. "I'm Father O'Ryan. I received your letter, Mr. Lawrence. Won't you please come into my office so we can speak? We'll be able to watch the children playing outside from my window, and it's always a sight that gives me joy. I suspect it will for you as well."

"Oh, don't waste your time, Father," Charlotte remarked wryly. "I've already tried. This one isn't a fan of joy."

Father O'Ryan confronted Charlotte with his withering mien. "You can wait here until we're done," he said, flicking his head at an uncomfortable-looking bench against the wall.

Charlotte opened her mouth to argue, but Nathaniel cut her off. "I'd prefer if she came along, if that's all right with you. She'll stay quiet," he added with a chuckle.

"I will?" she asked him, raising her brow.

Father O'Ryan gave a shrug and started down the hall. Feeling like an unwanted child, Charlotte clammed up and lowered her head penitently while Nathaniel sidled close to her side.

"It seems not everyone wants to be a part of your bevy of admirers," he said into her ear.

Forgetting she was a lady, Charlotte pushed him hard and hurried to catch up with the priest, leaving Nathaniel *and* his annoying laughter trailing behind.

Father O'Ryan's office could have easily been mistaken for one of the closets at Wembley House. Cramped and cluttered, it only had enough room for a desk and a couple of sparse chairs, which were both stacked with thick, drab-colored books.

Chuckling to himself, the priest murmured, "Please excuse me, Mr. Lawrence. My new office is currently under construction. In the meantime, I make do. The children love to tell me that cleanliness is next to godliness, but I like to remind them that the Lord is well aware that we are not perfect."

"So true. So true," Charlotte said sweetly. The priest didn't bother to acknowledge her as he cleaned off the chairs and offered one to Nathaniel. To his credit, Nathaniel waited for her to sit first, though he was wearing an irritating grin when he did it.

Father O'Ryan was oblivious to the exchange. He seated himself behind his desk and put on a pair of spectacles that only served to make him look younger. "I have to say, Mr. Lawrence" he began, "your father's donation was quite a surprise. Especially when we'd only just received a substantial gift from another benefactor. The Lord has blessed us, to be sure. Then again, he knows we are doing his work."

"Another benefactor?" Nathaniel inquired.

"Yes. I'm sure you noticed the roof when you came in. It's a bit of a vanity project—along with my office—but I want the children to be proud of where they live. If they are, hopefully, more will grow up to be like your father. He gave away his entire fortune; did I read that right in the letter?"

"You did," Nathaniel replied. "He split it up between many

charities, but the majority was allocated to St. Lawrence. I was actually hoping you could tell me why. He never said much about his years here, only that the priests were kind."

O'Ryan settled back in his chair, resting his long hands on his lean stomach. "I'm afraid I don't know much of your father. He was here before my time, and the priests that cared for him are long gone. However, if I might be so bold, it seemed like St. Lawrence himself had a hand in your father's charitable nature. Are you familiar with the story?"

Nathaniel shifted in his seat. "I'm afraid I'm behind in my religious history."

At that instant, a ball *smacked!* against the window. "This is new glass!" the priest yelled. He scurried up to check for any damage as several of the children hollered their apologies through the panes.

Charlotte took the moment to lean across the divide of their chairs. "Heathen," she breathed into Nathaniel's ear.

Quickly, Nathaniel crossed his legs as the priest returned to his seat. Charlotte frowned and stared into his lap quizzically. She had heard enough whispers to know what happened to men *down there* when they were aroused. Had she just done that to him?

She smiled to herself. At least something in the room liked the fact that she was around. The priest surely didn't.

"Where was I?" Father O'Ryan asked, placing his palms on his desk. "Oh yes, St. Lawrence. Well, the story goes that the prefect of Rome, a greedy man, asked for all of the saint's money and possessions. St. Lawrence denied him, instead giving everything he owned to the poor. In retaliation, the prefect ordered that St. Lawrence be tied on top of a grate and slowly roasted to death."

Charlotte lifted a finger in the air. "So, that explains the grate!"

"It appears that someone else is behind in her religious history," the priest said. "In any event. St. Lawrence had the last laugh in the end—literally. As he was roasting, he shouted out to his killers, 'I am done on this side, turn me over!'"

Nathaniel barked a booming laugh. Charlotte's hand flew to her bosom, and she gave him an odd glance. It wasn't *that* funny. For a moment there, she was worried he was having a fit.

"Well, I'll be damned," Nathaniel wheezed, finally getting a hold of himself.

"What is it?" Charlotte reached out and placed her hand on top of his. Just as she expected, he jerked away.

"It's nothing," he said gruffly, his face turning red.

Oh, this is fun. Clearly, he couldn't handle her touching him right now. Pity, since that only made her want to do it more.

Nathaniel cleared his throat. "Uh … yes … Well then, is that where he got his surname?" he stammered, cutting back to the priest. "My father, I mean. He was named after this orphanage?"

Father O'Ryan nodded. He twisted in his chair, picked an old ledger off the shelf lining the back of the room, and placed it on the desk. "As you probably know," he said, licking his finger to turn through the pages, "every orphanage is different. Father Adolphus was the headmaster when your father arrived here, and he believed that all boys that come through those doors should be given clean slates regardless of the names that accompanied them. Ah!" The priest stopped flipping. He arranged the book so Nathaniel could see it. "Here's your father. It says he was left in our care by the midwife who delivered him—a Mrs. Wellsfleet— on March 4, 1776. As you can see in the list, every child that came that year was awarded the surname Lawrence. I assume the name George was given because of the monarch."

Charlotte mirrored Nathaniel and leaned toward the desk to see the ledger better. Because the priest had placed it in front of Nathaniel, she had to lean over to make out the faint cursive. Though perhaps she might have leaned a little *too much*. She was practically lying on top of him and could feel his muscles tighten and clench underneath his clothes as the side of her breast rubbed against him.

Unable to help herself, Charlotte closed her eyes and took a deep inhale. She loved the way Nathaniel smelled. So clean. So new. So many men—her father included—doused themselves with perfume. They always gave her a headache. Nathaniel never would. Even if he stayed around longer than expected.

Charlotte heard Nathaniel make a little noise in his throat as he read the text, and her eyes popped back open. With his finger, he traced the scrawling pen that had recorded his father's arrival at the orphanage. Her conscience nagged her. Here she was playing games with him while he was learning about his father's tragic origin. She should have more compassion.

His beard twitched under his nose, and she watched as his nostrils flared. Was he going to cry? Was he overcome with emotion? The poor man! Charlotte kept forgetting that he'd so recently lost his father.

"You really need to give that pig a bath," he whispered under his breath. "It stinks. That's why you should have kept the animal at home."

Charlotte flinched back in her seat, instinctively covering Jolly's ears with her hands. Tomorrow. She'd have compassion tomorrow.

"Yes," the priest said dryly, his eyes zeroing in on her cherubic dog. "Why *did* you bring this beast inside my orphanage?"

Charlotte's armpits began to sweat. "I thought the children might like to play with him," she answered. The meekness in her voice made her ashamed.

"I'm sure they wouldn't," the priest said.

There was going to be no winning with this man.

Charlotte rolled her eyes. She returned her attention to the ledger, and something jumped out at her.

She placed her finger on the page next to Nathaniel's. "There are two George Lawrences," she pointed out. "This boy came six weeks earlier."

The priest stretched his neck over the ledger. "Yes, I can read," he said, before lobbing an apologetic smile at Nathaniel. "I'm afraid Father Adolphus wasn't the most creative man. You can see there are six Thomases from the year before. He had quite an affinity for Thomas Aquinas. It looks like the other George died just two weeks after arriving. Pity. So many babies come to us sick. The Lord's work can be heartbreaking."

"It's a wonder you can read all that," Charlotte remarked, squinting at the paper. "So much has been crossed out and written over. Not very tidy, was Father Adolphus."

She was certain that the priest's glare was hotter than the fire that had charred St. Lawrence on his grate.

"Everyone does the best they can. Food shortages were rampant at that time. As you can see," he added, "we took in more children that year than any other. I suppose my fellow priests were merely trying to keep up."

"Of course," Nathaniel said. "Forgive us."

"No, please forgive me," the priest said, grimacing at Charlotte before turning back to Nathaniel. "I'm not telling you what you really want to know, am I?"

"And what's that?" Nathaniel asked.

Father O'Ryan's eyes were large behind his spectacles, almost as large as his frames. "Clearly, you know that I met with the Duke of Wembley and his investigator. You know what they found."

"Are they …" Nathaniel swallowed visibly. "It seems too far-fetched to believe. It can't possibly be true."

The priest sighed, almost as if he already regretted what he was about to reveal. "I'm afraid so," he began. "You can find it here in the margins on the page. It gives the names of George Lawrence's parents and cites that they are deceased. Your grandfather was William Cordry, the same William Cordry who is the third cousin of the current duke. Your grandmother was Agnes Blunt. It also documents that they were unmarried; however, we now know that is not true. When the duke presents this information to Parliament—along with the wedding certificate he told me he has—I have no doubt your lineage and connection to the family will be secure."

Charlotte slid back in her seat. "I told you," she said, her tone a little on the high-and-mighty side.

"I just don't understand," Nathaniel murmured. "Why wouldn't this Father Adolphus tell my father who his parents were? He had no idea. It seems wrong, somehow."

Charlotte could tell the priest was trying not to bristle. It was obvious that men like him rarely had their decisions questioned. It occurred to her that an unhealthy amount of power probably resulted from that.

Father O'Ryan waved a hand in the air. "As I said before, when our little boys cross the threshold, they become blank slates, free and unencumbered from the sins of their depraved mothers. Only by taking on a new name can they truly start their new lives. We teach our boys that they are the stewards of their future. Only by hard work and determination can they earn their own legacy. It is an important lesson. Some believe having no past is a curse, but we see it as a blessing. Like St. Lawrence, they come to the Lord with nothing but themselves ... no money or earthly things."

It was Charlotte's turn to bristle. Father O'Ryan may be a man of God, but he was still a man, and was only too ready to place all the blame on women for having children out of wedlock.

The priest continued, "Please, do not fret over this. I understand this all must come as a shock, but all's well that ends well, yes? Rest assured that I promised the duke I wouldn't say a thing about your family until he makes it known." He flopped his spectacles on the desk. "You are one lucky man, Mr. Lawrence, but in times of confusion like this, one must keep heart and remember one thing."

Charlotte snorted. "And what is that? The Lord works in mysterious ways?"

Father O'Ryan shook his head. He stretched his arms wide before placing his hands behind his neck. "A feast is made for laughter, wine makes life merry, and money is the answer for everything. Come now, let me show you my new office. It's going to be quite magnificent. And then you can tell me when we can expect the funds to arrive. The Lord is so good, isn't he?"

Charlotte held her tongue until the priest slammed the door. Just as she'd expected, he did it rather aggressively as soon as she set foot outside the orphanage.

She stopped and stared down at Jolly's head, mulling over the politest way to say that Father O'Ryan was a tremendous ass. "He was … rather fond of himself, wasn't he?"

Nathaniel stood at her side, waiting as the carriage came around to fetch them. "Oh," he drawled, "you're just angry because he wasn't susceptible to your charms."

"You cannot be serious," she said. "It wasn't just me. That man hates all women."

"I doubt that." Nathaniel shrugged, nudging her with his elbow. "He probably just didn't approve of your throwing yourself at me."

"What?" Charlotte cried. "I did no such thing!"

The corner of his eye found her. "You sure did. Don't worry. I didn't mind."

Needing something to do, Charlotte placed Jolly on the ground to relieve himself. She wrapped her arms around her middle. "You could have fooled me. You practically yelped every time I touched you."

Nathaniel chuckled. "It was inappropriate! I felt bad for the poor, young man."

"Bad for *him*? He was horrible to me!"

"Yes, he was," Nathaniel finally agreed. "And for a few moments there, I thought I was going to have to jump across the table and punch the glasses off his face."

"Thank you!" Charlotte said, throwing her arms up in the air. "I knew I wasn't the only one who saw how abominably he behaved. How can you possibly pity him?"

Nathaniel ducked his head, expelling an audible breath from his lips. "Because," he said, "you're so beautiful it can hurt ten different ways to look at you. But it must hurt more for young Father O'Ryan. He can't even appreciate how those little wisps of hair curl around your forehead, or spend hours thinking which shade of blue matches your eyes, or even wonder if your tongue tastes like strawberries without thinking he's going to burn in hell for it. So, I feel sorry for him, even though he behaved like a bastard."

Charlotte's tongue felt three sizes too big for her mouth, and she couldn't get it to work. "It ... hurts to look at me?" she asked quietly.

Nathaniel chuckled bitterly. "Like being burned on a grate."

"Then why agree to marry me if I'm going to inflict so much pain?"

His smile was slow and lazy. "I'm not complaining. The second things get too hot between us, I'll just tell you to flip me over and work on the other side."

Charlotte burst into laughter, and she almost missed the funny look that came over Nathaniel's face as his eyes shot up toward the top of the orphanage.

She followed his gaze to the saint's engraving on the keystone. "What is it?" she asked. "What are you thinking about?"

His spine straightened. "The will."

"What?"

He whipped off his hat and ran a hand through his thick hair. "I know why he did it now. It's been killing me. I couldn't figure out why my father left me with nothing. I was worried he was disappointed in me somehow, but now I realize he was giving me another lesson. Now I know why he wanted me to come here, why he needed me to be the one to bring the money to the orphanage."

"Why?"

Before Charlotte could blink, Nathaniel grabbed her shoulders and pulled her against his chest. He fixed his lips on her so fully and completely, she had no idea he was kissing her until he abruptly pulled away.

Her hands came up to her mouth, and she blushed mightily.

"He wanted me to earn it," Nathaniel replied, smiling from ear to ear. "He knew me well enough to know I wouldn't be content until I did."

Charlotte vaguely heard their carriage stop in front of them on the street. It bewildered her to realize that the world could still move after something like that kiss occurred. "Earn what?"

Without waiting for the driver, Nathaniel swung open the carriage door and held his hand out to help her inside. With his bubbling excitement, he practically threw Charlotte onto her seat.

"Everything," he said.

CHAPTER EIGHT

"H E'S A VERY odd man. Attractive, yes. Maybe a little large, but he doesn't *seem* large. Does that make sense? His figure isn't hulking or terrifying. On the contrary, whenever he touches me, I can't help but think he's doing it honestly. He's not trying to seem gentle. He just is. I'm sorry. I'm aware that I'm going on and on, but you're such a good listener. I had no idea."

The alpaca munched its hay with large, comical chews as it continued its deadpan stare at Charlotte. She wasn't put off in the least. She'd been talking to the animal for the last half an hour and found it to be a somewhat cathartic experience. It was such a novelty to converse with someone who (unlike her father) wasn't in such a hurry to overtake the conversation with his opinion.

Charlotte shifted in her seat on the ground, finding a more comfortable position for her limbs. The animal jerked slightly, slowing its chews.

"You don't have to worry about me," Charlotte assured the alpaca. "I'm not going to try to touch you. Believe it or not, I know how you feel. People—men—don't necessarily touch me, but I can tell they want to—and usually try to when they think no one is watching. They don't particularly care if I want them to or not. It isn't about me. It's all about *their* experience, *their* joy. It's as if I was put here for their pleasure."

The alpaca bent its long neck to scoop up more hay from the

ground.

"That's why I've never been too keen on getting married," Charlotte went on. "It's so much pressure. Do you ever feel that way? Everyone talks you up as if you're some special being, when in truth you're just flesh and blood, like everyone else. My beauty will fade. It's nature. And naturally, my husband's attraction to me will likewise fade, because that's all he ever saw in me to begin with. And I will be blamed for it. I've seen it before. People talk about old beauties with disdain, as if they had a choice in aging. Women have so little control as it is that in forcing us to be judged primarily on our beauty, it seems like the world delights in setting us up for failure."

The alpaca swallowed her mouthful. Charlotte watched as the food traveled down the animal's throat and then came right back up again. Peter, the gamekeeper, had recently explained the strange occurrence to Charlotte, which involved the alpaca chewing, swallowing, and bringing its food back up again to chew more in order to digest it properly. The animals could do it up to seventy times during a meal. It was actually quite fun to watch, like following a little train moving up and down the tracks.

Charlotte brought a handful of hay into her lap and took her time, tying the ends together as if they were the threads of discombobulated thought. Each piece was a new attempt at trying to find the sense in her life.

"I don't think I could bear it if I fell in love with someone and that person tossed me aside. Look at my father. My mother died, and he hasn't been the same man since. People call it a weakness; maybe it is."

She dumped the hay on the ground and wiped off her skirt. Then she heard the rustling of a skirt and knew her time here was at an end.

"My lady," her maid, Anna, said from outside the stall. "They're calling for you."

"I know."

"You can't be late for your wedding," the maid replied softly.

"I know," Charlotte said again. "I'll follow in a moment."

Anna nodded and quickened her step back to the house, obviously not enjoying the smells of the stable as much as her lady.

With a sigh, Charlotte got to her feet, making sure to hug the wall of the stall so the alpaca didn't get spooked. "Thank you for letting me come in," she said, wading out into the aisle. "You won't mind if I come back, will you? If I need to talk every now and then?"

The alpaca blinked its long lashes. Charlotte nodded. She couldn't explain why, but she took that as a yes.

"ARE YOU SURE you don't want to wear the blue dress, my lady? It was recently made, and it does complement your eyes so well."

Standing in front of the mirror, Charlotte shook her head. Her maid sighed but said no more as she continued to do up the buttons along the back of her brown—and rather dowdy—dress. Charlotte couldn't remember how old it was, only that even with all the perfume in the world, it still smelled like the London streets on a miserably hot day. In other words, it smelled like she felt—used and dirty.

She hadn't started the day feeling this way. She'd woken up resigned, though not hopeless. Nevertheless, the mounting pressure of the evening ahead had weighed on her like a slow and steady snowfall on a delicate branch. It was only a matter of time before it snapped.

Charlotte couldn't even pinpoint when she noticed the load becoming more burdensome, although it was safe to say that the time spent with her fiancé this afternoon didn't help matters.

Did Nathaniel really believe that it hurt to look at her? Her beauty had never been described to her that way before, as if it were a torment rather than a gift. And why, after Nathaniel divulged that information, had her insides turned to warm honey? Why had it felt like every bird in the sky was singing just for her at that moment? Why had it seemed like every wish could be granted, every dream could be attained? Why had everything seemed utterly perfect?

Just because Nathaniel had looked at her with those deep, sad blue eyes and said something real? Just because he had proved that he desired her? Every man desired Charlotte. The only difference between Nathaniel and everyone else was that he would be her husband—and he would be living across the ocean.

She should be delighted by that fact. But she wasn't. Not even a little bit. Something had changed between them.

That would not do. That would not do at all.

Marriages in the *ton* were business arrangements—no more and no less. One wasn't attracted to one's husband. One didn't fawn over one's husband. That made life unnecessarily messy. And Charlotte hated messy. The sooner Nathaniel left for America, the better. Then she could move on with the life she'd always known she would have. She would be a duchess, a grand dame of the *ton*. She would rule the roost with no husband by her side to weigh her down. She would be the envy of every other woman who didn't have complete control over her own life. Charlotte would have her title, her estate, her son, and no husband to embarrass her, no husband to force his will on her, no husband to wonder about when he failed to come home at night as he should. Theirs was a perfect situation, and Charlotte wouldn't muddy it now with a giddy flutter in her stomach. She couldn't ruin it by staring at his beard longer than necessary, guessing what color was most predominant, and she certainly wouldn't put everything in jeopardy by wondering if he'd enjoyed their short, inconsequential kiss outside the orphanage as much as she had.

"Last chance," Anna said with a hopeful note in her voice. Her resourceful hands paused on the last button. "We still have time to put on the blue dress."

Charlotte studied herself in the mirror. Her long blonde hair had been swept back away from her face and secured in a tight bun at the nape of her neck. No curls framed her cheeks; no flowers or feathers adorned the crown of her head. She looked like a schoolmarm.

And it dawned on her.

What had she been thinking? Schoolmarms did not inspire lust. And lust was what Charlotte needed—not love. Lust would get the job done and provide an heir. The faster that happened, the faster Nathaniel could go back to America. Then there would be no more errant thoughts of kissing or hurt feelings. If love could break hearts, then lust would armor hers.

In an instant, Charlotte's mind was made up. She yanked at her bun, ripping the pins out until her hair fell in wavy curls down her back. Raking her fingers into her scalp, she fluffed at the tendrils until they radiated with life. Eve. The mother of us all. Charlotte needed to be as vibrant and earthy—and sinful—as the original woman.

"That took me close to an hour!" Anna whined, her eyes big with mortification.

"I'm sorry," Charlotte replied, reaching for the buttons on her back. "Quick, get me out of this. I want to change after all."

Anna hurried on the buttons, the frown still plain on her face. "So, you want to wear the blue one after all? Good choice."

Charlotte shook her head. "Not the blue one. I want the gold."

Anna gasped and jerked away from her mistress as if Charlotte was the snake in the Garden of Eden instead of Eve. "The gold dress? Not"—her voice lowered—"*the* gold dress?"

Charlotte nodded at her reflection, appreciating the flush coming back to her cheeks. Gone was the meek girl. She was no use to Charlotte. She needed a temptress. A woman of action.

"Yes," Charlotte replied, shimmying the old, used dress down her body, appreciating the dip in her hips, the undulation of her curves. "One only gets married once. Let's make it count."

"Your father is going to kill me," Anna replied sotto voce.

"My father is the least of your concerns," Charlotte returned with confidence, stripped down to her corset and petticoats. "He's no longer in control of this situation."

WHEN CHARLOTTE ENTERED the drawing room thirty minutes later, she got the response she'd been hoping for—from her father, at least. She was quite certain she would have heard his jaw hit the floor if the damn bird had been quiet. True to form, the macaw—enjoying the audience—went back and forth squawking about George being dead and what a pretty bird he was.

By his fierce scowl, Nathaniel was still the only person not used to the incessant noise. Jolly and the flamingo barely batted an eye at the loudmouthed bird, as did the sloth hanging by its three fingers on the back of the settee. The porcupine seemed disgruntled enough, though he was busy chomping on an apple underneath a chair and disinclined to react.

It was only when the macaw became immersed in whatever was going on outside the window that her father released his tongue. "Daughter!" he fumed, stamping his buckled shoes across the carpet. His blond eyelashes fluttered repeatedly as he desperately tried not to look at Charlotte's revealing dress. "What are you wearing?" he rasped. "It's hardly appropriate for a wedding."

Charlotte played the innocent. "What's wrong with it?" She spread her arms out wide and spun in a circle, making sure Nathaniel's thunderous eyes were glued on her. "I was told it was the height of fashion in France. You love the way Frenchwomen dress."

The duke's outrage toppled. She had him there. Still, not allowing his gaze to travel below her chin, he replied, "It's just cut rather low, that's all."

Charlotte chuckled. "Surely not as low as your ladies in Vienna?"

"What about the l-ladies in Vienna?" Nathaniel asked.

"You mean my father hasn't told you about his first trip to Vienna? Ask him about it sometime, along with his escapades in Barcelona, Rome, and Amsterdam. Well ..." She scrunched her nose. "Maybe not Amsterdam. I'm not sure if you have a strong enough stomach for it."

The duke lowered his head with a glower. "Amsterdam wasn't as bad as she's making it out to seem."

"That's beside the point," Charlotte went on, her hands on her hips. "I thought it was important for my new husband to see exactly what he's buying. Was I wrong?"

Her father's hurt expression stung Charlotte in the heart. Their predicament wasn't his fault—it wasn't *all* his fault. She would have to stop making him pay for it sooner or later, though today was evidently not the day.

The duke cleared his throat. He turned to Nathaniel. "I will get the priest. He's waiting for us in the library—"

"No," Nathaniel said. The vehemence in his voice made her shiver. "We'll do this *in* the library."

"The drawing room is the perfect place," the duke argued, but Nathaniel was already shaking his head.

He tossed a glare at the obnoxious bird perched on the top of its cage. "I want to be able to hear my vows." His focus then was pinned to the porcupine who was now rambling around his feet. "And not fear for my life the entire time."

"Fine," the duke answered. "Let's just get this done."

Charlotte followed behind the two men, smiling at the way Nathaniel's jaw clenched as he walked past her. She may be young, but she knew when she had an effect on a man. The gold dress was not something she would ever wear in public. It had been cut way too low, and she was in constant fear that her nipples would pop out with every breath. It cinched her waist to within an inch of its life and had enough beads and sparkles to challenge the queen's crown. Simply, it was a gown for standing out. And even though this wedding would only include her father and—no doubt—an exotic animal or two, Charlotte wanted to be at the forethought of her new husband's mind. Just for tonight, anyway.

She didn't recognize the jowly older priest who met them in the library. He broke into a fit of raucous coughs when he saw her, and Jolly responded in kind with high-pitched barks at the loud intruder.

"Is this house incapable of being quiet?" Nathaniel groused as he took his place at her side. He didn't touch her, even as their shoulders were close as they could be without skimming against each other.

Charlotte shrugged, and only then did her skin brush against his jacket. She could have sworn that he shuddered. "My father likes it loud. I think it's because he doesn't want to be alone with his thoughts."

Nathaniel *humphed*. "Well, we do not have that in common. There is nothing untoward or unsavory about my thoughts."

Her smile curved up on one side. She stared at his mouth, which was held thin and partially hidden behind his beard. "That's too bad," she replied.

Nathaniel sucked in a breath, and when her smile grew wide, he focused on her lips. She wanted to lick them, but even Charlotte deemed that too much. There was Eve and then there was Jezebel.

"Shall we begin?" the priest asked after he'd calmed himself.

As if in a daze, Nathaniel nodded, though it took him a few more seconds to rouse himself into action. He held Charlotte's arm and led her to the hearth, where the priest waited with his Bible clutched firmly in his hands. Even then, Nathaniel's touch was light—barely there—as soft and gentle as a tuft of dandelion.

He dropped her arm as they settled in front of the priest, waiting for his direction. Suddenly, all the confidence that she'd wrapped herself in vanished, and Charlotte felt the true effects of her dress. She had nothing to hide behind, no veneer to shield her. It was only her, taking the biggest step of her life toward a man she knew nothing about—not even his middle name.

The priest's voice was gruff and seemed to wobble from his jowls like a turkey. "We are gathered here today—"

"Ah, terribly sorry," the duke said, cutting in behind the couple. Charlotte turned to find him wearing a meek expression. "Since we started so late"—he threw a pointed look at her— "dinner is waiting for us. I think it would be best to cut to the important parts. We really don't have to stand on ceremony here. I'm sure you'll all agree."

Charlotte shrugged. What did it matter anyway? Even with all his plotting, dinner was still the most important part of this day to her father.

"No." Nathaniel barked the word so adamantly that Jolly's ears turned down.

The duke gave him a perplexed look. "No? Are you sure? Sole can taste rather gummy when it's been sitting for too long."

Nathaniel didn't respond. Instead, he faced Charlotte and took both her hands in his. A bolt of lightning ran up her arms at the intimacy of the action. As before, her hands were snug and hidden inside his, comforted and so very safe.

He caught her eyes and held their stare, speaking to her as much as her father, maybe even more. "This is my only wedding, and this is as true a marriage as any. I will hear it in its entirety and speak my vows to this woman, so she knows they are true. Get that peacock out of here. Don't let that damn bird in this room!"

Enamored by the beauty of his speech, Charlotte took a long second to realize that Nathaniel had changed tack so quickly and was now directing everyone to the peacock that was strutting through the entryway. Her father snapped to attention and ran over to the bird, waving his hands wildly to drive it back to wherever it came from. After a series of pecks and honks, it eventually got the hint and traveled back into the corridor.

"Now we can begin," Nathaniel said, nodding to the priest. His smile was adorably bashful as he turned to Charlotte once again. "It's not every day a man like me marries a woman like you. You'll forgive me if I want to stand here and hold your hand for as long as possible."

His cheeks burned, and Nathaniel nodded at the priest again, as if to signal that his tender words were over.

It was fortunate for Charlotte. Because she was in the midst of fighting back tears.

Her wedding was no place for emotions.

CHAPTER NINE

D INNER WAS … dinner.

Even though the duke was adamant that the sole had rested for too long, Nathaniel didn't taste it. He couldn't taste a damn thing—not the turtle soup, nor the raspberry pudding. Not with his wife sitting across from him looking like the most decadent thing he'd ever seen.

His wife. Would he ever get tired of thinking that? Would he ever hear it and not feel a jolt in his belly—and, quite frankly, much lower? She was his now, and Nathaniel would be damned if he knew what to do with her.

If she would only stop looking at him that way, then maybe he could start to think with something other than his raging balls. But Charlotte kept flickering her eyelashes at him, almost in a cat-and-mouse way. Whenever he caught her eyes, she averted her gaze, her cheeks suffused with delightful color. Was she flirting with him? It made no sense and threw him off his game. He didn't know this woman.

She giggled at just about every asinine thing her father said. Nathaniel liked her giggles—there wasn't much not to like about Charlotte—but he liked her throaty, masculine laughs better, the ones that were ugly and made her feelings clear. Her giggles seemed as manufactured as the gold dress she wore. A distraction. Nathaniel wanted the real Charlotte. Even though her dress showed so much skin, he couldn't help but feel blind as to who his wife truly was.

"Are you not hungry?" the duke asked, roping him back into the present. When Charlotte cocked one of her golden eyebrows at him, Nathaniel realized he was staring at her again. *Dammit!* She probably thought he was just another of the simpering puppies slobbering at his feet. Though she wasn't entirely wrong.

Nathaniel glanced at his plate. Other than a few bites he'd forced down, it was full.

"You didn't like the chicken?" the duke asked, frightfully disapproving.

"Oh, sorry, I don't even know why I put it on my plate," Nathaniel replied. "I don't eat meat."

The duke's fork froze in the air, just inches from his pinched mouth. "Ever?"

"No. Not for a long time."

He dropped the fork, and it pinged the plate with startling vehemence. "For religious reasons?"

"No."

"Political?"

"I'm afraid not."

The duke slammed back in his seat. "Then why on earth not?"

Nathaniel laughed, though none of this was funny—certainly not the ferocious look on the older man's face. He laughed simply because he didn't know what else to do. "I suppose I started when I read Pythagoras. He wrote a lot about meat corrupting the soul and how it made men wage war against another."

The duke scoffed. "I've never heard of such a ridiculous thing."

Nathaniel nodded. "You must forgive me. I was young and impressionable. However, after a while, I found that I felt better without eating meat—sharper, even."

"Such drivel," the duke replied, shoving a large piece of chicken into his mouth, followed by a bit of sole. He chewed it churlishly. "I don't see how you have any energy at all. Probably don't have enough to even create an heir."

"Father!" Charlotte said, the apples of her cheeks flushing pink. Finally, her practiced countenance vanished, and she glared at her father in a way that Nathaniel could truly appreciate.

"Oh, don't worry about that," he replied. He raised his brow to his wife, who turned her glare on him. There it was. There *she* was. The woman he knew. "I've never had so much energy in my life."

The duke scoffed again before taking a long sip of his wine. He splashed a little on his chest as he placed the glass back on the table. "I still think some beef would do you good. I need my heir to have a fighting chance."

"Believe me, I've got fight in me," Nathaniel said wryly, glancing underneath the table, where Jolly, the porcupine, and the tiny monkey waited for scraps to fall. "However, if I need meat, I know where to find it."

⇶⇷

THE ROOM WAS sweltering. Nathaniel stopped pacing, thinking that would help, but the sweat on his forehead seemed to only increase as the minutes passed. Where was Charlotte? Wasn't she supposed to come to him? Or was he supposed to go to her?

Nathaniel hadn't asked for that pertinent information when the duke dropped him off at his room after dinner. Now, he slumped on his handsome bed, feeling like the utterly ignorant fool that he was.

He swept a hand over his face and stared at the ceiling. Chuckling to himself, he wondered—not for the first time—how he'd ended up here. In this ridiculously old-fashioned yet elegant room, with furniture that was probably older than America, and bedsheets and drapes that were as flamboyant and finer than anything one could find at Versailles. He tried not to focus on all the split threads and minor tears. Even a little dilapidated, it was the kind of space that Americans envisioned when they thought of the peerage. Not a better class, but definitely a different one.

Nathaniel tore at his collar, unlacing his necktie and throwing it on the nearby desk. He unbuttoned the first five buttons of his shirt before ripping off his waistcoat as well, spilling it unceremoniously on the floor. He couldn't remember a time when he'd felt so nervous. The nightgown that had been cleaned and starched stared back at him from the chair. It wasn't his. He never wore nightgowns to bed, preferring to be naked. Someone had obviously searched his clothing and thought it was missing. Nathaniel wouldn't be caught dead in it, though. It reminded him of the duke as he'd stormed through the house last night, declaring he had an idea that would solve all their problems. Now the deed was done, and Nathaniel felt anything but saved. In all honesty, he didn't know how he felt.

Before he could explore his enigmatic feelings any further, he heard a movement in the adjoining room. Charlotte's room. A tentative knock sounded on the door. Nathaniel was just about to hop up from his seat when Charlotte opened it.

And took his breath away. Dressed in a white, silky robe that swept all the way to her feet, his wife entered his room as though she owned it, and him—which, he supposed, she did. Her hair hung past her shoulders as it had earlier, the long, loose curls swaying against her body like the tide on the shore. With her pale skin and her white gown, she reminded him of one of the vestal virgins of ancient Rome, meant to be adored and worshipped.

For all he tried, Nathaniel couldn't seem to find his voice. He sat there, watching her as she stopped in the middle of the room. It seemed to amuse her for some reason, his sparse things that littered the area. A solitary comb on the bureau. A book of Seneca's stoicisms on the table near the bed. The bed. Which he did not move from.

Nathaniel begged himself to stand. If he couldn't get his mouth to work, then he would have to force his legs. Slowly, he inched his limbs toward the edge of the mattress, watching Charlotte watch him with a hint of a smile.

Was she laughing at him? He would. He was being pathetic—beyond pathetic. Where had all his confidence gone? Nathaniel had no idea. It had vanished the second he saw her precious and bare feet.

That was a lie. His confidence had flown away the moment he realized that he was alone, and a door was the only thing separating him from his lovely wife.

His *wife*.

Charlotte mercifully broke the silence. "You didn't come," she said lightly, her voice as thin and provocative as her nightgown.

Once more, Nathaniel was struck dumb. How could three little words throw him for such a loop? Was it the way she'd said them—half accusatory, half shy?

Nathaniel combed a frustrated hand through his beard. "I was going to. I … I …" He drew a vicious inhale in through his nose. "I wanted to."

"You're supposed to come to my room," Charlotte said.

"Is that right?"

She nodded. "It is."

"Then why aren't you there still waiting for me?"

Charlotte shrugged, still holding the robe together with one hand just under her neck, though it was unnecessary. He supposed that her boldness wasn't as assured as she wanted him to believe. Her hands needed to be doing something. He understood that perfectly.

"I'm here now," she said. "I didn't feel like waiting anymore."

"And my wife always does what she feels like doing?" Nathaniel meant the words as a joke, a little teasing to break the absurdity of the situation. His nerves needed calming just as much as hers—maybe more. But Charlotte didn't laugh; she didn't even smile. Instead, her face wrinkled in consternation, her brow furrowing with the kind of thought that could only be dangerous.

Suddenly, her hands shifted, and her fingers poised on both sides of the collar of her robe. Biting her bottom lip, she began to mutter. "It's best to just get this over with."

And with that, Charlotte peeled off the thin garment, revealing herself—all of herself. Because his wife was completely naked. In the middle of his room. Looking at him.

Well, looking at the floor. Charlotte had tried to hold his gaze, but couldn't manage it for long. Nathaniel, for all his surprise, didn't have that issue. He could have stared at that resplendent woman forever—clothed or not clothed. Though *not clothed* definitely had its perks.

Charlotte's body was magnificent by anyone's standards. Her legs were long and defined by the kind of muscle that showed she was a woman who enjoyed a hearty ride. Her hips flared, her waist dipped, and her breasts were sure to fit luxuriously in the palms of his large hands. So many little details made Nathaniel's mouth water—the way her clavicle bones stretched along her skin to her shoulders; the way the valley between her breasts poured down her middle, pooling into the soft mound of her belly. She was both hard and soft, curvy and angular, plump and so very, very dangerous.

The fire from the hearth flickered against Charlotte's gold hair, casting a bronze sheen upon her skin. She was like a living, breathing statue, a prize any man would have risked everything to receive. Nathaniel couldn't help but feel unworthy of such magnificence. What had he done to deserve her other than possess the correct last name? He had not earned this gift, and yet what could a man do to ever earn something as startling as she? As far as Nathaniel knew, there were no more dragons left to slay.

Charlotte gave a little puff, and a tremor worked its way up her body. Nathaniel watched the enticing effect in its entirety before he thought to do anything about it.

"You're cold," he said, finally rising. He ripped the cover from the mattress and swung it around her shoulders, covering every inch of her skin. Charlotte's expression was anything but thankful, though she held the blanket in place as Nathaniel guided her to the edge of the bed.

Accepting a seat next to him, she opened her mouth to speak and shut it a few times before she actually began. "I'm sorry. Is something wrong?"

Nathaniel kept his arm around her shoulder and hugged her tight. "You were cold."

"No," she said, a hint of exasperation in her voice. "Is there something wrong with me?"

"No! Never!" Nathaniel blurted. "You just … I'm sorry …" He ducked his head, feeling like the most foolish man in the world. "You were naked."

Charlotte cocked her head. "I'm supposed to be naked, am I not? Or"—her face wrinkled with confusion—"is it different in America? Was I supposed to keep my clothes on? Or were you supposed to take them off for me?"

"No. Yes. I mean …" Nathaniel squeezed his eyes closed. Dear Lord, how could this get any worse? His words rushed out deep and gruff. "I would very much like to take your clothes off you."

Charlotte snapped her shoulders back to attention and leaned forward as if to get to her feet. "Oh, then let me put my robe back on and—"

"That won't be necessary," Nathaniel stated, tightening his hold to keep her from leaving.

"Then I don't understand," Charlotte began. "The whole point was to create an heir, yes? I thought this would be the best way, unless … unless … You don't want me … like that."

Not want her? Not *want* her? If Nathaniel stood up, he was afraid that he would terrify the poor girl with how much his body wanted her. His cock would never forgive him for all his stalling.

Nathaniel canted his body toward her, and he took both her hands, forcing her to relinquish the blanket. It slipped down over her shoulders, and Nathaniel could see the creamy mounds of her breasts peeking out. It would be nothing just to touch them, to swipe his fingertips over the downy skin …

He shook his head, gaining a grip on his lascivious imaginings. "I want you so much I don't know what to do with myself," he admitted.

"I know of something you can do." Charlotte scooted closer to him, and the blanket dropped off her shoulders completely, pooling at her hips. Frantically, he pinched the fabric up and over her again.

Nathaniel could feel his cheeks raging as hot as the fires of hell. He grimaced through a smile. "Yes, you're right. But I think it's a little early for that. We've only just met, and I thought we could get to know each other before we …" He clamped his mouth shut and nodded to the middle of the bed.

Charlotte's blue eyes were as round as pansies. "Have relations?"

Fuck. Nathaniel had wanted to say *fuck.* Thank God he'd stopped himself just in time. "Yes, of course. Have marital relations."

"Oh." Charlotte frowned. "I think there's a nicer term for it."

His heart was beating out of its chest. He desperately wanted to tell her *his* term for it. "And what's that?"

She smiled shyly, ducking her head. "Make love."

"Indeed." Nathaniel gulped. His cock twitched. For some reason, those two words from her mouth sounded even dirtier than the one begging to be screamed in his head.

He could only watch as Charlotte raised her hand and reached for him. With a curious expression, she tickled his beard, gentle and light, as if she were searching it for clues. "You married me in secret so we could beget an heir, and now you say you want to get to know me before we … make love. What would my father say?"

One day he would get her to say *fuck,* and he was certain he would explode in his pants when she did.

Nathaniel laughed uncomfortably as he shifted positions. "I'd hope we would agree not to tell your father anything that happens in this room. He seems a little too interested as it is."

Charlotte smiled. "I agree."

Her fingers traveled over his beard, and she placed them firmly against his lips. He took a deep breath. She smelled like oranges. He wanted to lick and suck and bite those fingers until she came in his lap. Was that even possible? He could make it possible.

"We won't tell my father a thing," she said softly. Her finger fell away, and Nathaniel knew he didn't contain his disappointment. "But now what?" she asked, turning back to the lonely room. "Should I leave? You must be tired. There's really no point in my staying here."

Nathaniel looped his arms around Charlotte, stopping her before she got the asinine idea to leave the bed. He fell back onto the mattress, taking her with him, and maneuvered their bodies until he lay on his back and she was snuggled up against his chest, her head just underneath his chin. The blanket skimpily covered her torso and shapely legs as they draped over his.

"There's no reason to leave," he growled as the side of her knee skidded against his cock. "Besides, what better way to get to know one another, yes?"

Charlotte nodded. Her hand rested on his chest. Nathaniel wasn't sure how he knew it, but it seemed like she wanted to touch him more. She felt restless. He realized he was holding his breath when her fingertips finally began to move. It was a lackadaisical motion at first, with her fiddling with his buttons, but it still was the most glorious sensation in the world. It felt … comfortable—which was odd, since this moment was anything but comfortable.

"And you'll tell me anything?" she asked.

"Of course," Nathaniel replied. "Anything you want to know."

Charlotte made a sound as if she was sucking on her tongue. She nodded again, and her fingers paused on his chest. "All right, then," she said cautiously. Her body went still, and Nathaniel was suddenly nervous about what was going on inside her mind. What Pandora's box had he uncovered?

In a million years he wouldn't have been ready for the question she lobbed at him. But he should have expected it.

"Nathaniel," she started slowly, sensual as all hell. He gulped. "Have *you* ever made love before?"

CHAPTER TEN

NATHANIEL SCRAMBLED OFF the bed, leaving Charlotte twisted in the blanket wearing little more than an incredulous expression. "What? Why would you ask that? Of course I have!"

Charlotte regarded him curiously. She was certain he wasn't telling the truth. It took her a while to figure it out, but it was the only logical conclusion. Either he was a virgin, or he didn't like women, and she could clearly see that wasn't the case. The bulge in his pants—pointing directly toward her like an eager arrow to a bull's-eye—answered that question.

She shrugged the covers off her shoulders and perched on her knees on the mattress. She crossed her arms and raised a brow at the poor, befuddled man. "You said you would tell me the truth," she said. "There's no shame in it. Many men go to their marriage bed having never known a woman."

Nathaniel tossed up his hands. "How would you know that?"

She didn't, but someone had to be the voice of reason here, and her new husband was much too irritable at the moment. "It's fine," she said, scooting toward him. Nathaniel regarded her like she was a lion going in for the kill. "I'm a virgin too. We'll learn together. We just have to get through it. You don't have to be afraid of me."

She reached for his shirt and pulled him forward until his knees hit the edge of the bed. Taking her chance, Charlotte threw her arms around his shoulders, plastering her breasts against his chest. Her nipples tingled at the embrace, shooting a spasm of feeling down her inner thighs.

What an odd man she was married to. On the outside, he appeared to be the epitome of manliness with his unyielding confidence and brutish behavior, and yet he refrained from alcohol and eating meat and held her with such sensitivity. Were all Americans so paradoxical, or just this one?

Even though their bodies were touching, Nathaniel stretched his neck away from her as if she was covered in a rash. "I'm not scared of you," he mumbled.

He said it to the wall, since he refused to look at her, even with his manhood jutting into her lower belly. Charlotte wouldn't be denied. She unleashed him just long enough to take his hands and place them on her hips. "Are you sure?" she asked with a sly smile.

Nathaniel gave no reply. His gaze was now pinned on his hands. She thought he might release her, but his hold increased, pressing the pads of his fingers into her skin. He looked like she had him stretched on a rack, and yet she knew he liked touching her.

"Have you ever held a woman like this before?" she asked.

"No," Nathaniel choked out, his eyes traveling up her body. When he got to her breasts, Charlotte saw pure hunger. "Never."

"Why? I heard Americans were prudish—"

"I'm not a prude," Nathaniel rushed out, kneading the flesh of her hips. She wondered if he even knew he was doing it. "I just … It's hard to explain."

"Try."

Nathaniel frowned. "I'm not used to things being handed to me. Even with my father … He started the business, but he wouldn't allow me to just take over, as everyone assumed he would. I had to begin at the bottom first, working as a wool comber before I became a buyer."

"What does that have to do with women?"

"I'm getting to that," he said, pinching her hip.

Was it her, or were his hands roving slightly behind her? He wouldn't dare palm her backside, would he?

"He kept me incredibly busy while I was younger," Nathaniel went on, "especially after my mother passed away. *Idle hands are the devil's workshop,* and all that. I never had time for women."

"Most men make time," Charlotte pointed out.

Nathaniel returned a lopsided grin. "I'm not most men."

"Oh, I've realized that." She played with the buttons on his shirt, slowly releasing a few before he could stop her. Curly brown hairs came into view, and she wondered if the hair on his chest was as multicolored as his beard. Would it be predominantly brown, or sprinkled with red and white as well? "I think most men would have taken off their shirts by now."

Nathaniel's smile fell. His neck wilted. "I hate not knowing things. I like to be prepared," he whispered. His words were soft and plaintive, almost embarrassed. "When something is just handed to you—and you don't have to earn it—something is missing."

He couldn't have hurt her more if he'd tried. Something was missing? *With her?* Charlotte had been tried and tested her entire life by the malicious vultures that only the *ton* could produce, and she had never once been found wanting. She hated to ask, but she couldn't stop herself. "What is missing, Nathaniel?" Her voice wobbled and her heart felt impossibly tight.

Nathaniel lifted his head, raised a hand to her cheek, and held her tenderly. "This has nothing to do with you. You are the most perfect woman I have ever seen."

"And yet you don't want me."

"I want to deserve you."

"Why?" she asked. "There's nothing to prove. You're leaving, so feelings don't matter. This is a business arrangement."

Nathaniel chuckled. "Sweetheart, I live for business, and this is nothing like a business arrangement."

Charlotte sighed, her anger getting the best of her. She

pushed out of his arms and left the bed. Finding her robe on the ground, she put it back on, then fluffed her hair out of the collar while glaring at the contrary man. "So, what now? Where do we go from here? You're simply going to make me wait until you're ready? For how long?"

Charlotte was losing her cool. What had happened? How had everything gone wrong so quickly? This was her wedding night. Was it so horrible for her to assume that she would lose her virginity in the process? She had expected the physical pain, not the emotional.

"Charlotte, sweetheart, come here."

"I'm not your sweetheart."

"Charlotte," Nathaniel said, drawing out the word. "Please don't leave. Come back to me."

Charlotte raised her head to see Nathaniel holding out his arms. He wasn't forcing her. Something told her he wouldn't force her to do anything. He merely wanted her to come to him. She'd been willing to do so much more only moments before. Why was this small stretch of space so monumental now?

Her shoulders bobbed up and down. "What's the point? It's been a long night. Perhaps we should try again tomorrow."

Nathaniel's jaw clenched. "No, now. I want to feel you again."

A dismissive noise escaped her.

His smile was wan. "I didn't express myself at all well tonight, did I? Here." He pulled out the chair and took a seat, slapping his lap. "Come sit, and I will tell you a story."

"I'm not a child."

His gaze narrowed. "I'm well aware," he replied gravely. If he'd said it any other way, Charlotte would have retreated to the safety of her room. Instead, the heat in his words created a tingle in her belly that signaled to her that all was not lost. There might be some life in the night yet.

Her feet were heavy as she padded across the divide, and she made sure to slap down in his lap with such force that he let out a groan. Charlotte smiled to herself. He was still hard. If she wasn't going to be comfortable, then neither was he.

"So, tell me this story," she said irritably. Surprising her, Nathaniel brushed her hair off her shoulders, leaving her neck bare to him. His fingers played with the sensitive skin just behind her ear. "We-well?" she stammered.

"Ah, yes," Nathaniel breathed, his words warm and hypnotic as he hugged her middle. "When I was growing up, I was constantly tested. My father wanted to make sure I was ready to move up the ladder. I was never treated better than anyone else. He wanted his workers to be assured that the best man would get the job, and not just me because I was his son. I had to prove myself again and again. I had to know my opponents, know my field, and always be two steps ahead. I was never allowed to rest on my laurels. I had to work harder, move faster, be better than everyone around me. It didn't take long for that attitude to become a habit, something that defined me more than my name or blood."

His fingers worked down her neck and landed on the top of her back. He tickled her in a lackadaisical fashion, and his skittering touch made it difficult for her to follow along with his words. His touch tripped down her spine, pulling the robe down with it. Charlotte let it go, and soon her front was as bare as her back. Using his other hand, Nathaniel reached for her breast, swiping his palm delicately over her nipple, back and forth, as one would lightly caress the petals of a rose.

Her lids dropped to half-mast as Nathaniel's voice hovered high above, somewhere over the sensual scene. "The point I'm trying to make is that I've always been the best. Nothing else would be tolerated. Not by my father, but especially not by me. Especially when I want something."

Illustrating his point, he plucked at her nipple, squeezing it between his thumb and his finger until the point hardened to attention. Charlotte squirmed on his lap, but he held her firm.

"Do you know the first thing I thought of when you took off

your robe? I didn't give a damn if you were cold. I wanted to fuck you. Don't tremble now. This is what you do to me. You make me think these savage things. I wanted to fuck you so badly. I still do."

Charlotte's eyes were completely closed now. She was sandwiched between Nathaniel's arms, and he was saying vulgar things that made her want to move. She didn't know how, only that she needed to.

"Why didn't you?" she asked, shocked that the words made it past her throat. Her hands balled into fists in her lap. "I threw myself at you."

"I know," Nathaniel said. He dipped his head to her ear and took it in his mouth. Charlotte's lips parted on a gasp as he tugged at her tender lobe, sucking at it with alarming need. "But I want to get it right. I need to get it right. I can't stand doing something and not knowing it was my best work. When I fuck you for the first time, I have to know that I'm giving everything to you."

His hand completely closed around her breast, and he massaged it with astonishing lovingness. It was the way he always touched her … with such gentlemanly suavity. And yet here he was using that vulgar word. Charlotte couldn't put the two ideas together, couldn't contemplate how he could be both men.

She squirmed some more, and he growled low in her ear. Her back arched under his lazy ministrations. "So how do we get there?" she asked in a purr. "How long until we get to that point?" Was she begging? Maybe. She didn't care. For a man with little experience, Nathaniel Lawrence was a fast learner. He'd already discovered how to make her wriggle.

He dipped his head and placed a chaste kiss on the side of her breast. She lowered her gaze to watch as he did it once more, just to the edge of her swollen, expectant nipple. When he raised his head level with hers, his smile was enchantingly satisfied.

"I think we've done well so far," he replied. "Though I don't think I could let tonight end without kissing you." He gripped her breast so tightly that she almost cried out. It also made her squeeze her thighs together, as if something in between them was dying to be set free.

Charlotte licked her lips. Kissing seemed so tame to what they'd been discussing. It also seemed innocently safe. She could use a little of that right now. "Kiss me, then, husband." She licked her lips once more and heard his breathing grow ragged. "See what you can learn from my mouth."

Nathaniel's face was poised above hers. "What do you want me to learn?"

Charlotte smiled, and her bottom lip skated against his. "That when you fuck me, I'll be ready—"

Nathaniel slammed his mouth against Charlotte, capturing her last word. She couldn't believe she'd said it, was almost afraid he would be turned off by the vulgarity.

Luckily, she'd been wrong. If anything, Nathaniel reveled in the depravity as he drank from her lips.

Charlotte had been kissed before, more times than she would like to admit. Some of the kisses had been taken—more like most of them—but some she had voluntarily given away like worthless fake coins at a fair. She had been biding her time, gaining experience as well as confidence. But nothing, not one of those episodes, had filled her curiosity like this one. Nathaniel Lawrence may not have been with a woman before, but clearly, he had spent some time in their company. The man could kiss.

He delved into her depths with the assured grace of a man who knew it took more than one person to create a worthwhile kiss. He measured his pulls with her own, using his tongue to mingle with hers, teaching and cajoling her to find a rhythm that worked for them together. He was sweet and playful, biting and nipping her skin so that they were smiling and catching ragged breaths when they weren't glued together. He held her tight, rearranging her body so that their chests were aligned and their mouths could cant in a harmonious blend of sensations.

Charlotte quickly became addicted to his body. Its size had frightened her at first, but now she pulled at his arms, tugged at his neck, so he would cover her as much as possible. She wanted him on her; she wanted to feel the weight of his desire and the pounding of his heartbeat, the swirl of his blood, the kneading of his muscles, the sharpness of his hipbones, the scratch of his beard. Nothing would feel like enough until she experienced all of him in one go.

But that would not be tonight. A kiss was all that was meant to happen.

"Charlotte. Charlotte, sweetheart," Nathaniel said, untangling himself from her arms. He had to say her name two more times before she decided to listen.

He leaned away from her, his hair mussed from her fingers, his lips red and bruised from her demanding kisses.

"If I don't let you leave now, I don't know what will happen."

Charlotte bounced on his lap, getting as close as she could. "That sounds lovely. Let's do that."

He smiled through a grimace, and immediately Charlotte's ardor felt like it had been doused with ice-cold water. What a horrible feeling. Now she knew how it felt to be all the men she'd casually rejected through the years.

She pounded a palm on his chest and stood up on her wobbly legs. Ever the gentleman, Nathaniel helped pull her robe up and over her shoulders. "Forgive me," she said. "You said you needed time. This was merely an … exploratory meeting."

His teeth flashed. "I like that." He chuckled. "Yes, an exploratory meeting."

"To see how we will get on," Charlotte added. "I think it went rather well, don't you?"

Not even trying to hide it, Nathaniel came to his feet, rearranging his manhood in his pants. "Indeed," he agreed. "I see a promising future between us."

"Much potential, indeed," Charlotte said, somehow not feeling foolish over this ridiculous conversation. They were like two old men finishing negotiations. She'd never shaken hands with anyone in her life but debated sticking her hand out now.

Charlotte stepped backward toward her door, only tripping twice on her feet. "I will leave you to it, then," she said, finding the tone of her voice to be incredibly odd. "Have a pleasant sleep."

"You as well, Charlotte," Nathaniel called out as she closed her door.

She slumped against the wood, no longer able to hold herself up. Emotion churned within her, ranging from confusion to excitement, anticipation to distress. Nathaniel was an enigma, and Charlotte was usually good with puzzles. What was her world if not one brilliant maze of intrigue and people pretending to be more than they were? Her father, for instance, showed one face to the world while hiding the other away. For the *ton* and all its vaunted members, duplicity was second nature.

But Nathaniel wasn't duplicitous. He was simply different. And as much as he wanted to learn about her, Charlotte couldn't help but learn as well. He was a man who needed to earn his keep. That notion was as foreign to Charlotte as Sanskrit. Didn't an apple taste just as sweet even if you didn't plant the seed with your own two hands? And did one need to kill the cow to enjoy the meat it gave? Dukes and earls and marquises and barons ... They took; they did not give. And they certainly did not have to earn their titles.

But, perhaps, that was why her family was in such a predicament. And although they didn't talk about it, other families in the *ton* were facing the same issues.

Charlotte had much to consider, and even after her head hit the pillow that night, it took hours for her to fall asleep. Her mind was too busy—busy learning and, more importantly, busy restructuring. Earning one's keep was a novel idea, after all. If Nathaniel was determined to do it, then so was she.

CHAPTER ELEVEN

NATHANIEL SPOTTED CHARLOTTE in the courtyard with her hand over her eyes, squinting toward him in the field. From his mount, he waved at her, though her return wave wasn't as congenial. It reeked of impatience.

"Where have you been?" she hollered as soon as he was within range. "I've been looking for you everywhere."

Before Nathaniel could respond, he heard hooves pounding into the ground behind him. He twisted in his saddle to see the duke coming up fast on his speckled gray horse. His color was high, and his mouth was set in a grim line. It was the fastest the man had ridden all morning.

"Where has he been?" the duke yelled, pulling up into the courtyard. With a natural grace, he dismounted next to his daughter before flinging the reins to the stable boy who had suddenly appeared at the ready like an apparition. "I'll tell you where he's been. He's been talking to the tenants! I never would have agreed to the ride had I known what he was truly about."

"I don't remember asking you to come, Your Grace," Nathaniel replied, matching the older man's icy tone. He was being unquestionably rude, but he'd had all he could take of the Duke of Wembley that morning.

And it was the truth. He hadn't invited the duke to join him. Nathaniel had, yet again, woken early, and planned to clear his head and frustrations with a ride. He hadn't intended to speak to the tenants, but he couldn't ignore them, could he? They were out and about, performing their morning chores on their patches of land, and Nathaniel had immediately felt a camaraderie at their resourcefulness. His curiosity was piqued, and he couldn't stop himself from asking questions. Simple questions of a purely innocent, inquisitive nature.

Apparently, according to the duke, that was not the *done* thing.

"My dear boy," the duke said, giving his daughter a hangdog look, "you cannot just bother the tenants with your mundane interest. They have work to do."

"I was asking about their work," Nathaniel grumbled, sweeping a leg over his horse to dismount. Charlotte's gaze went back and forth between the disgruntled men in an amused fashion.

"Yes," the duke went on, flapping his arms in Nathaniel's direction, "but they will never respect you if you do it like that. Look at the way you're dressed! It's not proper. You look like a common laborer. That's it. It cannot wait any longer. I simply have to take you to my tailor as soon as possible."

Along with everyone else, Nathaniel stared at his clothing. There was nothing wrong with what he was wearing! Yes, his boots could use a good shine, and he'd left off his necktie, but the rest was adequate and well made. Just because his coat wasn't every shade of the rainbow, that didn't make it common.

The words gritted out from between his teeth. "I don't need new clothes."

"Oh, yes, you do," the duke returned adamantly. "We are attending the Marquis of Sutton's small dinner party tomorrow night, and I will not have you making a scene of yourself."

Nathaniel scowled. He noticed that Charlotte was equally shocked by the news. "I thought I wasn't making my debut until the tournament. What's the hurry?"

The duke plucked at the white lace at his wrists. "The hurry, dear boy, is that I want others to deem you acceptable before we announce you as my heir. It's only fair to my daughter. Like I said, it's only a small party, nothing to worry yourself over. The more people know and see you, the more comfortable they will be with the future … *arrangement.*"

The arrangement. He meant the fact that Nathaniel would be living most of the year in America. He'd forgotten about that part. He'd been too busy thinking about the way Charlotte's luscious bottom had fit so well seated on his lap the night before. Christ, he was growing hard again at the memory. Why did he always have to be plagued with a cockstand when the duke was around?

He changed tack, switching to Charlotte. "Are you fine with this?"

She bobbed her shoulders. She was as buttoned up and prim as a nursery maid, but the catching of her hair in the breeze, the way she pursed her pink lips in thought, made him want to undress her right there on the ground and kiss the wits out of her.

"I suppose it's fine," she said with heavy consternation, dashing his erotic thoughts to the wind.

Nathaniel swiped a finger in the air, as sharp and dangerous as a blade. "But I will not wear new clothes. My ensembles are acceptable. I'm not a country bumpkin, as much as you like to think."

The duke planted his buckled shoes firmly in the dirt, spreading his legs in a fighting stance. The stalemate lasted for all of ten seconds before he relented. "As you wish," he said, falling back to the house. "But don't blame me when everyone talks behind your back."

Nathaniel lobbed a confused look at Charlotte. "How would I hear people if they talked behind my back?"

She cocked her head, regarding him as if he was from another time and place. "They'd say it loud enough for you to hear. They *want* you to know they're talking behind your back."

"And these are your friends?"

Charlotte shrugged. "The smaller the circle, the more limiting it is, and the *ton* is the smallest circle one can get. I'm sure it's not that different in Boston."

She had a point. Neither Nathaniel nor his father had much patience for high society, but that didn't mean they'd avoided it entirely. He'd heard viperish stories and terrifying rumors along with anyone else; he just chose to ignore them. He assumed he would retain the same privilege here. What could possibly change that?

He shook his head. His ride had meant to clear it, but now he felt just as discombobulated as when he'd woken up. And the woman he'd stupidly sent away from his room was once again in front of him with her searching gaze.

"Forgive me," he said. He tugged at his collar and realized he wasn't wearing one. People had told him London wasn't warm, and yet he was always in danger of sweating through his shirts when Charlotte was around. "You said you were looking for me?"

Charlotte's face came to life. It made Nathaniel's entire body feel impossibly light. "Yes. I was hoping you would accompany me today. Just a quick outing. Unlike my father, I don't think you have to change. Maybe put on a necktie."

Nathaniel's hand went to his throat. *Damn.* Once more, he could have sworn he was wearing one. His throat felt choked as all hell. Maybe he was growing on her. Perhaps she even wanted to show him off before the event tonight.

"Just let me wash up," he said with a quick bow. By the way that her eyebrows crammed together, he could tell it left much to be desired. He would have to work on those bows.

"Don't worry about all that. I'm sure the animals have handled much worse."

"Animals?"

She nodded. "You gave me an idea, Nathaniel, and now you will be the one to help me see it through."

NATHANIEL SURVEYED THE grim surrounding area and edged closer to the determined woman at his side. Damn propriety. There was no use for it in the East End of London.

"I have to point out, Charlotte," he said casually, disguising his growing trepidation, "that when you mentioned seeking out a menagerie, I'd thought you had something a little more refined in mind, like the Zoological Society."

With her parasol and bonnet, Nathaniel couldn't make out her expression, but when his arm brushed against hers, he noticed that she didn't move away. Perhaps he wasn't the only one wary of their environment. It wasn't like he had never encountered the seedier side of life. Boston could boast of an underbelly, and yet London's Ratcliff Highway was an unusual mix of burgeoning business and abject poverty. Smoke smothered the sky, the putrid smell of the Thames clogged the air, and street urchins and "working women" choked the arteries of the narrow road plying the tricks of their trades.

Needless to say, it was no place for a lady. Had Nathaniel known Charlotte had this in mind when she cajoled him from Wembley House this morning, he would have refused. Taking care of himself was one thing; keeping an eye on his billfold and Charlotte was another.

"The Zoological Society would have been lovely." Charlotte sniffed, peering inside the dirty window of yet another music hall. Nathaniel had counted four thus far, each more disreputable than the last. "But they only allow society members to view the animals, and my father doesn't care to be a member. I doubt they would accept him anyway. His love for animals has very little to do with science."

"Ah," Nathaniel said as he passed two ancient-looking men sitting on the ground outside what he could have sworn was an opium den. Charlotte smiled innocently at the men, and Nathaniel shook his head in wonder. If her father only knew what she was doing...

Suddenly, she stopped, looking up to the large sign pinned

above the window of another drab, nondescript brick building. *Bryson's Emporium and Menagerie,* it read it giant crimson letters. "This must be the place," she said over her shoulder, pushing the door open without waiting for Nathaniel's response.

If he thought the outside had an interesting smell, then the inside of the shop completely flushed out his senses with its unique and pungent aromas. It was like standing in the middle of an herb garden in a country he'd never been to or even heard of before. Spices lingered, and incense wafted throughout the cluttered space, giving the entire shop a hazy, dreamlike quality.

No shopkeeper came to assist them, leaving Charlotte and Nathaniel alone to witness the mysterious curiosities on their own. It was a daunting experience, since every shelf and table was littered with foreign items, ranging from exotic pottery and art to statues and models of all the various gods of the Far East. Nathaniel was afraid to turn too quickly and knock something on the floor, but there was such an explosion of newness and adventure that it was difficult to curb his eagerness. He saw the same excitement in Charlotte, who had closed her parasol and absorbed the glistening items in her purview like a sponge.

"Hello. Hello," came a jovial voice from the back of the shop, yanking the couple out of their curious stupor. "Welcome to my emporium! How can I help you today?"

A man emerged from between a set of bronze baby elephant statues and filled the room as if he was another of its peculiar curios. His head was bald and as shiny as the belly of the Golden Buddha that sat on the table next to him. He was dressed like a gentleman, with a sharp black coat and green-and-red plaid waistcoat underneath. His mustache fanned out wider than his face, reminding Nathaniel of a walrus without all of the blubber. The owner was a character and, by his exuberant expression, was well aware of it.

Nathaniel was not alone in being caught off guard. It took a few seconds for Charlotte to collect herself. "It's a pleasure to meet you, Mr. Bryson," she answered amiably. "I am Lady

Charlotte, and this is my—" She stopped abruptly as she turned to Nathaniel. Every inch of his body stood on its end as he waited for her to finish her sentence. They hadn't been married for more than a day, and yet the desire to hear her refer to him as her husband was as strong as anything he'd encountered before. He could be dying of thirst and still only ask for those words over a drink of water.

Alas, they were not to come. Charlotte blinked at him before returning to Mr. Bryson. "This is my associate, Mr. Lawrence. We have come to ask about some of your animals, but I think we might have come to the wrong place." Her brow furrowed as she twisted her neck around, searching the shop. "You must keep them at a separate location."

Charlotte's disappointment was noticeable, but Mr. Bryson's mustache only fanned wider with his gregarious smile. He waved them to join him further back in the store. "You're correct," he said, walking toward the curtain that he must have entered from. "I do have a warehouse where I keep many of my trinkets, but not my animals. My animals are never far from me. They are like my children, and I can't bear to be apart from them for long."

His hand poised on the royal-blue curtain as if he was ready to lift the veil on all the mysteries of life. Anticipation bounced from his slender body; it was infectious. Nathaniel was like a child again, waiting for the magician to lift the bunny out of the hat. Charlotte's hand clasped his, and he felt a jolt of energy shoot through his body.

Whatever was behind that curtain, they would experience it together.

"Are you ready?" Mr. Bryson asked with an alarming note of caution.

Charlotte nodded.

Nathaniel had visited a few traveling menageries in America, but nothing could have prepared him for this. The scale was beyond imagination. Behind that curtain was a connecting warehouse that looked like it could have held all the tea in

Britain. And it was filled with cages and compartments holding some of the most extraordinary animals that Nathaniel had ever seen.

Charlotte's lips parted in a silent gasp. For a second, Nathaniel forgot about everything but the way her lovely face opened up to the wonder. Stunned by her beauty, he simply watched as she took it all in. Her long lashes fanned her face; her cheeks and lips burgeoned with color; her chest heaved. Seeing something so glorious and new was one thing, but seeing someone else experience it was its own kind of miracle.

Which was why Nathaniel didn't try to stop himself. He leaned in and kissed his wife, needing to taste the fascination on her lips. It was a quick kiss, over much too soon, but he relished the surprise in her response, as well as the way she pulled at his mouth once she'd gotten over her surprise. When her hand touched his neck, he took it into his own, holding it at his side.

"Yes," Mr. Bryson said cheerfully, politely reminding the couple that he was still there, "this place does have that effect on people. Go. Go. Don't be afraid. Look around. Ask me anything. Just please don't stick your hands in the cage. We've lost quite a few fingers that way, I'm afraid."

For some odd reason, that made the couple giggle, and, hands entwined, they meandered into the menagerie like two children at their first fair, entranced and inspired by the natural world. No animal was too large or too small for Mr. Bryson. Lions and tigers and elephants enjoyed their spacious and (surprisingly clean) cages next to monkeys so tiny they could fit in the palm of Charlotte's hand. Colorful birds bathed and preened in little pools, and thick, well-fed snakes slithered behind glass enclosures that Nathaniel secretly prayed were locked tight. Horses and zebras and camels and even llamas munched oats and hay while swishing flies absent-mindedly with their tails.

They roamed the aisles, greedily taking everything in. But it soon became clear that Charlotte was searching for something, and Nathaniel finally understood why she had brought him to

Ratcliff Street today.

"Excuse me, Mr. Bryson," Charlotte called. The owner scurried over to them, passing out a few biscuits to some hungry pygmy goats in the process. "I was under the impression that you had alpacas." Nathaniel could sense her becoming discouraged. He squeezed her hand for extra fortitude. "Please tell me you have some. I've become rather interested in the animal."

"Of course. Of course!" Mr. Bryson said, turning on his heel.

Charlotte's feet lit up as they wandered to the far side of the warehouse. There, in the corner, sandwiched between two enclosures of big-horn sheep, four alpacas gracefully chomped on a mixture of grass and alfalfa. She released Nathaniel's hand and leaned on the bars of the cage, causing the alpacas to shift to the far side.

"Don't mind them," Mr. Bryson said, sidling up next to her. "They can be funny animals. It takes them a while to trust people—and other animals, for that matter. I've had to move them more than once. They don't love the sheep, but they deal all right with them. Cute little buggers, though, aren't they?"

"They are," Charlotte breathed in a low whisper that Nathaniel felt all the way down to his toes. Christ, couldn't he enjoy the menagerie without having lascivious thoughts of his wife?

The answer was a resounding no.

Charlotte straightened from the cage and squared her shoulders. Nathaniel had been in enough business meetings to know a proposition was coming. "Mr. Bryson," she said, "I would like to purchase your alpacas. I have two on my estate and would like to start a breeding program. Name your price."

Nathaniel winced. His father would laugh at anyone saying, "Name your price." One should simply declare what they were going to pay, starting with the lowest number imaginable. Then the negotiations could begin in earnest.

Mr. Bryson was obviously not ignorant to this, which was why he shook his head with feigned sadness. "My animals are not for sale, miss. As I said, they're my children."

"Oh, I see that," Charlotte replied. "And as a father, do you not want the best for your children? I have land as far and fecund as the eye can see. Your alpacas would live a grand life without cages."

"My cages keep them safe," he said. "Do you even know the first thing about alpacas? How does a fancy woman like you think you can breed them? Everyone believes they can make a fortune off their fur, but it's harder than it looks."

Charlotte's blue eyes crystallized under her dainty bonnet like she were a general surveying her opposition. "I know plenty about alpacas."

"Really?" Mr. Bryson crossed his arms.

"Yes, really," she returned. "I know they are naturally skittish animals."

"I just told you that," he said dryly.

"And I know they eat hay and grass and"—she peeked into the enclosure—"and some alfalfa."

Mr. Bryson cast a baleful eye at his animals eating hay and grass and alfalfa. "Go on."

Charlotte lifted her pointy chin. "And I know they like to spit."

"No." Mr. Bryson shook his head. "That's llamas."

Nathaniel was about to interject, but Charlotte beat him to it. "Ha! You're wrong. Alpacas do spit. That's how you know they're pregnant. They spit on the males, wanting nothing further to do with them. Smart animals, they are, I think. And when they want to mate, they kish next to the male—"

"Kush," Nathaniel corrected her.

Charlotte didn't hesitate. "They *kush* next to the male. Did you know that?"

Mr. Bryson regarded her curiously. "I might have, though maybe not in those words."

Charlotte smiled proudly. "I understand there's a lot more to learn, sir, but rest assured, I will do it. Now, as I said before, name your price."

Nathaniel groaned and stepped forward. The time to intercede had come. "What she means to say is—"

"Don't stop us now, Yank. We're doing quite well," Mr. Bryson interrupted, keeping his attention on Charlotte. He paused, chewing on the side of his mouth. "How much do you have?"

Nathaniel wanted to cry. His poor father was rolling in his grave.

Charlotte reached into her pocket and took out a small velvet bag. She dumped its contents into her palm and held it out to Mr. Bryson, who let out an appraising whistle.

Two diamond earrings, the size of English peas, glittered up at them.

In the end, Nathaniel had to hand it to Charlotte. His wife may not know how to negotiate, but she sure did know how to close a deal.

CHAPTER TWELVE

THEY WERE HER mother's earrings, and Charlotte handed them to Mr. Bryson without a single ounce of regret. Someday soon she would have to explain their absence to her father, and on that day, she would look him straight in the eye and inform him that he wasn't the only one who could spend their fortune on exotic pets. At least her purchases were for their greater good. The day he could explain the significance of the family porcupine or the sloth, she would heed his advice. Not a moment before.

Her body was weightless; it was like she was walking on a cloud all the way back to the carriage. Charlotte couldn't even be swayed by the countless dens of iniquity, nor the way Nathaniel crowded her body whenever a capricious character ventured past. The only slight ruffle in her feathers was his continued silence. Stony, it was. He hadn't even offered one peep since the sale. At first, Charlotte assumed that she'd impressed him with her undeniable business acumen. He'd thought he was the only one with a head for advancement and improvement, and she had proved him wrong.

Unfortunately, that line of thought only lasted one block. Nathaniel wouldn't even look at her. Straight ahead he stared, as if gazing at her might turn him into stone.

She tried to ignore him. What cause had he to be so angry

about? Charlotte had only followed his lead. Pound notes swam in front of her eyes. She would have a thriving alpaca farm in no time. It would be her money and her success that returned the estate to its former glory. Lady Charlotte—captain of industry, mother of alpacas … She quite liked the sound of that.

Was Nathaniel peeved because she'd stolen his idea—or, rather, borrowed it? Should she have discussed this venture with him first? Technically, her father had given Nathaniel his alpacas as a marriage gift—her sad dowry. Would he take them to Boston or leave them on the estate to live with her growing brood? Or worse, did he mean to take all the alpacas to Boston now? She hadn't thought of that. Women didn't own anything. Their husbands did. Had Charlotte just given her mother's earrings away for Nathaniel's benefit?

A sick feeling hit the bottom of her stomach. Suddenly, her brilliant plan didn't seem so brilliant. Why did marriage make everything so difficult?

A flurry of hysteria yanked Charlotte's attention away from her growing despair. "Oh, Lady Charlotte! Lady Charlotte!" A tiny fellow in a hat twice as tall as his face waved his hands spasmodically a few yards ahead of her on the street. "It is so fortunate that I ran into you. But what on earth are you doing all the way down here?"

Charlotte struggled for a welcoming smile as she heard Nathaniel mutter, "Now who the hell is that?"

"Mr. Hemsworth," Charlotte replied smoothly, "what a pleasure."

The short man bowed grandly, ignoring Nathaniel altogether. His rudeness might have been because Nathaniel was a good three times the size of the investigator. She'd only met Mr. Hemsworth a few times, and although he was an anxious sort of man, she had never seen him as jittery as he was at this moment.

Charlotte winced as he cracked every one of his little knuckles. "I called on your father this morning but was told he was out." The investigator craned his neck to look behind Charlotte.

"Is he with you?"

"I'm afraid not," she answered, trying to meet his eye. The poor man couldn't seem to settle himself. "Do you need me to convey a message?"

Mr. Hemsworth appeared pained at the suggestion, though he leaped on it right away. "I hate to ask it of you, but if you don't mind ..." He reached inside his pocket, taking out a letter. "Would you please make sure he gets this? It's just ..." His whole face turned pink. "I don't want to keep hounding him, but I did a great service, a monumental one, and he has yet to pay the bill." He leaned toward her, and she could see that the top of his forehead was soaked in sweat under the brim of his hat. "I told him I wouldn't say anything, that I would take everything I found to the grave, but he has to pay me. I don't work for free, you know. Can't afford to." He laughed awkwardly.

Nathaniel made an irritated noise in the back of his throat.

"Oh, Mr. Hemsworth, may I introduce Mr. Lawrence," Charlotte said, remembering her manners. "I think he might be the 'work' you are speaking about. It was your fortitude that found him in the first place. You are a brilliant investigator."

Mr. Hemsworth's eyes went wide as they settled on Nathaniel as if he'd just noticed the giant standing there. They each bowed, but Mr. Hemsworth became even more agitated and almost tipped over as he straightened.

"Very good, very good, then," the investigator said. He made haste to navigate around them. "So happy to see you both. Please, give my regards to your father. I must hurry. I have an appointment. Good. Yes. Um. Yes. Goodbye."

Nathaniel arched an eyebrow as he watched the man vanish into the bustling crowd. Slowly, he turned that eyebrow on her. "How in the world was that man able to track me down? He looks like he'd be afraid to question his shadow."

Charlotte shrugged, putting the letter into her pelisse. "And yet here we are."

Nathaniel nodded, taking her hand in his. "And here we are."

LATER THAT NIGHT, dinner was a somber affair. The cook was angry because she found out that though Nathaniel ate fish, he preferred to have it no more than twice a week; the duke was sulking because every time he wanted to toast, Nathaniel would only raise his glass of milk; Nathaniel was still peeved over something, and Charlotte was annoyed she couldn't figure out what it was.

She escaped to her room as quickly as possible and ordered a bath. A good soak was just what she needed to mull over her frustrations.

Her maid left the room after making sure that the tub was filled with steaming hot water, and Charlotte was just about to take off her robe when Nathaniel burst through their adjoining door, dismissing any ideas of pensive tranquility.

"Oh! I'm so, so sorry," Nathaniel stammered before giving her his back. "I didn't know you were in the middle of a … a …"

"Bath," Charlotte finished for him when he couldn't seem to find the innocuous word. She almost giggled. It was all so odd, since it was only last night when he held her breast in his hand. Was that why he was there? Charlotte blanched at the thought. From his sour mood this afternoon, she hadn't expected him to come to her. Had she read him wrong?

"Can I … help you with something?" she asked. His back broadened in response, and his head lifted, though he still didn't turn to face her. "I'm quite covered, you know. You can look at me."

He scoffed. "I'm trying to contain myself first."

Contain himself?

"I'm still furious," he continued.

"Furious? At me?" Maybe Charlotte had read him correctly after all.

Nathaniel swung around. The line of his jaw was straight and determined as he bore down on her. "You, my lady, are a horrible negotiator."

Charlotte didn't think she could have been more stunned if Mr. Bryson's entire menagerie paraded into her room playing musical instruments. With a strength she didn't know she possessed, she managed to unstick her indignant tongue. "I assume you are talking about my four new, lovely alpacas?"

He snorted.

"Well then, I have to disagree with you," she countered haughtily. "Mr. Bryson had no intention of selling the animals, and I convinced him to anyway. So, I walked away with exactly what I wanted. That would mean the negotiations went to plan."

Nathaniel raked a hand over his head, sending his dark hair out in a tufted mess. Now wasn't the time to tell him that he reminded Charlotte of his father's porcupine. She might tell him later, though, if he annoyed her enough. "You showed him your cards too early," he argued. "You could have got those alpacas for much less. Never, *ever* go up to a man you want something from and tell him to name his price! It's bad business."

"But it worked!"

"Because you were lucky!"

Charlotte smacked her lips. She hadn't felt particularly lucky in a long time. "You're just upset that I thought of it first."

Nathaniel threw up his hands, pacing the room. The man was a ball of energy, always needing to move. "*I* thought of it first," he replied testily. "You *stole* my idea for the alpaca farm."

Charlotte rolled her eyes. "You gave it to me, and now you're mad that I did it without asking you for help."

"No, I'm *furious!*" Nathaniel said, looming over her.

Without thinking, Charlotte backed away, and he swiftly ate up the space. She had no doubt this was how he intimidated many men, but his body didn't scare her. The thick cords in his neck, the vein beating in the center of his forehead, the fierce gleam in his eye—it all only made her want to fight more. Because Charlotte had spent her life surrounded by animals who blustered but had never actually hurt her. Nathaniel was just like the peacock, fanning his feathers for glorious effect to get his point across. She was not impressed.

"Why?" she asked calmly. "It was my money, not yours. This had nothing to do with you."

Nathaniel blinked. Twice. And gulped. "That's where you're wrong. You gave away your mother's earrings. Maybe ..." A faint blush covered all the skin his beard could not hide. "Maybe I would have wanted our daughter to receive those one day. Now, I will have to keep an even greater eye on you. I won't have you taking from our children's inheritance just to satisfy this drive. You need lessons in business, and I will give them to you."

Our daughter. Our children. Nowhere in that explanation was there any mention of an heir. Was that a slip of the tongue? What kind of a future was he envisioning, and when had he began forming it in his mind?

Charlotte's stomach did a little flip. Why did she suddenly feel so unbearably warm?

She closed her eyes, regaining her concentration. "You will teach me about business?"

Nathaniel blew out a long exhale as if he couldn't believe what he'd offered.

It was too late for that. There was no way Charlotte was going to let him take it back.

"I suppose," he grumbled, putting his hands on his hips. "If I must be forced to take those insipid duke lessons with your father, then you will have to listen to me speak about what I know."

"But you don't take my father seriously," Charlotte pointed out.

"Are you saying you will take *me* seriously?"

"Yes." The one word burst out of her like a volcano. "I want to learn. I want to know how to make this successful."

She looked down at her hands twisting together in front of her. Embarrassment and shame clogged her throat as she tried to make him understand. She couldn't look at him when she began to speak again.

"I know my father is relying on you to send us money, but I don't want to just laze around waiting for you to save us." Her chest tickled with insufferable flutters. "I want my—*our*—children to know that I helped earn all this for them. I want them to know that I wasn't just some delicate English rose who never found her own voice." Charlotte shrugged, locking her gaze with his. "Surely, that can't be that hard."

Nathaniel studied her for a long moment before answering. "It will be incredibly hard."

Charlotte's stomach flipped again—but not in the good way.

"But," Nathaniel went on, "I have a feeling you will do it. You are capable."

Charlotte had been called many things in her life: beautiful, angelic, heavenly, and as lovely as a summer day. But nothing compared to Nathaniel's simple words.

"Thank you," she said softly. A plume of steam rose from the bath. It would turn cold soon, but that didn't matter. Charlotte was ready to work. "So," she said, echoing his stance and resting her hands on her hips. "Shall we get started? I know it's late, but one lesson wouldn't hurt. I am ready."

Nathaniel chuckled, scratching his beard in thought. Charlotte didn't mind the laughter; she knew he was taking her seriously. In an instant, his eyes alighted and a lopsided smile came to his face.

"Fine," he said, walking next to the tub. "We'll start with negotiating. People think there's nothing to it, but it's truly an art. You want something, and you want to get it by giving the least amount away."

Charlotte nodded. "Should I be taking notes?"

"No need. I have a feeling you'll remember this lesson."

She frowned. That was rather presumptuous of him.

Nathaniel continued, "You see, the key is that you need to keep your opponent on their toes, keep them guessing and off balance. It's your job to convince him that he wants what you have more than you want what he has."

Perhaps Charlotte was concentrating on his words too much, or maybe it was the easygoing way he explained everything, but she didn't think it odd when he shrugged off his jacket and tossed it on the back of the nearby chair. Nor did she take note when the waistcoat met the same fate.

"Let's play a game," he said casually, working on his necktie. Charlotte dumbly watched him slide it to the floor. "Are you ready?"

A shiver of doubt ran up her body as he pulled his linen shirt out from his waistband and unbuttoned it to the middle of his chest.

"I … I don't know," she said, barely able to hear her words over the thumping of her heart.

Nathaniel's smile was pure rake. "I'll take that as a yes," he said before pulling the shirt up and over his head until his torso was completely bare in front of her.

Charlotte always thought she would be the kind of girl that turned away at the slightest hint of impropriety. After all, that was how her reputation remained so untarnished in the *ton*. And yet, as Nathaniel unveiled his body to her, she did not falter. She drank in his body like he was nectar and she was the industrious bee.

Calling him big would be an understatement. *Big* implied bulk and a lack of finesse and grace. Nathaniel's body type was completely different to the lithe, blue-blooded men Charlotte had grown up with. Still … there was an elegance to his design. The muscles and tendons that rippled under his skin had purpose. The white scars that licked at his forearms most definitely had stories. Here was a man who had earned this body. And Charlotte would not prohibit herself from admiring the journey.

Nathaniel raised his brow. "Now, I want something right now, and only you can give it to me."

"What's that?"

"I want to touch your body," he replied matter-of-factly. "If I tell you I would do anything to touch you, you could ask me for something wild, like the moon."

A giggle formed in her throat. "And would you get it for me?"

His stare was brazen. Charlotte felt it in the marrow of her bones. "I find that there is very little I wouldn't do for you."

Oh.

Nathaniel waved a dismissive hand in the air. "But strike that comment now. Pretend I never said it."

How could she do that?

"We will negotiate," he went on. "I will *not* ask you to name your price. Instead, I will act uninterested. I will pretend that you are just another woman in a long list, and if you say no, then I will merely go on to the next."

Charlotte wanted to cover her stomach. It felt like someone had just punched her in the gut. "But I know that's not true."

"Do you?" Nathaniel cocked his head, before looking down at the bath. "You know, this looks refreshing." His hands went to the waistband of his trousers.

Alarm bells went off in Charlotte's head. "What are you doing?"

With a flick of a button and a slip of a few pieces of clothing, Nathaniel stood before her completely naked. And again, she stared … mostly. She focused on his long legs—his lower legs. Her courage couldn't seem to lift her gaze any higher.

Charlotte had never seen a man's private parts before and, quite frankly, hadn't thought she ever would. Men didn't usually show themselves so cavalierly, did they? She'd always believed that if married couples had to be naked then it would be under myriad sheets. Americans were supposed to be Puritans! But there was nothing prudish about Nathaniel. And his rascally smile confirmed it.

Thankfully, he stepped into the tub, submerging himself in the water. It was her tub and not meant for someone for his size, but it covered all but his knees, which stuck up from the surface.

"I'm taking a bath," he said pleasantly enough, as if they were discussing the weather.

"That's my bath!" Charlotte couldn't think of anything else to say. Her mind was completely gone, and her body had turned to honey, liable to pool on the floor at any minute.

"You can have it after," he said, reaching for the soap. He took his sweet time, cleaning his sinewy arms and chest, lathering the dips and valleys of his rough-hewn skin with astonishing attention.

Attention that Charlotte no longer had.

Of course!

The man thought that he was so smart. This was all a part of his ridiculous lesson. He was doing exactly what he'd told her to do: keeping her guessing. Keeping Charlotte on her toes. Well, she was definitely that. She was quite literally balancing on her toes to peek into the tub as Nathaniel took the soap under the water to clean … there.

When he was done, he placed the soap back on the side table and slapped his knees. "Now," he said, flashing his teeth like the wolf that he was. "How about you come over and sit on my lap like a good girl and let me touch you?"

Charlotte was incredibly proud she didn't start ripping her clothes off. She'd been ready for him. "You didn't offer me anything," she said, crossing her arms.

Nathaniel lifted his chin, squinting at her. *In approval?* "Do I need to?"

"Yes."

He screwed up his lips to one side. "*One* of your mother's earrings."

Charlotte jerked back. She hadn't been ready for *that*. "You'd get them back for me?"

"I'm getting them back regardless. Whether I give them to you is up to you."

Charlotte grinned. She couldn't believe she was enjoying this. "Both earrings *and* an alpaca."

Nathaniel snorted. "You set a high value on yourself."

She uncrossed her arms and began a leisurely amble around the tub. Balancing her fingertips on the lip, she meandered around him, letting the belt of her robe fall free to the floor. She could feel his eyes on her, feel the hunger he generated spark against her skin. She was naked underneath her robe and wondered if she had the courage to let it fall to the floor again.

"If I don't, then no one else will," she drawled lazily as her robe parted. Glancing down, she could see the swell of her breasts peek through the opening. "I'm not called the rose of the *ton* for nothing. Men from far and wide have come to me and asked for my hand. Asked to whisper in my ear to smell my perfume, to hold my hand to see if it looks as soft as people say, to look at my hair to judge the shade of the yellow."

Charlotte stopped. Placing both hands on the lip of the tub, she leaned over the edge to peer into the water. Through the translucent surface, she allowed herself to gaze idly at his manhood, to openly leer at the one thing that men loved to boast about.

With a sly smile, she turned her head to him. Nathaniel was watching her closely. He now hugged the tub at his sides, and the muscles clenched and stretched his sweating skin tight.

"I turned all those men away because I know what I am worth," Charlotte said softly. "The question is, Mr. Lawrence, do you?"

Before she could blink, Nathaniel had his arms around her and was pulling her into the water. She landed on top of him, and he wasted no time maneuvering her legs so that Charlotte straddled him. She sat up in time for his mouth to crush hers in a kiss that burned straight through her skin into her soul.

With his hand behind her neck, Nathaniel stormed inside her mouth, lapping her with his tongue, taking no mercy on her inhibitions. There was a time for caution, but this was not it. All of their pent-up frustrations and confusion crashed against one another as they slaked their need.

Charlotte couldn't imagine anything more carnal. The water slapped around them as they grappled for one another, making every movement slippery, every hug slick and inelegant. She was a wanton. But she was not out of her mind. This was *his* lesson, and she would not let him forget it.

Ripping her lips away, she breathed heavily as Nathaniel turned his attention to her neck, kissing and licking down the silky path with utter abandon. When he reached the valley of her breasts, he took one of her nipples into his mouth without warning, and she gasped. It was like a lightning bolt had been let loose inside her, pinging against her walls, searching for a way free.

Charlotte clenched her thighs tight against his as odd sensations coalesced in her lower belly. His kisses were ruthless, his tongue unyielding, as he feasted on her. And still … still Charlotte found clarity in the passion.

"Two earrings and two alpacas," she stated firmly against his ear. Punctuating her point, she bit at his lobe, doing what he had done to her the previous night. It had made her want to jump out of her body. By the way his hips bucked into her, she was satisfied that he felt the same way.

Nathaniel's lips paused on her skin, and his breath scalded her. She could hear his thoughts running, hear him trying to remember what she was even talking about.

His hand traveled down her side, sinking into the water. She felt his fingers run down her belly until they reached the apex of her thighs. "Two earrings and one alpaca," he growled. His voice was so ragged that Charlotte's nipples strained further. But she smiled. Because she had him right where she wanted him.

His fingers moved once more, and just as the tips skidded across the seam of her cleft, Charlotte edged away, giving him nothing. She held his head in her hands and licked his bottom lip.

He closed his eyes and groaned.

"Both alpacas and both earrings," she repeated. She rocked her pelvis against him for extra measure. Charlotte had no idea where she'd learned to move like that. It just felt right. With him. As natural as his naked body pressed against hers.

She rocked her pelvis once more, touching his hand against her core before she quickly retreated. Until he broke.

Nathaniel ducked his head into her breasts. "Fine. Dammit," he said. "Both earrings and both goddamn alpacas. Now open up for me, sweetheart. I need to feel you now."

Charlotte didn't gloat. She didn't have time to. The moment he slid his fingers over her, it was like she'd completely left her earthly body. She forced herself to relax on his lap and give herself over to his touch. Nathaniel was tentative at first—for her sake or his, she did not know. He stroked her gently, getting the lay of her land, parting the folds of her sex with adoration.

With just those tiny movements, it felt like someone was massaging her entire body from her toes to her head, such was the way it encapsulated her whole self.

Nathaniel attacked her lips again and held her mouth captive as he finally sank one finger into her. Charlotte wanted to resist at first. The feeling was so incredibly foreign, and yet with just a few tender flicks, a couple gentle nudges, Nathaniel had exposed something inside her that she had never dreamed could exist. A welling of emotion crested as he continued the assault on her senses, filling her mouth and her core, creating a rhythm that drove her to distraction. Charlotte clawed at him, squeezing him with her arms and her thighs, sucking on his neck, begging—yes, she actually heard herself begging—for him to finish something that she wasn't even truly aware had started. She was only certain that a deed had to be done, and that Nathaniel had to be the one to do it. This was his lesson, after all.

They moved faster against one another, and the water splashed over their bodies and out of the tub. Once his fingers found the spot that made her cry out, he kept them there. He couldn't have stopped if he'd tried. Charlotte had latched on to his wrist, forcing his hand to stay between her and give her what she wanted. A feeling was there—*almost* there—balancing on a precipice of a need that was so strong, she thought it would tear her in half. It frightened her, that need. At that moment, with this man, she would do anything for it. Anything for him.

When it came—when she finally broke and burst through—Charlotte screamed with terrified delight, astonished that a gift like that feeling could be given. That it could be earned with the right amount of give and take.

Charlotte collapsed onto Nathaniel, naked, wrung dry but still wet. He held her, patting her back, shaking ever now and again with quick tremors that vibrated straight to her heart.

When their breathing had slowed, when Charlotte had the wherewithal and strength to lift her neck, she asked, "Did we both get what we want?"

Nathaniel snorted and shifted underneath her. His manhood was hotter than the water and still incredibly hard. Charlotte didn't know what that meant, but he didn't seem to mind. He returned a tired grin. "I feel satisfied, do you?"

Charlotte nodded shyly and placed her head back on his chest. She yawned while he caressed the hair down her back. "I think I might like business," she said.

Nathaniel chuckled, kissing her head. "You might be good at this negotiation thing after all."

CHAPTER THIRTEEN

I T TURNED OUT that the Duke of Wembley's idea of a "small dinner party" was vastly different from Nathaniel's. He lost count early, but concluded that there were close to fifty people mingling throughout the Marquis of Sutton's palatial home, and they all had questions about the American who had been invited into their midst.

The duke was in his element and did a laudable job ignoring Nathaniel's glares while simultaneously introducing him to all and sundry. Nathaniel didn't try to remember all the names that the man threw at him. Instead, he stayed mostly silent, nodding here and bowing there whenever the duke elbowed him in the side. He was clearly not made for the type of small talk that this crowd desired; however, Charlotte's father thrived on it. The old peer reminded Nathaniel of a snowball getting bigger and bigger the faster it rolled down a hill. The more attention the duke received, the more he craved. If a friend finished one drink, then the duke would finish two. It wasn't so much a competition between aristocrats, but rather an excuse for excess.

As the night wore on and the duke's laughter became louder and his arms waved wider and his footsteps stumbled more often, Nathaniel was able to recognize the truth of his bizarre behavior. The Duke of Wembley wasn't so much the life of the party, but rather a relic of a past one that he hadn't realized had been over for many years. From his garish and antiquated clothes to his ostentatious comportment to his old and rehashed stories, the duke was from another time and place, and the others … tolerated him. His acquaintances tittered at his jokes and afforded him the respect a duke apparently deserved, but pointed glances were made over champagne glasses. Conversations were cut short, and smiles were forced as the duke regaled one and all of better times.

Everyone noticed, and yet no one said anything. It was just as Charlotte had told Nathaniel. Whispers were made behind the duke's back—none very discreet—but his ears were too clogged with the rags of the past to hear.

But Nathaniel heard. And so did Charlotte. She, however, hid it better than he did.

From the duke's side, Nathaniel watched his wife from across the ballroom, resplendent in blue. Her veneer was as icy as the shade of her gown. Not unfriendly, not dismissive, just mercilessly stoic. She waded in and out of conversations with a dancer's agility, giving and taking just the right amount, never saying too much, never smiling too grandly, and never laughing too loud. She was a professional tightrope walker, keeping the perfect balance of propriety, countering her father's undiluted willfulness.

Everything about Charlotte was in moderation—everything except her beauty. There was no tempering that. But, Nathaniel noticed, even that was handled cautiously. When they'd left Wembley House in the carriage, he determined that Charlotte's dress was the finest that he'd ever seen, tantalizing with its delicate flounced lace sleeves and ornate flowers secured at the apex of her bosom. But now, seeing her with all the other ladies in her set, she appeared demure—muted, even.

Nonetheless, Nathaniel still had a hell of a time keeping his eyes off her. Unfortunately, so did the other red-blooded men in the room. That was another reason Nathaniel couldn't be bothered to remember all the earls, dukes, barons, and marquises parading around him, attempting to make him feel inferior with their pointless crests and ridiculous signet rings. Nathaniel's entire focus was securely on Charlotte. The only married woman standing in a sea of single ones. And he couldn't do anything about it except fume as other men coveted what was his, circling her like depraved vultures.

Three hours into the night, Nathaniel's vision began to cloud. The acrid stench of red wine circled his head like a low fog.

"For pity's sake, boy," the duke slurred in his ear, "just ask her to dance and get it over with. That will hardly set tongues wagging. Oh, damn, too late. Lord Mason has already gotten to her." The duke stumbled into his side. Nathaniel resisted him until he accepted the fact that the duke was using him as a column to prop himself up. "You have to act fast around here. My daughter is very popular and rarely alone at these events."

Nathaniel's neck popped as he stretched it back and forth. The duke pounded him on his back. "No worries; you can just try to jump in on the next waltz."

"How many waltzes are there?" Nathaniel asked, surveying the room of circling figures.

The duke chuckled. "Four, maybe five."

Christ! Nathaniel wasn't physically capable of watching Charlotte dance with four other men. He wanted to strangle Lord Mason as it was. The silly fop with the overly pomaded hair was leering at her with suggestive eyes and holding her so close that she had to turn her face to the side so as not to hit his chin with her forehead. But the worst part was that she kept talking to him! Most of the other couples on the floor maintained a dignified silence as they hit their steps. Not Charlotte. She was chirping away, more spirited than Nathaniel had seen her all night. What could she possibly have to speak about with the greasy, skinny Englishman?

"Just wait off to the side and ask her to dance when Mason releases her," the duke said. "*If* he releases her." He finished his champagne with a triumphant smack of his lips that made

Nathaniel's dismal reply difficult to hear. "What did you say?" he yelled, spraying spittle onto Nathaniel's ear.

"I said I can't waltz!" Nathaniel growled, casting wild glances to each side to make sure their conversation was still relatively private. He felt like an animal in Mr. Bryson's menagerie, caged in by a sea of curious onlookers.

"Of course you can waltz. Everyone can waltz, even Americans!" the duke replied, seeming astonished despite his adamant claim.

Nathaniel lowered his head, his frustration for the night knowing no bounds. "I never learned," he rasped. "I never thought it was important."

The duke chuckled, raising his empty glass toward his loquacious daughter. "I bet you'd agree it seems awfully important now."

IF LORD MASON lowered his hand any further down her hip, Charlotte was going to scream. She'd already stepped on his foot more times than she could count, trying to get him to stop staring down her dress. The flowers she'd strategically placed at her bosom were not providing the coverage she thought they would. Or maybe Lord Mason was more of a degenerate than she'd assumed.

Stop it! she told herself. *You must focus! The dance is almost over, and you haven't closed the deal. What would Nathaniel think?*

Since when did she care so much about what Nathaniel thought? From the moment he came into her life? Or since she rode him half-naked in her tub? Honestly, it was a toss-up.

"What could possibly be circling around in that head of yours, Lady Charlotte?" Lord Mason purred. "You're becoming as pink as one of my father's flamingos."

How would he know? He hadn't looked at her face since the music began. Charlotte glanced down. *Oh, right.* Her chest was just as flushed as her cheeks. *Vile man.*

She giggled. "I don't think I've ever been compared to a flamingo before. I forget that we have so much in common. Your father collected animals as well, didn't he? And wasn't he a member of the Zoological Society?"

Lord Mason's swarthy façade swiftly clouded over. "Indeed," he returned tightly. "My father loved his animals, even more than people. Do you know that I'm still stuck with them? One hundred and forty, all living on my estate. I don't know what to do with them. My mother refuses to let me dispose of them, but she has no idea how much it costs to feed the lot. The wretched beasts eat better than I do."

Charlotte fought to hide the disappointment in her voice. "Oh, so your mother is … attached."

Lord Mason scowled. "That's putting it mildly. She says the ridiculous things are all she has left to remind her of my father. Funny, isn't it, how she doesn't consider *me*?"

He snorted over his own joke and raised his chin as the music faded. He almost looked relieved to lead Charlotte off the floor. It appeared that discussing his impotence regarding his estate wasn't half as fun as leering down her gown.

But Charlotte wouldn't be discarded so easily, and held his arm. "I'm open for the next waltz, my lord. I had such a lovely time and would love the chance to speak more."

His face lit up. "Is that so?" He inched closer to Charlotte, tickling the hair around her ears with his wine-soaked breath. "If *talking* is what you want to do, there are other quieter places to *do it*. Places where the others won't interrupt us. Places where you won't need to speak so much, and you will let me appreciate your beauty." He played with the flowers at her bosom, stroking the petals boorishly.

Even though it felt like an army of ants was crawling up her skin, Charlotte closed the gap between them. *Keep your opponent on their toes.* "I would be amenable to more *talking*," she began, swallowing the bile rising in her throat. "If we could also discuss your alpacas."

Mason jerked his hand back as if he'd discovered poison ivy in between her breasts. "Alpacas? Who the devil wants to talk about those silly beasts?"

"I do." Charlotte batted her eyelashes coquettishly. "I hear you have three. I would love to buy them from you—for my father, of course. As a present. He absolutely adores them."

"They're strange creatures, aren't they? Every time I try to get close, they run off. They have to be some of the stupidest animals I've ever met."

Or maybe they can't stand the smell of your hair?

"Then we're agreed," Charlotte continued. "You don't want them, and I do. Let me take them off your hands. I am so happy we talked. You have no idea how happy it makes me to know I am doing you such a favor. It almost feels like we are becoming great … friends."

Charlotte let the word drop from her mouth as smooth as honey and placed her hand on his arm, pressing into his jacket with more-than-friendly assurance. She smiled to herself as his breathing grew uneven. Lord Mason's tongue appeared abnormally heavy, as if he was having a difficult time keeping it in his mouth.

Indecision and adoration took turns battling for supremacy on the lord's mottled face. After a pause, he shook his head. "I don't know … My mother would be furious with me. I don't think I can make this decision without informing her first."

She pawed him more. Lord Mason's nose hairs whistled as he drew in a breath. "It must be difficult for her. I understand," she said regretfully. "But you are the earl now, correct? For only the last four months. How exciting that must be." She straightened her shoulders as she turned to the dance floor. "I wish *I* could be an earl. Be one of the most important men in the land, so strong and important. So virile."

Charlotte felt a body come up behind her, and she immediately went rigid. Lord Mason didn't notice; he was too ensnared in the hypnotic vision she was laying out for him. However, once she heard the timbre of the voice, there was no mistaking who had joined their party.

"That sounds so funny to me," Nathaniel cut in, sounding anything but amused.

Charlotte rounded to find him standing over them, his expression dispassionate and bored. He bowed and smiled to Lord Mason, and there must have been a trick of the light, because his teeth seemed unnaturally sharp to her—predatory.

"I've heard you always wanted to be a duke," Nathaniel went on. He picked a speck of dirt off the arm of his coat and flicked it to the ground. "Surely they are the strongest and most superior in the land, save for the queen, of course."

Charlotte rewarded him with a glare before fixing her consideration back on Lord Mason. The man blinked a few times, in danger of breaking out of her spell.

"I've come to ask you if you need a refreshment, Lady Charlotte," Nathaniel added briskly.

She waved a hand, keeping her attention on Lord Mason. "Thank you, I'm fine."

"We're talking," Lord Mason replied importantly.

Nathaniel's entire frame seemed to crowd the earl. "Oh, are you?"

The clipped words snapped Lord Mason's mouth together like a steel trap. Charlotte thought the poor man shrank four inches in an instant.

Damn him. Nathaniel was ruining her plan!

"Yes, we *are*," Charlotte said, pinning him a weighted look. "Lord Mason and I were just talking about the dirty and foul alpacas that are running rampant on his estate. Did you say they bite, my lord? Yes, I heard that too, but alas, my father will not see reason. Again, how lucky you are to be your own man and be able to get rid of them."

Despite her efforts, Lord Mason continued to wilt in front of them. He slowly began to backtrack. Charlotte refused to look at

Nathaniel, but she assumed his expression was about as jovial as a box of hungry rats.

"Quite. Quite," the earl responded. "Perhaps we can speak on it some other time, my lady."

"Oh." Charlotte's spine stiffened. "Of course. This was nothing. No matter," she replied breezily. For added effect, she brought out her fan and fluttered it near her bosom, rustling the flowers the earl had so recently molested. "I just thought you were ready to make real changes to *your* estate. I've heard that about you—that you were an earl who wasn't afraid to do what he wanted. Be his own man." She cocked her head and addressed Nathaniel. "That's what really sets the English apart, isn't it, Mr. Lawrence? Our peerage system is second to none. Our lords are the successors of the warrior knights of the past."

Her smile could have curdled milk. She returned to Lord Mason. "You are not involved in the Eglinton Tournament, are you, my lord?"

"No, n-o, no," the earl stammered. "My mother didn't approve of spending the funds on the armor and equipment."

She paused, allowing his anemic words to float around them, before she worked pity into her smile. "That's right. I think I heard that. Pity. No doubt you would have made an exemplary knight. I'm a lady-in-waiting to the Queen of Beauty. Did you know that?"

"Yes, my lady," Lord Mason said. "Everyone knows that. It's all anyone talks about … How beautiful you will look on the day, that is."

Charlotte exhaled a resigned breath. "Yes … well … I'm sure I'll see you there watching in the stands with the others in the … audience."

She curtseyed to Lord Mason and allowed Nathaniel to lead her away.

They had almost made it to the refreshment room when Lord Mason caught up with them. "You're right, my lady," he said grandly, blocking her path. "We are true friends. And since I am my own man, I see no reason not to give the insufferable animals to you for free. I will have the alpacas dropped off sometime this week."

"Oh, no, no, please," Charlotte cried. "Let my man pick them up. I don't want to inconvenience you!"

Lord Mason put up a palm, silencing her. "Not at all," he stated. "It would be my pleasure. You are doing me a great service by taking over the burden of these animals. You are too selfless as it is. I will hear no more of it."

Charlotte lowered her head demurely, curtseying extremely low. With that, Lord Mason turned on his heel, stomping across the ballroom with his ego fully restored. He'd even recovered the missing inches in his height.

Charlotte waited until Nathaniel escorted her out of the room until she allowed herself to gloat. Three more alpacas! She'd have a herd in no time.

Nathaniel led her to the refreshment table and handed her a glass of punch. He watched her with a puzzled expression as she took a long drink. Negotiating made her parched!

"I know I don't have to say anything, Mr. Lawrence, though I will," she said, incapable of hiding her glee. "The teacher is becoming the master, don't you agree?"

Nathaniel's disgruntled sigh made every second spent in Lord Mason's company absolutely worthwhile. "Oh, please. That was hardly difficult. The man clearly wanted you more than he wanted the damn alpacas. It was too easy for you."

Charlotte's laugh was throaty and full. He couldn't stand the fact that she'd pulled off the acquisition without his help! But he was wrong. All wrong.

"Lord Mason didn't want me—" She shook her head as Nathaniel lifted one disbelieving eyebrow. "I mean, he didn't *only* want me. He's a young earl, and his mother has held him by the collar for most of his life. He won't sit without her telling him to. All I had to do was pull on that thread and it all unraveled."

Was she glowing? Charlotte's entire body felt like it was

glistening under Nathaniel's appraising eye.

"And the tournament?" he asked. "What is so damned special about it? For the life of me, I can't comprehend why everyone is so excited to dress up in ridiculous armor and prance around a field like penny actors."

It was so like a man to disparage what he did not know without trying to understand it first. "You don't *want* to comprehend it," Charlotte said, lifting her nose in the air. "So, I will not waste my time. Suffice it to say, it means a lot to people like us."

"And not like me?"

"Well, no," Charlotte said. "Americans don't have the history that we do, nor do they care for it. Everything over there is about what's new and big and bold and fast. Everything is moving forward. All business."

Nathaniel's slow smile sent a shiver up her back. "Ah, my lady. But I thought you were coming to appreciate the intricacies of business." He was only looking at her in that arresting way he did—when his gaze lingered just a little too long—but it was as if he'd reached inside her clothes and skimmed his fingertips down her frazzled skin. In this room full of people, there was only them.

Charlotte ducked her head shyly. "I cannot deny that I am beginning to see the benefits of our business meetings," she said, knowing full well her chest was as red as her face again. Unlike Lord Mason, Nathaniel did not leer. He didn't even gloat. His expression was soft and pensive, like he was as bashful about their nighttime escapades as she was.

He reached out and took the punch glass away from Charlotte, placing it on the table next to them. "I think I'm done with this party," he said. "I find I am in the mood to teach."

Charlotte's legs almost went out from under her. Her pulse was beating wildly, but she could only feel it in her inner thighs. She wanted him to feel it there as well.

"It's still early," she said, biting her lower lip through her smile.

"But you're married to an American now," he replied. "We

are early to bed and early to rise."

Charlotte *tsked*. "And what would my poor father have to say about that?"

"Not a damn thing if all my 'rising' produces an heir."

Charlotte hid her face behind her fan. Such talk! She was well versed in polite flirting, but this was on a whole other level. She absolutely loved it.

Nathaniel was obviously proud of himself as well. He gave her a true smile that managed to change his entire façade. His cheeks bulged high and red above his beard, and his blue eyes shone like polished jewels.

It was only now that Charlotte realized how badly she'd treated Lord Mason. When she'd batted her eyelashes, the poor earl had no chance. She was in the same predicament with Nathaniel. Like a moth to a flame, she was drawn to him, completely dazzled by his true self. And ready to throw caution to the wind and leave the party with him. Why not? It would go on without her, as parties always did.

A crash of glass sounded from across the room. Charlotte jerked her head toward the disturbance to see men storming to the far wall coming to another man's aid. In a sea of black coats, it didn't take Charlotte long to find her father's deep purple in the middle of it all. Lodged between friends, he was mumbling incoherent nonsense as a couple of the servants knelt in front of him, cleaning up the mess of his broken drink. Onlookers snickered at the duke's slovenly behavior, but no one did a thing to take the man away from the party. Instead, the Marquis of Sutton made a special motion of bringing her father another drink as if he was presenting Excalibur to King Arthur himself.

Tiredness enveloped Charlotte. And like she'd been caught in the rain wearing nothing but her chemise, she felt heavy and overburdened, with no shelter to be found.

Nathaniel draped her hand over his arm. "Let's get your father and go," he whispered.

Charlotte shook her head, already knowing how this night

would play out—how it always played out. "No," she replied flatly. "He won't leave yet, and if you try to make him, he'll make a scene." She took a fortifying breath and masked her face with a pleasant smile. "You go. I'll wait for him. Besides, there's so much dancing left, and people will talk if I leave."

Nathaniel frowned, casting a dark glare around the room. "Who cares if they—"

"I care," she cut in sharply. "You don't understand."

"You keep saying that," Nathaniel said, his voice edged with hurt. "Make me understand."

The duke's cackle rained loudly over the room. The broken glass had been forgotten. He was back in form. From the corner of her eye, Charlotte saw him sling an arm around the Marquis of Sutton and retreat unsteadily back into the ballroom.

"I have to stay," she said. It wasn't an explanation, and it wasn't what she'd meant to say, but it was all she could get out.

Nathaniel continued to stare at her. Under his scrutiny, she felt like one of Mr. Bryson's caged animals.

"I can't leave him like this," she went on. "I can't leave here letting everyone remember him like this."

Nathaniel shook his head. "But what can you possibly—"

A gentleman cut in. "Lady Charlotte, I hear the waltz starting up again. I do believe it's my lucky turn?"

Charlotte knew she should feel relief at that moment as Lord Jerginson appeared next to her side. His youth and excitement to dance with her were no match for the caution he should have felt interrupting Nathaniel. But all she felt was defeat. There were no winners tonight.

She swallowed her hurt and gave him her hand. "If you'll excuse me," she told Nathaniel before her partner whisked her out of the room. "I have responsibilities."

She wanted to say it again, but she didn't: *You wouldn't understand.*

CHAPTER FOURTEEN

LATER THAT NIGHT, Nathaniel found himself back in the stables. He crouched in the stall, scooting his feet closer to the alpaca in the corner. The animal's eyes were closed, but its breathing was fast and loud, leading Nathaniel to believe that it was only biding its time. She wasn't ready for him yet.

Still … Nathaniel held his hand above the sweet girl's back, hoping that she'd finally allow him to pet her. He didn't know why he needed it so much. He'd gone out to the stables every night since he moved into the duke's home, and every night the alpaca had rebuffed him. Nathaniel felt rebuffed by everyone tonight. He didn't think he could take any more.

He was close. So close. Lowering his hand, he could make out the long, scruffy fibers that stuck out from the rest of the fur. This show of trust would do so much for his flagging confidence. Holding his breath, he shuffled his feet closer. But then there was a twitch. The alpaca shuddered and pitched its ears away from its wooly face, and its eyes burst open.

However, it didn't bolt. It didn't even stand. Its whole frame went tense as Charlotte appeared at the stall's entrance, still in her blue gown and fancy slippers, looking as worn out as Nathaniel felt.

She folded her arms and leaned against the stall's entrance, a tired half-smile on her face. "You weren't in your room."

"I'm here." To Nathaniel, it should have felt silly, stating the obvious, but since something needed to be said, it seemed like the safest option.

Charlotte nodded and came into the stall. Her movements were quiet and plaintive as she took a seat opposite the alpaca, who accepted all this with only a slight shift in its position on the floor. "Make any progress?" she asked, nodding to the animal.

Nathaniel lowered his hand back to his side, giving the animal the space it craved. "I thought so," he admitted gruffly. "Though not as much as I wanted. She's still wary of me."

"Give her time," Charlotte replied. "She'll trust you."

"Will she?"

Charlotte's gaze flickered to the ground. She picked up a long piece of hay and wound it around her finger. "My father wasn't always like this," she said softly, twisting the hay around and around until the tip of her finger turned pink. "The servants told me he got worse after my mother died. He was always a reckless spender, someone who obeyed his wants like a gluttonous child. But I suppose my mother had a calming influence on him." She lifted her eyes to meet his. "Unlike me. He never listens to me. He never listens to anyone. He drinks and dances and falls out of carriages and then forgets it all the next day. He's not a glutton—I don't believe so, anyway. He's just … sad, lonely, and has these energetic fits. So, he buys things thinking it will make him feel better."

Nathaniel's heart hurt for the little girl who must have grown up so isolated in this gigantic house. Nathaniel had also grown up without a sibling, but his father kept him at the office so much that for the longest time, he believed the workers were his cousins. Lawrence Textiles had been his family. Charlotte had the animals, but other than Jolly, none of them could speak her language.

"How do you cope, Charlotte? What makes you feel better?" he asked.

A corner of her mouth crept up, and the dimple in her cheek appeared. "When people are looking at me and not him. It's the one good thing about my beauty. When I'm in the center of a room, dancing or laughing, I can command all eyes. And for a moment, one moment, those people can forget about my father's embarrassing antics and remember that Wembley House used to be a place of honor, a home of one of the oldest lines in this county."

"You would have made a fine duke."

"Yes," she agreed. "I would have."

Nathaniel laid his head against the wood, bending one knee into his chest. His wife's unflinching persona was beginning to make sense. He'd thought her proud at first—maybe a little aloof. However, it was much deeper than that. The perfect rose persona was a mask she wore for necessity. She was just as much of a character as her father, only she understood that she was actually playing a part.

"So that is that why you stayed?" he asked. "To draw attention away from him?"

Charlotte shrugged, tossing the hay back with the rest. "I suppose. It's not hard. People have always appreciated looking at me, so I allow myself to be available. For better or worse, these people are our friends, our circle. You may leave in a few months, but I am stuck with them. My child is stuck with their children. My father might not be able to control himself, but I can, and I will uphold my family's honor till the day my child can do it for me."

Nathaniel blew air out of his teeth. "That's a heavy load. Some might say too heavy."

"Not me."

She was speaking the truth. Nothing was too heavy for this woman who had been subjected to burdens for most of her life. She ran Wembley House. She managed her father. And now she was dealing with him.

Only, Nathaniel didn't want to be another burden. He didn't want his visits to be something that Charlotte had to deal with, nor did he want his leaving for America to be something she had to continually explain. He didn't want to stay in England, but the idea of a whole ocean between them seemed unconscionable. Something had to break, but they were both hellbent on being strong.

"Is she pregnant?" Charlotte asked, interrupting his thoughts.

Nathaniel blinked a few times before scrutinizing the alpaca. "I haven't had a chance to see her with the male yet, but I think it's probably the case. Peter, your gamekeeper, informed me she's much bigger than she used to be and eating more than before. He suspects we can expect a baby at any time."

Charlotte's expression was positively effervescent. Suddenly, he had an urge to kiss her, knowing full well that he would be able to find out what happiness tasted like.

"Splendid," she said. "I can't wait."

"Nor I," he said, staring at his wife.

Charlotte yawned. "I should go," she said, climbing up from her seat. She dusted the hay from her skirts before casting a hesitant look his way. "Will you … will I see you tonight … later?"

Nathaniel's stomach flipped at the hopefulness in her voice. But something stopped him. Something told him that he would be sitting in that stall for hours to come. His mind was too busy for anything else. "I don't think so," he returned. "Not tonight."

"Ah," she said quickly with a perfunctory nod. "Of course. Have a good night, then, Nathaniel."

"You as well, Charlotte."

She smiled, but her mask was back in place, and Nathaniel felt like a stranger again. Charlotte started for the door but turned back toward the alpaca. Reaching out, she caressed the animal's ear. "And congratulations to you, my little dear. I'm sure you'll make a wonderful mother."

With that, Charlotte left, not noticing Nathaniel's mouth as it dropped open or the way the alpaca watched her go, with stars of trust in its little eyes.

THE DUKE OF Wembley opened one bloodshot eye. "Christ on a cross!" he screamed, rolling out of his bed, landing with a *thump!* on the chilly floor. "What the hell are you doing in my room at this hour?"

With his hands clasped behind his back, Nathaniel waited patiently for the blustering to end before he answered. It took longer than he anticipated. "I need your help."

"Ha!" the duke responded, staggering to his feet. He righted the limp cap on his head. "I've been trying to give you help for days, and all you do is throw it back in my face. What's so important now that you have to wake me from my sleep?"

Nathaniel issued a long sigh. He hadn't woken the duke. He'd wanted to—badly—but had simply been standing in the room for the past fifteen minutes. He *had* been biding his time in the drawing room; however, that infernal, loudmouthed bird drove him swiftly away. It was for the best. The duke's room was private. And Nathaniel needed privacy.

"I apologize if I haven't given you the right amount of respect or appreciation regarding your lessons," he said, only receiving a rude snort in response. "However, I would like to rectify that."

The duke wiped a tired, pathetic hand over his lined face. The youthful morning sun was no friend to the old. "I believe the initial lesson that I gave you was to sleep in and stop bothering the staff. You have a young wife and an heir to produce. Something tells me you're not focusing on your first ducal duty. Why is that?" Without waiting for an answer, the duke swiveled his head in all directions. "There. Over there," he said, nodding to something behind Nathaniel. "Hand me that glass. I'm parched."

Nathaniel didn't budge. He knew what was in that glass, and he couldn't risk it. "I need you sober this morning."

The duke was incredulous. "I'm sober every morning. Well … most mornings … The majority of some mornings." His shoulders sank. "Listen, boy, I don't remark on your odd drinking habits, so you better not start remarking on mine. It's not your place."

Nathaniel yearned to point out that the duke most definitely did whine about his non-drinking habits at every chance, but decided now wasn't the time. "I need you to teach me how to dance."

"Dance, you say?" The duke's eyes gleamed with knowing. "You didn't appreciate all those men pawing on your wife last night, did you?" His cackling ended in a phlegmy coughing fit. He wiped his mouth with his sleeve. "You should just get used to it, dear boy. Your wife will always have plenty of attention—especially with a husband who can't be bothered to live in the same country."

The duke was baiting him. Nathaniel knew it. And it was working. "I don't think you want to speak about the attention my wife receives."

"What does that mean?"

"It means she receives plenty because of you—and none of it is good." Nathaniel went on as the older man stewed in his words. "You drink and act the fool at those parties and have no care what it does to Charlotte. I won't be a source of embarrassment for her. I may leave, but I won't desert her to those cruel whispers as you do—"

"You have no idea what you're talking about!"

"Oh, don't I?" Nathaniel retorted gently. "Tell me one thing about last night. Just one. Is there anything you remember?" As the duke remained silent, Nathaniel laughed bitterly. "Here, let me make it easy for you. What color was your daughter's dress last night? Any man there could wake up and tell me the answer. Let's see if you can."

The duke punched his hands into the mattress. As the seconds ticked on, his face became redder and redder. "What does it matter if I can't remember?" he exploded. "She knows I love her; she knows everything I do is for her. I found *you* so that she could stay here and be the duchess she deserves to be. I am not a monster!"

"I never said you're a monster," Nathaniel replied. Perhaps he should have waited for the duke to have his morning tea, even if it was usually laced with alcohol; this wasn't going as smoothly as he'd planned. "I was just explaining why I need your help. When the time comes, I don't wish to be someone she's constantly answering for. I don't want her to be a source of gossip and ridicule."

The duke scoffed. "People don't gossip about dukes and duchesses." When he saw Nathaniel raise his brow, he rolled his eyes. "Well … it doesn't matter if they do. Dukes and duchesses are beyond such petty slights. They are above it."

Nathaniel pressed his lips tightly together. "Are you?"

"Of course I am!"

"Then why didn't you petition the queen about the title? Why didn't you do as Charlotte begged and ask the queen to reconsider the line of succession? You didn't have to find me. I never would have known about the blood between us."

"Because I already know what the answer would be!" the duke lamented. "Charlotte is only a woman—"

"A smart, capable woman."

"—who shouldn't be burdened with the running of the estate! It's hellish, believe me. The accounts, the managers, the properties." He rubbed his hands furiously over his face. "Money. Money. Always having to make sure there's enough money. I wouldn't wish it on my worst enemy."

Nathaniel chuckled. "And yet you gave it to me."

The duke cast him a gimlet eye, pointing a long finger at Nathaniel. "Forgive me for thinking an American businessman would be up to the challenge."

"Oh, I am," Nathaniel said. "But so is she. I just think she would have appreciated it if you saw it too."

"What do you want me to do?" the duke asked. His shoulders hunched, and he became smaller, like he was melting into the plush mattress. "What's done is done. You're married. You are my heir. I can't change that, nor do I want to."

"Well, that brings me back to my point nicely," Nathaniel said. "I'm giving you free rein."

"To do what?"

Nathaniel grinned. "To change me into a duke."

CHAPTER FIFTEEN

CHARLOTTE TOLD HERSELF she was busy. She told herself she had too much on her plate to care that Nathaniel had become something of a ghost. In fact, both Nathaniel and her father had turned into apparitions around the house. Over the following week, she counted herself lucky if she saw even one of them at the dinner table at night.

"Duke lessons," they'd tell her grimly whenever she asked what they were up to. Whatever that meant. Since Nathaniel was still not drinking alcohol or eating meat, she had no idea what her father could be teaching. His areas of expertise were primarily gluttonous, since he had no head for figures or schedules.

Case in point: on one of those afternoons, Charlotte ventured into his office, which—true to form—was a flat-out mess. Stacks of ledgers crowded his desk along with letters that her father hadn't bothered to open. Most of the names on the letters were ones she recognized, creditors her father had grumbled about over dinner, as well as a few from the investigator, Mr. Hemsworth. She remembered that she'd forgotten to tell her father that she bumped into the investigator while out with Nathaniel. She would have to tell him soon. Mr. Hemsworth didn't seem the type to fade away easily, and he would, no doubt, make trouble if he didn't receive his payment. The last thing Charlotte needed was more people gossiping about her father's lack of funds ... *her* lack of funds. They'd managed to get this far without their friends knowing the extent of their poverty, but it was only a matter of time.

Charlotte sighed, tracing a hand over the layer of dust on the edge of the mahogany. The duke trusted his estate managers, but clearly, he did not take an active role. Would he care or even notice if she did? Her involvement with the managers had stayed at a polite distance; she only stepped in when it was necessary. Perhaps it was time to be impolite.

She rounded the desk and took a seat in his giant armchair, letting herself settle into the cushion. Immediately she felt awkward, like an imposter, and yet the more she sat there, the more the room in front of her came into clarity. As a child, she'd always thought of this formal space as completely off-limits, where great men did important things. No place for a young girl. Now, she saw it for what it was—a mirage. A place where a once-great man surrounded himself with things that would make him appear important.

There were books in Greek and Latin lining the shelves that Charlotte knew her father could not read. There were paintings of historical events on the paper-lined walls that the duke would be hard-pressed to explain. The environment was ripe for greatness—if one only chose to be great.

Well … her father had made his choice, and it was not that.

A jolt of music woke Charlotte from her musings. She quickly left the office and followed the sounds to the drawing room. To her astonishment, she found her large husband and her tiny father, arms enclosed around one another, bickering like an old married couple while their butler, stiff-laced James, played a lively waltz in the background.

"I can't do this with him staring at me," Nathaniel muttered.

"Leave my monkey alone. He likes to be on my shoulder. Besides, it's not his fault you're terrible at this. You are ruining my shoes!" the duke whined. "If you step on me one more time, I'm going to make you buy me new ones."

"You're holding me too tight," Nathaniel shot back. "How can I avoid your baby feet if you continue to hug me like a drowning man who can't swim? I swear that monkey is laughing at me!"

Charlotte cleared her throat. And then did it again, since they couldn't hear her over their griping.

At the sight of her, Nathaniel jumped out of the duke's arms, immediately falling back to the window, investigating the outdoors with a ferocious intensity. The macaw stared at him, for once with its beak closed. Its one saving grace was that it adored music. If someone was at the piano, then the bird was mercifully quiet.

The duke held no embarrassment at all, and nor did the marmoset on his shoulder. "Oh, my dear. How lovely to see you. Did you need something?" he asked pleasantly.

Her father seemed different to her. There was something off, though Charlotte couldn't put her finger on it. He was looking at her the same way he always did, wearing the same jewel-toned clothes, his comportment exceptional. However, his gaze struck her. Was it more intense … sharper?

She shook her head. "I just heard the music and wanted to see what was happening."

He waved a blithe hand. "Oh, you know … duke less—"

"Yes, duke lessons," Charlotte cut in.

She stared at Nathaniel, who was still at the window. She had a difficult time understanding his distance, and it was becoming increasingly more difficult not to take it personally. Since that night with the alpaca, they hadn't spent any time alone. He hadn't come to her room, and she'd been too afraid to go to his— afraid that she was doing the wrong thing, and afraid that he would turn her away. She wasn't sure why she felt that way. He'd been nothing but completely courteous to her whenever he saw her around the estate, and yet the uncomfortable feeling was still there. She couldn't shake the notion that he didn't want to be around her. And for the life of her, Charlotte couldn't understand what she had done to make him behave that way.

"I should go," she said when she realized that Nathaniel was not going to face her. "I am going to watch the knights practice this afternoon. It's their last one before they quit for the country. I should probably get there early in case it's a crush."

The duke nodded. "Good idea, my dear. Take the carriage—and take Nathaniel as well. It will be good for him. I spent the morning regaling the fellow of all the illustrious knights in the Cordry line. I daresay he will probably be champing at the bit to go out and show the others up on the lists."

"Hardly," Nathaniel scoffed from the window.

Charlotte shook her head. "Aunt Mary asked to accompany me. Besides, I couldn't bother Nathaniel will this. I'm sure he'll be bored by the spectacle—"

He spun to face her, and Charlotte gasped.

His beard …

Was gone.

He reminded her of one of the alpacas right after they'd been shorn. He was smooth and baby soft and oddly two-toned, with the bottom of his face a slightly paler shade than the top half. He was also incredibly handsome with his strong, square jaw on full display, and the hollowness of his cheeks added another dimension that he surely didn't need to get her attention.

"I like spectacle," Nathaniel said, ignoring her response to his naked face. He shoved his hands in his pockets and rocked back on his heels as if he was suddenly self-conscious. "I would accompany you … if you would like me to."

The duke slapped his hands together. The marmoset did the same. "There. It's settled. My feet need a rest anyway. I'll see you when you return. I'll have Cook plan a special dinner tonight. I'm sure you'll be hungry."

Charlotte's stomach growled as she left the room, not giving Nathaniel another look. Her next thought surprised her with its cheekiness. *I'm hungry* now.

"OH, LORD," NATHANIEL said without a shred of sympathy, "that definitely looked like it hurt."

Charlotte leaned over the wooden rail that separated the crowd of onlookers from the practice grounds, checking to see if Lord Royce was hurt. He'd been practicing with the quintain, a piece of equipment consisting of a pole sticking up from the ground with a crossbeam laid across its top. On one end, a dummy hung for the knights to tilt their lances at, while a bag of sand balanced it from the other end. Instead of making a hit in the center of the dummy, poor Royce had missed to the left, causing the bag of sand to swirl around and knock him on the back of his head as he passed. In an instant, he was off his horse and flying through the air, landing facedown in the dirt.

Charlotte couldn't draw breath until Lord Royce finally picked himself up, patting the dust off his armor with frustrated strokes. "It's harder than it looks," she said without glancing at her unimpressed companion.

"It doesn't look that hard," Nathaniel returned evenly.

Charlotte rolled her neck from side to side, alleviating the stress and tension that had been building all afternoon. She wouldn't respond to that ridiculous comment. What could an American know about the hardships of being a knight? Most of them could barely ride horses at an acceptable level—an *English* level. It was so easy to sit and judge, especially on such an idyllic day in St. John's Wood.

On the surface, Charlotte could understand Nathaniel's ambivalence. The practice had turned into quite the show. Carriages were crowded all around the large garden behind the Eyre Arms Tavern, where the knights had chosen to practice. Canopies had been erected for the knights, banners were waving, and tiered benches had been erected for the onlookers to enjoy the event in comfort. It was a spectacle, and, to the untrained eye, shared similarities with a carnival act.

Charlotte knew better. She'd been watching the men all summer. Though the knights tried to hide it with their confident smiles and the plumes on their helmets, what they were attempting to create was difficult and not a little bit dangerous. Even with their blunted lances and strict rules, anything could happen.

But again, she wasn't going to waste her time explaining that to Nathaniel. With his smug quips and ever-ready criticisms, he was not in the mood to be lectured, and he certainly wasn't in the mood to enjoy himself. Charlotte had no idea why he'd volunteered to come with her today.

Perhaps he merely wanted to show off his fancy new chin.

Once more, Charlotte pretended to squint past Nathaniel down the field, where a group of knights were practicing their sword skills, and spied on his bare face. Her reaction to his skin was so strange to her. She wanted to peel off her glove, rake her finger across those angles, and feel the difference only a little shave made.

Whose decision had it been? Had her father been behind it? Odd that it didn't make Nathaniel look any less dangerous, any less brooding. The intensity of his stare still gave off that effect. He remained rough, in an unpolished-diamond sort of a way. But beautiful, remarkably so, and Charlotte was not the only one who noticed that afternoon.

Most of her fellow ladies-in-waiting were sneaking their own share of glances at her husband, even though their attention should be squarely on the field. But how could Charlotte blame them when even their Queen of Beauty, Lady Jane Seymour, had a difficult time battling her curiosity?

Every time Lady Jane twisted her long, graceful neck their way, Charlotte would lower her parasol a few degrees to the right to block her sight path. By the end of the practice, Charlotte had waved her dainty umbrella so much that her wrist was sore.

When she'd accidentally hit Lady Diana Davenport in the

back of the bonnet with an absent-minded flick, Charlotte apologized profusely, saying that she thought she saw a bee. Lady Louise, the Earl of Somerset's sister, flanked Diana's other side and was the only one who laughed. Lady Louise was a strange girl, though Charlotte was grateful that at least someone found the humor in the ridiculous situation.

Nathaniel checked his pocket watch once more. He should have asked her. Charlotte could have told him what time it was— five minutes since the last time he checked.

Her fingers tightened around her parasol. "You didn't have to come, and you can leave at any time."

"I'm enjoying myself," he replied in the exact tone of a man bored out of his mind.

"I still don't know why you came."

She felt him angle his body toward her. They were in a sea of people. His body wasn't touching hers any more than the others around her, and yet it still felt as if he was covering her like a blanket.

"I came because I wanted to spend time with you," he said softly. The words were issued so matter-of-factly that Charlotte's throat seized. "Is that such a bad thing?"

"I-I thought you only had time for my father these days," she replied, her anger brimming to the surface. Lady Diana angled her head to them and Charlotte *tsked*, lowering her parasol to block her view. She leaned into Nathaniel. "You seem to be spending all your time with him."

His lips curved into a smile. Without the beard, it seemed bigger now—and more infuriating. "Jealous?"

"Ha! Hardly."

"Trust me," he replied. "You don't want to sit through these duke lessons."

"Then why are you?" Charlotte countered. "I told you that you didn't need to. You won't even be here that long."

Nathaniel's mouth tightened. She felt him take her elbow. "Charlotte, we need to talk about that—"

"Lottie, is that you? I feel like I haven't seen you in ages. Are you enjoying the day?"

Nathaniel released her elbow, and they both turned to watch as the Earl of Somerset, Lord Charles, swaggered up to the rail. He took off his helmet and held it underneath one arm as he ran one hand through his sweaty, golden hair. It had to be the wind, but Charlotte was positive most of the women surrounding her let out a lusty sigh.

Charlotte loved Charles. Had always loved him, though not like the others around her. She'd spent many happy summers with the earl, as their parents had been friends. He was a good sort, always up for fun and a laugh. Yes, he was also handsome, but Charlotte had never fallen under his spell. Maybe it was because he'd never shied away from acting like a rambunctious boy around her. She'd had a front-row seat as he'd eaten worms, jumped headfirst into mud ponds, peed on every shrub in her father's garden, and slept with the pigs after a new litter was born. Life was an adventure for Charles, and she'd loved experiencing it with him when she was younger. But Charlotte had to grow up. And Charles didn't.

"It's hard to keep my eye on you out there, Charles," she said happily while he rested his two long arms on the barrier. "You're everywhere all at once. Aren't you hot in that thing?"

A lock of hair fell over Charles's tan forehead as he surveyed his armor, which clung to his body like he'd been dipped in silver. "You know, actually … I am." Roguishly, he flicked his head so Charlotte would come closer. "But don't tell anyone," he whispered loudly. "Knights aren't supposed to complain. We're much too courageous and honorable for that sort of thing."

Charlotte laughed, but it was drowned out by Nathaniel's disgusted snort. She'd forgotten he was there. Charles just had that effect on people. When the Knight of the Sun was around, all the light centered on him.

He straightened away from the rail, his smile frozen on his face as he tossed a look toward Nathaniel. Neither man had any intention of introducing themselves, and Charlotte didn't have the faintest idea how to even start. Luckily, a call from Lord Craven pulled Charles back onto the field, and the awkward encounter was over before it started.

"Lottie, huh?" Nathaniel said, staring straight ahead.

He caught that, did he? "It's just something my friends called me when I was a girl."

"Well, *Charles* seems mighty friendly."

"Indeed, he is …" She narrowed her gaze at him. "With everyone. He's a favorite."

"Is he *your* favorite?"

"Of all the knights on the field, I would be happy if the Earl of Somerset came out on top, as many would."

Nathaniel's Adam's apple jumped over his collar. His stony silence was interminable. "I wonder why your father didn't find a match for you and this earl then," he said eventually.

"You know why."

And he was being a bastard bringing it up now. Men like Charles needed their wives to have a dowry. That was why so many of the peerage considered marrying heiresses without a title. Love and friendship were all well and good, but they didn't keep the estate running. In a land of peers, money was still king.

Nathaniel ran a hand over his mouth, but Charlotte still made out the vulgar word he'd released. "And these men think they have honor," he spat.

Charlotte squeezed her eyes shut. "Please don't," she said. "You have no idea what you are speaking about."

"Oh, don't I?" He gripped the rail. "I know any man that passes up a chance to have you is a fool. And all these men are bloody idiots. They ride around acting like they've just sacked Jerusalem but have no idea what hard work is. My father came from nothing and still had the strength to pull himself out of the gutter and make something of his life. Any of these men would have folded at the first hardship."

"You know nothing about these men," Charlotte replied icily.

"I know they've been given every advantage, and instead of doing something with it, they spend their time doing"—he flung his arm with disgust toward the field—"*this.*"

Charlotte was at a loss. What did Nathaniel expect them to do with their time? Purchase alpacas, like her? They didn't need to! "Just because they were born with titles, that doesn't mean they don't know hard work. They understand duty"—she lowered her voice—"unlike some others."

"And what's that supposed to mean?"

Charlotte whipped her parasol to the side before Lady Peverly could bring her ear any closer. "It means you have a duty—one duty—to perform, and then you can go and let us all resume our lives. And you haven't done it. I don't know why." She shrugged. "Maybe you don't like me; maybe you are scared—"

"Scared!"

Charlotte turned to the field, looking straight ahead. She never made scenes, and here she was behaving like a fishmonger's wife in the middle of the *ton.*

"Now isn't the time," she murmured. "Later."

"Ha! Nice try, sweetheart. We're leaving, we're going to talk about this when we get home, and I'm going to show you just how *not scared* I am to do my duty."

CHAPTER SIXTEEN

"**G**ET IN," NATHANIEL ordered her.

"Don't push me!"

He sighed, following Charlotte into her room. "I didn't even touch you. Stop being so dramatic."

She rolled her eyes as she stood at the foot of her bed still holding that silly parasol in her hand. Would she use it on him? She looked angry enough.

Though … so was he. Nathaniel had managed to keep a lid on it in the carriage on the way back to Wembley House, but the steam had only continued to grow.

Afraid? How could she say that about him? The only thing he was afraid of was disappointing her—and not in the bedroom. Nathaniel wanted her to be proud of him, or at the very least, not embarrassed. Boredom had reigned supreme these last weeks as he'd listened to her father wax on and on about being a duke, which to Nathaniel only seemed to mean sleeping late and putting every emotion on display so no one ever wondered what he needed or wanted.

And he'd let the silly man cut his beard! Or, rather, Nathaniel had allowed the silly man to oversee a servant cutting his beard. It itched like crazy, which made absolutely no goddamned sense, since his face was now as naked as a baby's ass!

And it was all for Charlotte. All so she wouldn't look at him the exact way she was now—with utter disappointment.

Well, if Nathaniel had to have sex with his wife to make her happy, then that was precisely what he was going to do. Damn her feelings. Damn being considerate.

Damn him.

Because Charlotte was right.

Nathaniel *was* fucking terrified. How did one … initiate the act? Ordering Charlotte into a room with a bed was as far as his muddled mind took him.

She continued to stare at him expectantly, then dropped the parasol to the floor with a demonstrative *thunk.* "Well? You brought me here. What are you going to do with me?"

Did the woman have to be so damned forward? Nathaniel had heard that Englishwomen were delicate with their boatloads of lace and heavy-handed decorum. This woman—*his* woman— liked nothing better than to challenge him.

"Take—" He cleared his throat. "Take off your clothes."

In the blink of an eye, Charlotte had her arms straining behind her back. Gritting her teeth, she worked at her buttons before eventually unleashing an exasperated sigh. She stalked over to Nathaniel and twirled around, offering her back. "Help," she said.

Nathaniel blinked, grateful that she couldn't see his hands shake. He raised them and unfastened each button. His actions were clumsy, taking much too long, but he couldn't keep his eyes off the long swath of skin he unwrapped as he worked. Just at the top of her back, above the neckline of her chemise. He'd seen every inch of Charlotte the night of their wedding, and yet this stretch of creamy, pale skin appeared more intimate, since she wasn't aware he was looking. Three freckles called out to him. In a sloping line across the top ridge of her scapular, they reminded him of the stars of Orion's Belt.

As he came to the end, Nathaniel was unsure of his next move. Fortunately, Charlotte made it for him. As her dress fell off her shoulders, she spun around. Nathaniel had thought his command might shock some hesitance into her, but as usual, he was mistaken.

Charlotte's hands worked efficiently. She shoved the gown to the floor. As she stepped out of it, she unlaced her corset and threw her chemise up over her head. In the time it ordinarily took Nathaniel to toe off his shoes, she was naked for him once more, save her stockings and her bonnet, which was still tied delightfully around her chin with a thick blue ribbon.

"I thought that was going to take longer," Nathaniel rasped. Immediately he frowned. That hadn't been what he meant to say at all. Though, in all honesty, he didn't know *what* he'd meant to say.

You are a goddess incarnate seemed too poetic. And Charlotte didn't look in the mood for poetry.

Her cheeks were saturated with a delicious pink, along with the rest of her body. Her breasts were high and firm, her nipples a dusty rose. Nathaniel's hands tingled. They remembered how it had felt to hold those gorgeous breasts, the lovely weight of them.

Charlotte's patience had reached its limit. Her gaze fell to the floor. She crossed her arms, cupping her elbows in her hands. "It's your turn," she said, her voice betraying a slight quiver. "I may be a novice, but I'm almost positive you have to take *some* of your clothes off."

That forced a chuckle out of Nathaniel. "Some?"

Charlotte shrugged, crossing one leg over the other, hiding the springy patch of dark blonde hair between her legs. Nathaniel wanted to kiss her there. Would she let him? Would he have the courage to ask her? Did husbands *need* to ask?

Only one way to find out. "Lie on the bed," he said. Was it just him, or was his voice getting so deep it was becoming harder to understand?

Charlotte heard him and, with slow steps, did as he ordered. She untied her hat from her head and lay on the bed quietly as Nathaniel finally went to work on his clothes. He'd heard of some men who kept their nightgowns on when they met with their wives in a show of deference to the ladies' feelings. Only, Nathaniel didn't wear a nightgown, and nor was it nighttime. There was little hiding when the late-afternoon sun slanted so vigorously through the large windows, casting everything in a bronze glow. Perhaps he should keep his linen shirt on?

Nathaniel ripped off his jacket and waistcoat and fumbled with the buttons at his waist, finally getting his trousers off with an irritated yank. He hoped to God Charlotte wasn't watching. He almost fell twice during the clumsy process.

"Is something wrong?" she asked from the bed.

Nathaniel's head shot up. Charlotte was staring up at the ceiling, tapping her fingers on her lower belly. Her legs were stretched out but sticking together. What he would give for her to separate them an inch. He was too much of a coward to do anything about it, but he sure as hell would have enjoyed the view.

"Nothing's wrong," he answered, shutting his eyes. "I just … I just …" Nathaniel exhaled a defeated sigh and dropped his hands to his sides. "I don't know what I should do."

Charlotte picked herself up, leaning on her elbows as she regarded him with a studious air. "I think once we get started, it will make itself known."

He ran a hand through his hair. "No, not *that*. I know how *that* works." *In theory, not in practice.* "What I mean is …" He waved his hands toward his torso. "Would you feel more comfortable if I kept my shirt on?"

Charlotte's eyebrows lifted as she tried to stifle a smile. "I'm naked."

"I can see that." Nathaniel breathed heavily, his chest almost collapsing from the effort.

Her smile was no longer contained. "Don't you think it's only fair for you to be naked too?"

He didn't wait for another word. His undergarments were off in seconds, along with his stockings and shirt. However … he was done standing. He approached the bed, enjoying how Charlotte's eyes grew larger the closer he came. He climbed onto the mattress and went straight for her, sliding on top of her body, abrading her virgin skin with his coarse, dark hair.

He groaned. She squeaked. They both shuddered.

Nathaniel placed an arm on either side of her and held his weight on his elbows. Instinctively, Charlotte separated her legs, creating room for his pelvis, cushioning him as they waited.

And waited. His balls were on fire. He'd never felt his cock so ready and wanting, and yet he held back. Because he was ready. He was always ready where Charlotte was concerned. Only … it was obvious she wasn't.

Nathaniel tried to smile, but he wondered if he looked insane, because she didn't relax one inch under him. It was like lying on a plank—a smooth board, but wooden nonetheless. "Let's take this slow."

Charlotte's face immediately clouded over, and she bucked her hips into his awkwardly. Nathaniel bit his tongue at the unexpected action and dropped his head onto her shoulder. *Holy fuck!*

"I'm tired of taking it slow," she said, pouting. "I'm ready. Please, let's just get it over with."

There it was again. *Get it over with.* Nathaniel hadn't the heart to tell her he wanted to do this for the next few hours—the whole night, if she'd allow him. There was no *over* when it came to them.

And that realization—that commitment to his wife then and there—gave Nathaniel the courage he so desperately needed. It also gave him permission to enjoy himself. This was a joyful act. Loving was as close as two people could ever come to the divine. Because in becoming one, they created something new. Something pure and whole.

He placed a chaste kiss on the side of Charlotte's neck. When he found that her frown only deepened, he grinned. "Let me tell you how this is going to go," he said, wrapping one of her long curls around his finger. "We are going to be honest with one another. We are going to touch each other, play with each other, and tell each other what we want. It's probably going to be awkward and weird and odd, and I'm going to fumble things terribly, no doubt. But I'm also going to make you feel good, just like I did in the tub that day. And you are going to do the same to me. We are going to take our time and try to get it right."

Charlotte's innocence shone back at him. Timidly, she reached up and cupped his shoulder. "And if we don't?"

"Then we try again. And again. And again. Until we get it right. And the trying will be just as fun."

Charlotte bit the inside of her cheek, still not convinced. "I hate not getting things right the first time," she muttered.

Nathaniel chuckled, kissing the frown off her face. "I don't. Accept it as another rule of business. How can you learn if you don't fail? Every good businessman has failed a few times in his life. He is better for it. Let me show you." He slid down her body, kissing the lovely path between her breasts. "If I bite you … here … then I will know if you like it or not." He took a nipple in between his teeth and gave it a sharp tug.

Charlotte gasped, instantly placing her hands against his chest, pushing him away.

"There," he said proudly, then blew on the offended sharp point. "That was a failure. Now I know you don't like it that hard. So I'll try this instead." He kissed the nipple gently and took it into his mouth, swirling his tongue around the skin, caressing it with all the love and tenderness that beat within him. His heart was thundering in his ears, but he could still hear Charlotte gasp. The sound was different this time, more exultant, and when her hands came back to him, they pulled at his hair, bringing Nathaniel closer.

"That's my sweet girl," he said against her skin. "You've never been afraid to be honest with me before; don't stop now. Tell me what you want."

"What do *you* want? You have to be honest with me too."

Her voice trembled.

Nathaniel raised his head and saw Charlotte had her eyes closed and her chin tilted to the ceiling. The arch of her neck made him want to be a little *too* honest. "I want to fuck you, Charlotte, until you scream my name," he said.

Her eyes popped open, and Nathaniel dropped his forehead onto her belly. *Stupid fool.* There was honesty, and there was *honesty*.

"You can call me Lottie, you know," she said shyly.

Nathaniel shook his head. "Lottie is a girl's name. I want to fuck my woman."

"Do you think we can do that tonight?"

He choked out a gruff laugh. "In all honesty, I don't really know." His words vibrated against her softness.

He felt a flutter around his ears and looked up to see Charlotte's hands outstretched, cradling his head. She brought him back to her and kissed him sweetly on the lips. "Let's try," she said, and it sounded like a dare.

Nathaniel answered with another kiss, deeper and more forceful, skimming his tongue over her lips until she opened wide for him to plunder her, to swallow away the last bit of resistance and fear. She wrapped her arms around him, encouraging his need—encouraging her own—circling her legs around his pelvis, clinging to Nathaniel as if he was her lifeline.

His hands began to move. At first, Nathaniel had control, but that naïve thought quickly fell to the side. They acted of their own accord, exploring the fecund richness of her body, repeatedly failing until Charlotte directed them to success. She only wanted them in one place.

When Nathaniel's hand reached the apex of her thighs, Charlotte let out a little puff of air, a soft sound that told him he'd reached the right destination. He petted her swollen folds, wetting his fingers with her heat, luxuriating in the way her body danced against his with languid movements that made him feel dizzy.

Nathaniel did not suffer delusions. He knew he wouldn't last long when he was inside her. Fucking her was a lovely idea—and he'd get to it in time—but this first encounter would be fast and furious. He wanted Charlotte to cry out in fulfillment as she'd done in the tub—as she desperately yearned to do now.

As his fingers entered her tight sheath, she grabbed his wrist, squeezing his sides with her inner thighs to keep him in place. She arched against him, working herself slowly, using him to crest the wave again. Nathaniel sucked on her skin, trailed his tongue over the salty skin of her ribcage, but the moment he felt her gyrations quicken, the moment he heard her breath come quicker and higher, he slid his fingers out and replaced them with his mouth.

Charlotte's torso popped off the bed. "Holy Mother!" she yelled. Nathaniel swept the flat of his tongue over the swollen length of her seam. She tasted like the ocean, like the briny freshness of swallowing an oyster right from the water. And as Nathaniel feasted on her, he was reminded of the lotus eaters who ate and drank from the flower that kept them peacefully oblivious to life outside of their island.

Charlotte was his island. He stroked her flower, licked it until she shuddered and thrashed, pressed her heels into the mattress and raised her pelvis, clenching her ass as she came with a ferocity that made Nathaniel forget his name and every other care that took him out of this moment. There was only his wife. Only now.

"Nathaniel," she whispered, releasing her fists from his hair, dropping back on the bed in a collapse of wonder. "That was … That was …"

"Be honest," he said, kissing his way back up her, licking his lips on the way so as not to miss any part of her. If her body was a plank before, it was a feather now, supple and springy as he positioned himself at her entrance.

Her inner thighs tensed, but her voice betrayed none of that tension. "It was miraculous," she replied. "I should be furious at you. You made me wait so long for that. Had I known—"

"You would have questioned my sense of duty sooner?" A bead of sweat fell from his forehead onto the swell of Charlotte's breast. He couldn't wait much longer. He desperately had to be inside her, and yet he liked when they talked like this—so free and unencumbered. It seemed important now, maybe even more important than slaking his need.

Having said that, Nathaniel *really* fucking needed to slake that need.

Charlotte's face became serious. She caressed his brow, capturing his gaze. "I'm ready … if you are," she said.

The tip of his cock wept at her entrance. He could only nod as he slid inside her, one blessed inch at a—

"Mr. Lawrence," a voice boomed from the door. A flurry of pounding followed the desperate call. "Mr. Lawrence, it's time."

Of all the rotten timing. Nathaniel's arms shook with the strain of holding himself above Charlotte, and the muscles of his forearms bulged erratically from the supreme effort. "We should have told your father we weren't coming down for dinner tonight," he rasped.

"Tell him we're busy," Charlotte said, pulling him down so that he lay flat on her chest. She began kissing his neck with giddy laughter that made Nathaniel feel like he could do anything, even tell a duke he wouldn't be down for dinner because he was too busy making love to said duke's daughter.

Charlotte curved her pelvis, trying to take more of him inside her, but he resisted. He couldn't do this with the butler waiting for his reply. "We don't want dinner tonight," he called out, then laughed at Charlotte's increased giggles.

James wasn't to be deterred. "It's not time for dinner," he replied irritably. "The gamekeeper is here. He said you asked him to tell you when the alpaca was showing signs."

Signs?

Charlotte's kisses stopped. "Signs?"

"Yes, signs," James answered, not mentioning that it was her who had issued the question. "Peter said it could happen soon …

the uh … accouchement."

"Unpacking," Nathaniel murmured. At Charlotte's questioning look, he added, "When an alpaca gives birth, it's called unpacking."

"Oh," Charlotte said, biting her lip. "We should go."

It was official. Nathaniel's cock hated him and would never talk to him again.

He gripped Charlotte's side, loving the fleshiness of her hips, loving the way she'd gripped him when his tongue was inside her. He closed his eyes at the beautiful vision. "These things can take time."

Charlotte's smile was heavy with pity, but she persisted. "They can also go fast. And I want to be there. And you do too. We can finish this later."

She kissed his cheek and scooted out from underneath him. The shock of cold air to the top of his cock caused Nathaniel to hiss through his teeth. He heard Charlotte rustling around her room, searching for her clothes. "Hurry up," she said as he collapsed on the bed.

"Give me a minute," he returned.

"We may not have a minute."

"I don't care," Nathaniel groaned. "I need one anyway."

CHAPTER SEVENTEEN

A s CHARLOTTE WATCHED Nathaniel's eyelids droop, she wished she could have given him back that minute—even an hour. The "unpacking" wasn't going as quickly as she would have hoped. Having never been a part of any kind of birth before—animal or human—she was at a loss for what to expect. In her naiveté, she'd assumed the baby would present itself the moment she and Nathaniel entered the stables.

The alpaca mother had not agreed.

"Are you sure she's in labor?" Charlotte asked, forgetting that she'd asked Peter the very same question two hours before.

The old gamekeeper laughed, crossing one foot over the other as he leaned against the outer stable wall, watching the alpaca roam the field, munching on the grass. Dinner was long over. The moon was high and full, and the wait seemed endless.

"Most definitely," he answered in a deep voice that caused Nathaniel's eyes to snap back to attention. Her husband had taken a seat against the barn once it was apparent that the alpaca didn't want to stay in her stall that night. Charlotte knew next to nothing about labor; however, even to her, the animal appeared uncommonly unaffected by the birth.

"See how she keeps moving?" Peter said as the alpaca sat down and then popped back up again to eat more grass. "She's uncomfortable, and I'm guessing this is her first baby. She's unsure of herself."

"Should we be worried?" Nathaniel asked, taking the words out of Charlotte's mouth.

Peter shook his head. "I don't think so. I have no experience with alpacas, mind you, but animals have been birthing babies long before we got involved. If she needs help, she'll let us know."

Charlotte's stomach lurched. She sincerely hoped the alpaca didn't direct its sweet, desperate eyes to her. Her help might be paltry, indeed.

Nathaniel gave her a reassuring smile, which helped to settle her nerves. Since leaving her room, they hadn't said much to each other, but that didn't mean communication was stagnant. The last few hours had been full of half-smiles and blushes, little touches and sighs. She'd fully expected embarrassment's unwanted influence to creep over them during the wait, but so far, they'd been lucky. The heat that swarmed Charlotte every time Nathaniel glanced at her with his hooded eyes wasn't the result of shame or bashfulness. It was born of the pulse that quickened when he reminded her of the joy that they'd experienced. The joy that still awaited them.

"There she goes," Peter said, breaking the taut string between the pair. Charlotte watched as the alpaca became more distressed, which still wasn't much. Her belly vibrated slightly and her muscles flexed and clenched near her backside. It seemed a trick of the moonlight when a tiny head emerged from her, covered by a filmy white sack.

"Is that good?" Nathaniel asked, his expression tight. He shoved his hands into his pockets, almost like he was hiding his loss of control. "Is that normal?"

Peter's smile was kind, and it relaxed Charlotte's rampant heartbeat. He explained to the novices that the baby was still covered in its birth sac, and when it broke, the baby would take its first breath.

Charlotte's own breath intensified as she watched the mother go to work with a nonchalant air. How amazing to be witness to something's first breath of life.

Even with the wonder taking place, her attention found its way back to Nathaniel, who regarded the proceedings with a mixture of awe and horror. Would he be there when she gave birth to *their* child? What if he didn't make it back in time? What if business kept him away?

A shroud of loneliness fell upon her as she thought of experiencing that moment by herself. The gift seemed too important and life-altering to bear on her own.

"Its legs!" Nathaniel shouted in disbelief.

Charlotte turned her focus back to the birth to find two little hooves had burst the watery sac, bringing the head and neck with it. For long minutes, the mother remained unbothered—eating, even—as half of the baby hung from her, coughing the water out of its lungs.

Those sounds were more than the new mother expected. Curving her long neck to look behind her, she yelped as she noticed the baby, as if she hadn't even realized she was pregnant. In a panic, the alpaca began to twirl in a circle, trying to rid herself of the surprise.

Charlotte stepped lightly to the distressed animal, putting her hands up and offering soothing noises. "Shh, shh, girl," she said, stopping short of getting too close. The mother had grown used to her, but Charlotte still wanted to respect her space. "It's all right, dear girl. It's all right. You're just going to be a mama now. You can do it. Just relax. Shh."

Charlotte could feel Peter and Nathaniel's eyes on her, but she kept her concern on the new mama. Suddenly, two of the alpacas that Lord Mason had had delivered the day before came out of their stalls. Very interested in the proceedings, they ventured to the mama and began to sniff her. Along with Charlotte, their appearance seemed to settle the alpaca, and she stopped twirling and went back to munching.

Charlotte let out a long sigh, and the next few minutes went by without a hitch. Before she knew it, a baby alpaca was on the ground, wet and scrawny, all legs and neck as the mother looked on, proudly surrounded by her fellow ladies.

"They're congratulating her," Charlotte whispered while the other alpacas nudged and licked at the baby and the mamma.

Nathaniel came up next to her, placing his arm around her shoulder, and kissed the side of her head. "They're welcoming the new addition," he said, his voice similarly tinged with reverence.

Peter checked the baby, making sure the sac was completely off the nose and eyes, and the three of them watched in silence as the wee alpaca fought to take its first steps. So many firsts in one night for one little life.

Charlotte held Nathaniel's hand on her shoulder and laid her head on the soft spot underneath his chin. A spot that seemed reserved just for her. "We should leave them now," she said while the baby began to look for milk. The mama finally decided to lie down, exhausted by the ordeal, and let her baby feed.

Nathaniel nodded. After sharing their goodbyes with Peter, they headed back to the house, lost in a daze, holding each other in the same fashion. Her head on him. His arm around her. No more words were needed when nature decided to speak.

The house was quiet. Their footsteps echoed as they tackled the marble stairs. Something buzzed inside Charlotte the higher they climbed. All sense of tiredness vanished; it was like a fire was lit in her blood and all thoughts of sleep evaporated in the heat.

When Nathaniel stopped outside the door to her room, she looked at him closely. His hair was a mess. Half of his shirt was hanging out of his trousers, and a thin layer of whiskers covered half his weary face. But his eyes were bright … and hopeful. He was as alive and hungry as she was.

Charlotte wasn't ready for this night of firsts to be over.

Nor was Nathaniel.

Moving at the same time, they crashed into one another against the door, their lips finding each other in a blaze of passion. Charlotte threw her arms around his neck as the one small working part of her brain pondered why he didn't touch her in the same reckless manner. She was answered when she heard the doorknob turn and felt the door open behind her.

Nathaniel caught her just in time before she stumbled into her room. He captured her laughter in his mouth with another searing kiss, then kicked the door shut with his boot.

Then there was only the kiss. He placed his hand behind her head and tilted her at just the angle he needed to plunder her mouth, coaxing her open with the tip of his tongue, sweeping it inside again and again as Charlotte fought to keep up. They couldn't seem to get enough of each other. They couldn't seem to move—stuck standing, locked in an embrace, too involved to do anything other than take.

When Charlotte felt the door against her back once more, she realized that they'd finally moved. Only, it wasn't in the right direction. The bed was on the other side of the room. She wanted to point that out, but then figured Nathaniel was well aware of the layout of her room. He wanted her there. And, for some reason, that heady thought made her chest tingle even more. Because that was what she'd wanted all along, wasn't it? She wanted Nathaniel to want her. She wanted him to take her. Just as much as she wanted him.

As his lips broke from hers, Charlotte could feel her buttons ripping off and pinging off the floor. "I can't make it to the bed," he said between ragged breaths. "I need you now."

A little stunned, Charlotte could only watch as he undressed her, his trembling hands saying more than any words. Her dress fell to the ground and cold air burned her chest. She hadn't put her corset and chemise back on before they'd gone out to the stables; she was completely bare to him. He didn't stop and stare as he'd done before. The time for adoration was over.

Locking his eyes with hers, he worked on the buttons of his trousers, releasing them in the same hurried fashion. His energy was frenetic and arousing; Nathaniel was always so measured and in control. His lack of restraint had her pulse quickening, and her own patience on the thinnest tether.

She needed to touch him. She needed the connection so she didn't lose her nerve. Cupping his face, she kissed him again, swallowing his exhale. Charlotte opened her mouth, sucking in a breath as she felt Nathaniel caress her between her legs. His fingers massaged her, and she tried not to be embarrassed by the wet sounds she heard.

"I'm going to take you now," he said, wrapping his arms around her behind. Before she could utter a response, he hoisted her up against the wood, wedging his body in between her thighs. "Let me know if this is too much."

"It's not too much," she responded instantly.

Nathaniel's head dropped to her neck, and she felt his hot breath as he chuckled. "Wait until we start before you answer the question."

Holding his neck against her, Charlotte shook her head. "I don't need to. I just want you to—" She felt him at her entrance, insistent and pulsing.

"If you say, 'Get this over and done with,' I think I might cry," he replied.

Charlotte worried he might be irritated, but he kissed her collarbone after he said it, all while pushing into her.

Her muscles were unused and unwilling at first, but Nathaniel remained persistent. On the third try, he thrust home. "Sorry," he rasped, his head still tucked into her. "I wanted to be a bit more elegant."

Even through the sting, Charlotte laughed. There was nothing elegant about making love against the door with her toes barely grazing the ground. But it was effective. And the deed was done.

She tried to block the thought from her mind; however, she couldn't stop herself from comparing the act to what had happened earlier. Earlier had been mind-blowing. A mixture of the sacred and the divine. A harmony of—

Oh.

That was interesting.

Nathaniel pulled out of her and pushed back in, slow and uncertain at first, his thrusts shallow and experimental, as if he was trying not to hurt her. Charlotte had been treated like she was made of glass her entire life. She didn't want that from him. She wasn't sure what she wanted, but it definitely wasn't that.

"You asked for honesty before," she whispered, watching the goosebumps rise along his skin as she cuddled her head to his ear.

Nathaniel's sigh was sharp and … defeated? "I did," he muttered, holding himself halfway inside her. She could feel the supreme effort it was costing him. His arms were unyielding, his muscles so tight they could snap.

He was waiting for her answer.

"Harder," Charlotte said softly.

His head shot up, and the abrupt motion planted him even deeper inside her. Charlotte's head fell back against the door, and her eyes snapped closed with the utter bliss.

That was most interesting.

Eyes still closed, she said it again. "Harder."

Charlotte could hear him thinking. "I don't want to hurt you," he said.

"You won't hurt me," she said, not able to hide her exasperation. "You would never hurt me."

Nathaniel's hand floated around to her waist, and he squeezed. In that touch she felt his indecision and fear, his innocence, as he pondered the correct thing to do. Charlotte forgot that he had also been a virgin—though not anymore.

Slowly, he withdrew. For a startling second, Charlotte thought that he was leaving her entirely, until she felt him thrust back into her—harder, but not as hard as she wanted.

She smiled, meeting his gaze. He was watching her, looking for any and all signs she could give him. She hooked one leg around his arse. "Better," she said.

His smile warmed her heart. She wanted him to quit worrying so badly.

"But not great?"

"Be great," she replied, pumping her pelvis toward his at the moment of his next thrust. Charlotte couldn't stop as she cried out in pleasure.

There.

That was better than interesting.

"More?" he said, entering her again, not waiting for an answer. With every push, he understood more, became more in tune with what she needed and asked for. It wasn't long until their pace picked up into a frenzy as they pounded into one another, searching for that elusive high. Their kisses were sloppy, their motions even more so, but the wildness was thrilling and seductive, teasing her breaking point until Charlotte burst.

Nathaniel must have been watching her the entire time, because the moment she began to scream, his mouth captured hers and he drank her pleasure as he released into her, nailing her into the door with a lack of grace but a newfound assuredness.

He pressed into her for a long moment, shaking every so often as Charlotte regained her senses. As he let her drift back to the floor, her inner thighs tinged with discomfort. Not pain, though.

When Nathaniel unpeeled himself from Charlotte, his smile took her breath away. It wasn't the smile of a man who'd just had sexual relations for the first time, but that of a husband who had just made love to his wife.

He reached up and tugged on a lock of her hair, staring at it as if it held all the answers to the universe. "That was worth the wait," he said, and his blush was evident even with his high color.

Charlotte's lids felt heavy. Everything about her felt heavy. She thought she could sleep for days. But that idea held no appeal. She ran her hands up Nathaniel's chest, loving the feel of the crisp hair against her fingers. It was still difficult to believe he was hers. And after experiencing so much loss lately, knowing that everything she owned was in jeopardy, she was gripped with fear. Losing Nathaniel was untenable. Now that she had him, she couldn't bear to let him go.

She moved away from the door, skirting around his large figure. She could feel his eyes on her as she walked toward the bed, and swayed her hips because she could.

"It was worth the wait," she agreed, her words as cool as the sheets she slid upon. Lying on the bed, she held her head in one hand. "It certainly wasn't a failure."

Nathaniel placed his hands on his hips and cocked his head. "You're right. But it wasn't *perfect*, was it?"

Charlotte squinted and pretended to think. "Now that you mention it, it wasn't perfect."

"Not at all."

"Not by a long shot." Nathaniel grinned and stalked toward the bed. The way his muscles all worked in perfect harmony reminded Charlotte of a panther, all languid and smooth. At the edge of the bed, he shook his head regretfully. "Looks like we'll just have to keep trying until we get it right."

Charlotte smiled when he grabbed her foot and dragged her to meet him. "Again and again?" She giggled.

Nathaniel nodded sternly, leaning over her. "And again and again. Didn't I tell you failing could be fun?"

CHAPTER EIGHTEEN

"CHRIST ALMIGHTY, ARE you still packing?"

Charlotte jumped at the expletive and twirled away from her growing pyramid of bags to catch Nathaniel standing in the doorway to her room. His expression was playful, yet still irritated, as he leaned against the frame, his arms casually crossed. The poor maids moved in a rush. He was all bluster, but their feet definitely skittered quicker across the floor whenever he came up to complain. Which had been a lot. In Charlotte's estimation, it had happened at least four times throughout the day. Almost as if her husband couldn't bear to be away.

Her body sizzled at the thought.

"You were just here an hour ago," she replied with an exaggerated huff. "How could we possibly be done in that time?"

Nathaniel rolled his eyes and strolled into the room like a bored child. He came to the bed, inspecting a few articles of clothing passively before flopping into the chair next to her vanity. Charlotte couldn't contain her smile at seeing the large man sitting in something so dainty and feminine, especially wearing a scowl that could frighten the dead.

"We're only going to Scotland," he returned petulantly. "I packed less to cross the ocean."

Taking pity, Charlotte came over to him. The second she was close enough, Nathaniel laid his head against her belly and she wrapped her hands around his neck. It amazed her how far they'd come. It had only been a week since their night together, and so much had changed. Touching was the biggest development of note. Her husband was incredibly tactile. Nathaniel liked to have a hand on her no matter where they were or who they were with. She'd almost yelped when he reached for her under the table at dinner one night. Then she realized he only wanted to hold her hand. During dessert. It turned out that Charlotte didn't mind eating her blancmange using her spoon with her left hand. She preferred it now.

She smoothed his hair away from his forehead as he tilted his head at her. "Of course you packed less. You weren't going to be a lady-in-waiting to a queen of a medieval tournament."

His laugh rumbled through her body. "I was traveling to meet a duke about becoming a duke. I'd say that was mighty important."

Charlotte scrunched her nose. "Yes, but you didn't believe him at the time, so that hardly counts. My role requires clothes—and lots of them—as well as jewelry and accessories you've never dreamed of. My responsibilities will be endless."

Nathaniel's hands snaked their way around her middle. As he buried his face into her abdomen, he breathed deeply, as if searching for signs of himself. They wouldn't be hard to find. Their nights were filled with passion and only each other. Charlotte had been forced to take naps during the day to keep up. She wasn't complaining. She liked that his scent lingered on her skin. It kept her satisfied when the sun was high.

"What about your other responsibilities?" he asked in a voice that made her insides feel like honey. "Your … wifely responsibilities."

Charlotte's face went hot. She craned her neck to see if her maids were listening to this conversation. By their tiny smiles, they definitely were.

"Nathaniel," she whispered. He looked up at her, all round eyes and innocence.

"What?"

She shot a weighted glance at the others in the room.

"Out, please!" he called at once.

Everyone turned to face him, wondering if he'd lost his mind. There were a few hours of daylight left and the party was leaving for Eglington's castle first thing in the morning. Every moment counted.

Charlotte tried to make him see reason. "They can't possibly leave—"

Reason was not to be seen. "Out, please," he repeated, his tone incredibly ducal. Those lessons with her father must have been going well, Charlotte concluded.

The maids flew out of the room. Nathaniel didn't even wait for the door to close before his hands disappeared underneath her skirt and cupped her backside tightly. "It can't be helped, Charlotte," he said while he kneaded her flesh. "I simply can't be around you and not think about this."

Charlotte sighed. Her head dropped back and she stared at the ceiling, all the while screaming inside because she was secretly pleased as Punch. "I don't have time for this," she said, rather unconvincingly. His fingers had crawled around to her front, and he was trailing silky fingers up and down her inner thighs. "There's still so much packing left, and I have work to do in my office. I purchased two more alpacas, you know."

"I know." The sound was muffled, but she still heard the pride. That might have made Charlotte wetter than anything. She adored Nathaniel's pride in her venture and loved the fact that he let it be hers alone. He didn't meddle; he didn't pry. She was the ultimate decider. That was not to say that he wasn't busy in his own right—or invested in her success. Ever true to his father's message, Nathaniel had been intent on earning his own fortune. Most nights he was out dining and picking the brains of other engineers and industrialists who had expertise working with alpaca wool using the latest technology. As soon as Nathaniel found the space for his factory, he intended to launch a mill that specialized in the exotic wool.

But that studious, somber, ambitious gentleman was worlds away from the man she held in her arms now. There was no time or place for the future in this room.

When Nathaniel inserted one finger inside her, Charlotte's legs almost buckled. She had to stop this before she lost control. By experience, she'd learned that happened in the blink of an eye. "I can't," she said, trying to squirm out of his arms to no avail. "I have—"

Nathaniel's smile turned impish. "Work to do. I know. I'll be quick, I promise."

"You always say that, and you never are."

It was a losing battle. Her heart was already beating outside her chest and her body was humming with electricity. She wanted this just as much as he did. *But no!* She had to be the responsible one. There was simply too much to do. "You can wait."

"I can't," he said firmly.

"It takes too long to get dressed again."

His head came up. "Who said anything about getting un-dressed? I think it's time for another business meeting, hmm? We'll focus on efficiency."

"Efficiency?"

Nathaniel returned a firm nod. "Indeed. The key to any good business is that it can work quickly but effectively. One must know the end goal before one begins in order to make the most out of the resources."

That stumped her. *Work … effectively … resources …* "Those aren't the most romantic words," Charlotte replied dubiously.

"I beg to differ. No matter. I'll just show you what it's all about."

Charlotte caught a glimpse of his rakish grin before her hus-band pulled her into his lap. Nathaniel tucked his head into the crook of her neck and took another lengthy exhale. "God, I love it when you smell like sex."

She squirmed in his lap, her shyness overwhelming her. "I do not smell like … sex … Do I?"

"Oh, yes. It is so fucking delicious. I want to eat you."

She should reprimand him for using that vulgarity in her presence, but the word shot all the way to her toes. "Just hurry," she whispered.

Nathaniel went still, then reached for his buttons, undoing them with sure fingers.

"Don't worry," he said into her mouth as he swept in for a kiss. "I'll get this over and done with. I'm horribly efficient that way."

⟫⟫⟫⟨⟨⟨⟨

IN THE END, it was not fast, and certainly not over and done with. What was more, Charlotte didn't believe her husband accurately depicted *efficiency*, though she decided arguing was unnecessary, since he had brought her to climax twice.

It was an hour later when she finally unwrapped herself from Nathaniel's slumbering body and ventured toward the office. At least he'd held true to keeping their clothes on, although that probably wasn't the best decision in the end. Charlotte caught a glimpse of herself in a passing mirror. She was so ruffled and wrinkled that it appeared as though she'd slept in her clothes— which had almost been the case. Though, Charlotte had to admit, she also looked … happy. Supremely so. The blonde curls framing her face might be limp and ragged and her face might be red and blotchy, but it seemed like a moonbeam was inside of her, shining out in all directions.

Charlotte didn't pause to knock on the office door. Her father wouldn't be there; he never was. She charged into the office, taking a seat behind the large desk. She'd contemplated swapping the chair for a smaller one but ultimately decided against it. She liked the fact that everything in the room was grand and masculine. The more time she spent there, the more it felt like she was growing into it. Her body and boldness were morphing to fit the atmosphere.

Nevertheless, the room still held shades of her father. The desk stared back at her, almost taunting her with its piles of ledgers and unopened letters, like an impudent mini-tornado of procrastination.

Charlotte's anxiety rose at the cluttered sight. She couldn't work like this. Not if she was going to start an alpaca farm in earnest and get the estate's finances under control.

What would a good duke do? she asked herself.

A good duke would answer his damn letters.

With a groan, Charlotte snatched a handful of unopened missives that were stacked precariously on the desk's edge. Just as before, the majority of them had been sent by her father's investigator. It seemed that Mr. Hemsworth was still pleading to be paid in full. Charlotte couldn't wrap her head around it. Her father had told her that he'd sent the investigator a sizeable chunk of what remained of her dowry. Mr. Hemsworth couldn't be quibbling for that much more. Surely there was something she could do to put the bill to rights. Maybe, after the tournament was finished, she could sell the gowns she'd commissioned in order to pay off the investigator's fees. It was not like she would need the costumes anymore. She couldn't imagine participating in many more medieval tournaments—not with Nathaniel in her life. His interest in Eglinton's event continued to be lukewarm at best.

She found her father's paper knife in the drawer and was just about to slash open the most recent letter when she heard a muffled shout coming from outside. Charlotte headed to the window and saw her father—decadently dressed, as always— marching away from the grounds toward the pond … dragging another man by his collar.

"What in the world!" Charlotte dashed from the office and out the back door, chasing after the struggling pair.

Strength—or muscles, for that matter—wasn't something she usually attributed to her father, but he was in rare form because he showed no problems dealing with the other man, even when his captive lurched to the ground in their tussle. The duke kept going, towing the screaming gentlemen so hard that muddy trails marked the grass in his wake.

"Father! What are you doing? What has this gentleman—"

Charlotte's scream broke off. Ignoring her, the duke picked up the man and held him by his lapels at the edge of the pond. It was then that Charlotte saw that it wasn't just any man ... but Mr. Hemsworth.

The investigator's face was mottled and sweaty, and his hair was in complete disarray. When he noticed her standing a few feet away from them, his panicked eyes latched on to hers. "Lady Charlotte! Lady Charlotte, help me. Talk some sense into your father!"

"Go back inside," her father said with astonishing calm, still facing away from her. "This is none of your concern."

Mr. Hemsworth clawed at the duke's hands, but they remained firmly attached to his coat. His tiptoes were balanced precariously along the weedy edge, inches from the murky water. "Oh, yes, it does involve her!" The duke began to shake him like a rag doll, and words warbled from his mouth. "Why don't you tell her? Tell her about what you've done and how you refuse to pay me for the help I gave you."

Charlotte stared in disbelief, creeping closer despite her reservations. Could this insanity just be over a little money? "Tell me what?" she asked cautiously, reaching her father's side. His face was as red as Mr. Hemsworth's, and although he was clearly angry, he was also just as panicked. "What do you need to tell me?" she repeated.

The duke's lips turned white as they formed a vicious line, barring any explanation from spilling forth.

"Tell her!" Mr. Hemsworth goaded him. "Tell her that you used all of her dowry to pay off the priests at the orphanage. Tell her that Mr. Lawrence is no more the heir than I am. Tell her that I worked night and day for you to find the American and haven't seen one pound for all my effort. Tell her!"

The duke yanked Mr. Hemsworth close to his face. "If you don't shut your mouth, I'll drop you. All it takes is one whistle from me and the alligator will come. Just one whistle. That will keep you quiet forever."

The blood rushed out of Mr. Hemsworth's face. His lips trembled. "You're lying. There's no alligator." He looked at Charlotte. "Is … is there?"

"No!" she cried, though Mr. Hemsworth didn't seem to find her very convincing, especially since she scanned the water while taking a few steps away from the edge. "He's trying to scare you."

"Do you want to take that chance?" the duke said icily. "If you do, then keep talking."

Mr. Hemsworth's face crumpled, and he burst into tears. Then he released an onslaught of words so quickly that Charlotte only registered them after her father pushed the investigator into the water. She heard words like *forgery*, and *George*, and *dead*.

The duke brought two fingers up to his mouth and issued a shrill whistle that made the hair on the back of Charlotte's neck shoot up. Again, she peered into the water. Was her mind playing tricks on her? Was there something walking across the surface?

Her father didn't wait. He turned his back to the pond, leaving Mr. Hemsworth to deal with the aftermath. Charlotte didn't have time to waste on the flailing, drenched man—especially since she was absolutely (mostly) sure there was no alligator. She chased after her father, speaking over the high-pitched screams of the investigator who was high-stepping out of danger.

"Stop!" she said, reaching out for the duke's arm. With a frantic tug, she managed to finally get him to stop and face her. "Explain this to me," she said slowly, still holding on to some bizarre belief that everything could be fixed with one of his convoluted stories. But Charlotte was not a little girl anymore, and her father's anecdotes had been old and tired for years. "Is

Mr. Hemsworth speaking the truth? Did you use my dowry to pay the orphanage?"

The duke was good. He barely blanched at her statement. And yet there was a moment, a split second, when Charlotte saw a twitch. Just one little twitch that made the floor drop out from under her.

"You shouldn't be listening to the words of a crazy man."

"And you shouldn't be keeping secrets from me," Charlotte said. They were the same height, and she could meet her father right at eye level. What she saw broke every bit of her into pieces so small that she didn't think they could ever be put back together. "What did you ask the priests to do?"

The duke grimaced at her harsh tone. "It's nothing," he said softly. "What's done is done. You don't have to worry about it."

"*What* is done?"

He shrugged. "You're married now," he said. "And you will be a duchess. The orphanage—and its paperwork—is essential to Nathaniel's claim on the title. Don't go looking for things that will put that in jeopardy."

Charlotte stumbled back, clutching her chest as if he'd struck her. What was he saying? That the orphanage's ledgers were debatable, or worse … forged? That Mr. Hemsworth was telling the truth?

Once the idea stuck in her head, Charlotte couldn't get it out. Yes. It made so much sense. Her father hadn't found the heir.

He'd *created* him.

Nathaniel had been right. The duke had been lying this whole time, and Charlotte was an accomplice.

Instantly, she broke for the house. She had to get to her husband. She had to tell him before he found out from another.

"Where are you going?" her father asked, snatching her forearm. Charlotte jerked and struggled, but he wouldn't relinquish his hold.

"Let go of me!"

He pulled her so hard that she almost banged into his face.

Charlotte tried not to look, but the pain and hysteria of his countenance sucked her in like quicksand. She'd never seen his pupils so dark; they swallowed up the whites of his eyes with frightening effect.

"You can't tell him," he rasped. "No one must know. Only us. I handled everything. No one is the wiser. I had to settle with the orphanage first, but I'll pay off Hemsworth when I get the funds, and then he won't make any more trouble. I did this for you. Why are you threatening to put everything in jeopardy?"

"You didn't do this for me! You only wanted Nathaniel's money, and when he wouldn't give you that, you wanted a child to pass on your name to. I am so stupid. I should have known you would do something like this! You never cared about me. You only care about your precious family name."

The duke laughed grimly. "I saved you! We barely have a penny to that name. I saved your future. You could have ended up a poor spinster, or worse, married to some second-class—"

"What?" Charlotte challenged, raising her chin. "Say it. A businessman. An American manufacturer. Well, that's exactly what happened, Father. So congratulations. You've failed me once again."

"It doesn't have to be this way," he pleaded as Charlotte whipped her arm away from his hand. "You can stay quiet, and we can have everything we want. It can all end well."

"No. It can't."

"He'll leave, you know." The dire words stopped Charlotte from walking into the house. "Once he knows, he'll think you were behind it, and he'll be furious and leave. You won't be able to stop him. How will you live through it if he demands a divorce? How will you handle the shame and embarrassment he will rain down on this family?"

Charlotte let out a pitiless sound and turned toward her father. "A lot easier than if I don't tell him at all."

CHAPTER NINETEEN

NATHANIEL WOKE TO an empty bed. With a lazy grin, he took his wife's pillow and snuggled it close, burrowing his nose into the softness, breathing in her lingering scent.

He wouldn't get up just yet. For starters, he was hard again. And secondly, he thought that maybe if he stayed, then she would come looking for him and be able to help with the first problem.

Nathaniel chuckled at his lascivious thoughts. He couldn't have been sleeping for more than an hour, and he was already itching to find her again. When would it end, this aggressive yearning? Did it have to? He'd gone twenty-eight years without having a woman. Now, it seemed, he couldn't go sixty minutes.

The door banged open and the object of his fascination flew inside. Her hair was still deliciously tousled, and Nathaniel's cock immediately thickened as he confirmed that her appearance was all because of him.

"Look who couldn't stay away," he teased, feeling as carefree as a young boy. He patted her vacant side of the bed. "That's perfect, because I have use of you, wife—"

Charlotte's expression forced him to stop. Finally, he noticed how worried she was, the way her brow sank low on her face in agitation.

"What is it? What's wrong?"

Charlotte twisted her fingers together in front of her, opening her mouth and then closing it again. "I have to tell you something," she said, finally dragging her bright eyes to his. She'd been crying. Nathaniel had just hoped that she'd been happy to see him.

He nodded, sitting up in bed. Reaching out, he untangled her hands and kissed one of her palms. "Tell me, sweetheart, before you make yourself ill."

She shook her head. "I don't know how … You have to believe me … I didn't know until now."

"Know what?"

Nathaniel's blood went cold. He'd never seen her this disturbed. He couldn't imagine what had made her so upset. Charlotte was always so cool and collected, so in charge. The only thing that ever threatened that was her father's actions.

And that was when his voice almost locked in his throat. "Charlotte. Just tell me. Honesty, remember?"

Her head fell onto his shoulder. "I don't want to tell you. If I don't tell you, then we can still have a chance."

Nathaniel caressed the back of her head. "My love, we're married. We have every chance in the world."

Don't we?

When his wife raised her head, the look she gave him cut straight to his gut.

Don't we?

NATHANIEL ORDERED CHARLOTTE to stay home. He didn't want her to accompany him to the orphanage that night. There was no telling what he would do. Charlotte had never seen that side of him, and he didn't want her to witness it now. He made an excuse about her packing, but she readily ignored him. She wouldn't be left behind.

As the carriage hit every bump and hole in the road, Nathaniel became more furious. Why hadn't he fixed the damn old conveyance by now? He'd had the time. But he knew the answer, and it only made his insides boil more. He'd let himself get so carried away in his ridiculous "duke lessons" that he'd forgotten who he was. He'd forgotten to do his due diligence.

What in the world had he been thinking? He'd just taken the duke's word for it—surveyed a few old pieces of paper and considered them a bible. Bible. Ha! That was an interesting word for it, considering whom he was going to go accuse of downright lying to his face. This priest better be up on his confessions, because Nathaniel wasn't sure if he'd be breathing after their meeting was over.

"Stay in the carriage," he ordered Charlotte gruffly as they pulled up outside the building. But the damn woman was out before he could shut the door.

"This pertains to me as well as you," she said, pulling at her gloves. "We will confront him together, as a team."

Nathaniel didn't know why, but her little speech managed to calm the fire in his blood. Maybe it was because she still considered them a pair. He needed that as he felt his castle crumbling around him.

He pounded on the door of St. Lawrence's and was quickly escorted to the priest's office to wait for him.

His new office had been completed, and was as splendorous and airy as the old one had been cramped and dingy. Nathaniel's hope sank. The clues had been there all along, but with Charlotte shining next to him, he hadn't wanted to see them.

"Ah, Mr. Lawrence, Lady Charlotte, how lovely to see you again, and so soon," Father O'Ryan said behind them as he came into the room.

Nathaniel stood, issued a curt bow, and didn't go back to his seat. He was too jumpy. If he sat any more, he might rip the arms off the chair.

"This isn't a social visit, so I will get right to it," he said firmly, watching the pleasant smile fade from the young priest's face. "I want to see the ledger again. And I want to know why the Duke of Wembley sent you so much money. At our first encounter, you mentioned another benefactor. It was him, wasn't it? Why did he feel the need to give you so much when he hadn't given one lick before?"

Father O'Ryan's spine straightened. He placed his two gangly arms on the table as if trying to keep it from floating to the ceiling. "Mr. Lawrence," he drawled, shaking his head, "I don't know who you've been speaking to, but—"

"Just stop," Charlotte said. "We know."

The priest shot her a murderous glare that made Nathaniel want to jump over the desk and pummel him. *Later.*

Softening his expression, Father O'Ryan turned back to Nathaniel. "Many men reach into their souls and decide to give back to the church. It happens all the time."

Charlotte laughed. "Not to my father." She settled back in her chair with calm assurance. "He already told me everything. You don't have to lie for him. Just show Mr. Lawrence what he needs to see."

The priest's words seethed through his teeth. "I already did before."

Charlotte echoed his nasty tone. "Do. It. Again."

With a sigh, the priest reached behind him for the ledger. He *thwacked* it on the desk and proceeded to find the page in question. Nathaniel leaned over him, practically breathing down his scrawny neck.

"There!" he said as the priest almost skipped over the page. "That one. The one with two George Lawrences."

The priest's fingers froze, poised at the corner of the page, before he let it drop.

Nathaniel pointed at the George Lawrence who had a slash through his name. The one that had died soon after arriving at the orphanage. "That's it, isn't it?"

George is dead. George is dead. George is dead. The idiotic parrot's verbal onslaughts chimed in his brain.

"George is dead," he whispered. "The rightful George is dead." He looked up to the priest, who was growing redder and redder. "The duke asked you to switch the names. The rightful George, the real heir to the Duke of Wembley, died when he was a baby, but the duke saw the opportunity to find a new one: my father, especially when he found out how rich he was."

The priest slammed the book shut. "You are delusional. The orphanage—the church—would never condone perfidy such as that."

"Really?" Charlotte asked. "I find it quite easy to believe, especially when a roof was involved. Costly things, roofs can be." She skimmed her hand over the shiny wood on the arm of her chair. "And offices."

The priest reclined back in his seat with a closed-mouth smile. "You'll never prove it. The documents are there. The duke was careful."

Nathaniel growled, helping Charlotte from her chair. "Not careful enough, it seems."

"You're only hurting yourself," Father O'Ryan called, stopping the couple before they left the room.

"Oh, I think I'll be hurting others as well," Nathaniel murmured with pure menace. It wasn't an idle threat, and the rush of blood to the priest's face showed that he knew it. "As I'm sure you'll remember, I am in charge of my father's very large charity endowments, and they haven't been disbursed yet. If there comes a time when I need your honesty, you'll do well to remember that. As I told you before, I am not up on my Bible, but I remember one pertinent line: *The Lord gives, and the Lord takes away*. Does he not, Father O'Ryan? And that's a lot of money to take away."

NATHANIEL HAD ONE more person to speak to. One more set of

eyes he needed to peer into and try to understand what hid behind them. There was a reason he'd saved this meeting for last.

The Duke of Wembley had threatened Nathaniel—threatened to be something more in his life. The duke had stepped into a void that Nathaniel hadn't realized was even there, become a father figure that he didn't think he needed. In the weeks he'd spent in England, Nathaniel had grown to like the unusual aristocratic—more than like him. Even with all their differences, the duke had showed him another side of living, one that didn't revolve around stuffing as much work into a day before collapsing at the end of it.

The duke had been exasperating, head-scratching, and bewildering at times, but he'd also shown kindness, patience, and an ability to change. It wasn't only his drinking that had slowed, but also his spending habits. Nathaniel couldn't think of one thing the duke had wasted his money on lately. He'd actually sold a Rembrandt, which had delighted Charlotte to no end. And he'd given her the money to purchase more alpacas. Nathaniel would never forget the look on her face when the duke had told her. He'd gifted her something greater than diamonds or silks. His actions had shown a selflessness that Charlotte had forgotten existed.

But how could Nathaniel reconcile that man with the one who'd been such a Machiavellian figure in his life? The duke had pressured his only daughter to marry him, knowing that he wasn't the true heir. Was he really so sure that no one would ever find out? Try as he might, Nathaniel didn't understand that kind of hubris; perhaps his duke lessons hadn't progressed far enough yet.

The duke was waiting for them in his drawing room when they returned from the orphanage. The first thing Nathaniel noticed was that the macaw's cage was covered with a dark blanket. Maybe he was being considerate, or maybe the duke understood that hearing *George is dead* repeated wasn't the best idea for the discussion ahead.

Nathaniel turned to Charlotte, thinking to ask her to leave and give the men privacy, but the tilt in her jaw made him stifle the words immediately. Then again, why should she leave? Hadn't she been as duped as Nathaniel? For better or worse, they were now a family. And as a family, they would have to find a way out of this mess.

The duke sat in his chair by the hearth. His clothes were impeccable; his dark blue velvet coat reminded Nathaniel of liquid against his pale skin. But it also made the older man look close to death, especially as his head hung low between his shoulders.

The man was broken. Did Nathaniel have it in him to break him more?

Charlotte did. "It's done," she said, strolling into the room. She stood in front of her father, waiting for him to lift his head. "Nathaniel knows, and the priest confirmed it."

"He did, did he?" her father replied to his shiny, buckled feet.

"In his way," Charlotte answered.

"Well," the duke drawled with a long, ragged sigh. "You can't hate me for trying."

"Oh, yes, I can."

The vehemence in her words shocked Nathaniel into moving. He went to her side. Taking her hand, he gave Charlotte a small squeeze. He wanted her to look at him; he wanted to plead with her to take her time. Words—especially vicious ones—had a horrible way of staying around long after they'd been said. But her sights were stuck on her father.

The duke finally held his head up. The bags under his eyes were as heavy as the tuft of white hair sticking up from his scalp. "I'm sorry, my boy," he said to Nathaniel. "You have no idea how sorry. I wanted your name at first. I thought that was enough. But the more I got to know you, the more I realized that I just wanted *you*. You would have made a brilliant duke."

Nathaniel snorted. "We both know that isn't true."

The duke's chest rumbled with painful laughter. "Better than me, anyway." He planted his hands on the arms of his chair and rose to his feet. The movements were slow and stilted, as if he'd aged a decade since the morning. "I haven't taken the documents to Parliament, so you're all saved from the embarrassment. And I can speak to the priest who married you. I will have him burn the marriage certificate. All of this can just be a dream. Bad or good, it doesn't matter."

He picked up the poker next to the hearth and stabbed at the logs that were dying with the fire. Nathaniel flinched with every punch. He'd never encountered the duke so low. He didn't know what to say.

It was so anticlimactic. As always, the duke had a plan, even regarding his amends. Nathaniel just had to collect his things and get on a boat bound for home. No one in this city would even think of him, just as he wouldn't give a second thought to them.

Except Charlotte. Always Charlotte.

Out of the corner of his eye, Nathaniel saw her follow her father to the hearth. Like a specter, she watched him while he continued to poke at the fire, not moving, hardly even breathing.

Damn you, man. Look at her! Look at your daughter and see how much you hurt her!

But the duke didn't have the strength, nor the dignity. Nathaniel tried not to judge him too harshly. Dukes were only men, after all.

Charlotte's first words wobbled out of her throat, but she soon regained control, resulting in an awesome intensity. "Do you want to know what the worst of it was, Father?" she asked. A line of tears dropped from the duke's face onto the floor. "That you were so willing to lie for Nathaniel, but you weren't willing to tell the truth for me. All I asked is that you speak to the queen. All I asked is that you try to convince her to amend the title. And you refused because you were too embarrassed, too proud. So, instead, you embarrassed me."

The pain on her face was gut-wrenching. Nathaniel longed to pull her into his arms and take her far away to a place where the lines drawn weren't cast in stone. Or to a world where she had a father that would fight for her.

The duke placed a shaking hand over his mouth. To Nathaniel, it seemed like that was all his energy would allow. "I'm sorry," he said. "I failed you. I always fail you."

"No, Father," Charlotte said gently, losing some of her ire. Her face became pink, and tears pooled on her bottom lids. She was barely hanging on. "You failed yourself. You didn't *believe* in me. And I don't know if I can forgive you for that."

The duke snorted, lifting his gaze. He squinted at his daughter, and Nathaniel was reminded of the time he'd told Charlotte that it physically hurt to look at her. Her beauty was just too great. But the duke's contemplative stare was more than that. He was looking deeper, maybe even deeper than he ever had before. "*You* would have made a brilliant duke."

Charlotte didn't hesitate. "I know. And I'm glad you know it now too. But it's too late."

Her father paused. "Is it?"

"I'm leaving." She turned to Nathaniel with a nod. He returned it, though he had no idea what she was talking about. "My husband is going back to America, and I am going with him."

The duke momentarily forgot that he was supposed to be on his best behavior, because his face clouded with a ferocious scowl. "You don't have to be a martyr, Charlotte. I told you, I can erase the marriage. You can stay here with me, and we can fight this. Help me fight this."

Charlotte showed him her back, returning to Nathaniel. She took his hand in hers, giving him the same squeeze that he had given her earlier. Nathaniel felt it all the way to his heart. He hadn't expected this. He'd known he wouldn't leave her, but he thought a logistical discussion would happen. The fact that she'd already made up her mind to follow him across the ocean, leaving everything she'd ever known or cared for behind, humbled him to the extreme.

Humbled and disconcerted him. Nathaniel couldn't understand the uneasiness in his gut.

The duke was as confused as Nathaniel felt. He continued to watch his daughter, bitter resignation painting his face, dragging the tired lines and sagging skin even further down. "So that's it," he lamented. "I make one mistake and you're leaving me?"

Charlotte filled her lungs. "Your conniving was almost perfect, Father. You thought everything would go as you planned. But you couldn't control one thing."

"And what was that?"

Her smile was sad. "That I would fall in love with my husband."

CHAPTER TWENTY

CHARLOTTE WAS READY for a barrage of questions from Nathaniel, but his first threw her.

"Why are you unpacking?"

Her fingers stalled over her bag, and she turned to find him at her door. It was such a familiar sight, but this was the first time that shivers didn't run down her spine when she saw him. She was too overwhelmed, overcome … She was still too damn angry!

"What does it look like I'm doing?" she retorted. "I'm packing … or, rather, unpacking and then packing again. I want to leave soon as possible, and I don't want to lug all this medieval nonsense across the Atlantic."

Charlotte heard him enter the room, his footsteps soft and gentle, as if he was trying not to upset her further. Little did Nathaniel know that his consideration only fanned her flames! She didn't want soft and gentle. Nothing about her *or* the situation was soft and gentle. Charlotte wanted loud and furious. She wanted to yell and fight.

Only not with Nathaniel. He didn't deserve this. He didn't deserve any of it.

"Darling?"

He'd never called her that before. Charlotte wasn't sure if she liked it. She was afraid anything he called her at this moment would be burned into her head as happening on the worst day of her life. The worst day of both of their lives.

Which reminded her …

Charlotte whipped around, fists landing on her hips. "Why aren't you upset like me? You should be angrier, punching the air and threatening to tear down this useless house one brick at a time. How can you stand there so calmly? It's driving me crazy."

"I'm sorry," he said, annoyingly soft again.

Charlotte picked up a cape out of her luggage and slammed it back down onto the cluttered bed. "Don't apologize. You didn't do anything wrong. It was all him … and me, because I should have kept an eye on him. I knew he wasn't to be trusted."

She felt him at her back. Nathaniel placed his hands on her shoulders. "He's your father. You're supposed to trust him."

Charlotte snorted.

"And I *am* mad," Nathaniel went on, "or was mad, but not anymore."

She sighed, releasing most of her tension. How did he do that? Just one touch and she felt enormously better. It was a gift— *he* was a gift.

"What changed?"

"Did you really forget what you said back there?" Nathaniel punctuated his question by kissing the back of her neck. "Were you trying to get back at your father, or do you truly intend to come back to America with me?"

Charlotte closed her eyes. She'd thought he'd mention the other statement she'd made to her father. The one about loving him.

"If you're on a boat, then I'm on a boat. It's as simple as that," she replied matter-of-factly. "Do you think I'll like Boston?"

She loved the way Nathaniel's chest felt when he laughed. "Probably not," he said. "It's cold."

"It's cold here."

"Not like it is there." He hesitated. "And they don't particularly love the British."

"Why not?"

Nathaniel wrapped his arms around her, resting his chin on the top of her head. "There was this little war about seventy years ago. I don't know if you heard of it, but it had to do with independence—"

"Oh, that," Charlotte said, waving a hand in the air. "Aren't you all over that yet?"

"It was pretty important to us." He laughed.

"Well, you Americans just have to deal with this British girl, because I am going, and you can't stop me. They will learn to love me as I will learn to love them, as …"

Nathaniel's arms tightened. "As?"

Charlotte twisted in his embrace until she could look him in the eye. He waited patiently for her to speak. She would never be able to thank him enough for that—not only listening to her but believing that what she had to say was worthwhile. So many people took the time to stare at Charlotte, never stopping to think that whatever came out of her mouth could be as worthwhile as her beauty.

She swallowed down her fears. This was Nathaniel. Her husband. The man she could tell anything. "As you learned to love me," she said.

Nathaniel blinked as if her words were a wave that just knocked into him. Then he raised his arms and held her face. "I didn't have to learn anything. Falling in love with you was as natural as breathing. I only had to spend a day in your presence to know that I never had a chance."

Charlotte's heart fluttered. "Really?" she asked, biting her lip so she could contain her smile. Nathaniel wouldn't let her. He claimed her mouth in a lingering kiss that melted away all her resistance.

"Yes, really," he said into her mouth. "Loving you was the most effortless experience of my life. Why do you think I married you?

Charlotte jerked away. "Because my father offered you the

chance of a dukedom."

Nathaniel was shaking his head before she even finished speaking. "I wanted *you*. I let the dukedom come along."

He was still holding her face, and Charlotte placed her hands over his. "And now you *only* have me."

"That's all I ever wanted," he said before pulling her in for another long kiss that said more than any declaration of love. Charlotte felt that kiss all the way to her feet and back.

When he released her, she let out a shuddering exhale. The fury she held for her father could still be found within, but it was wilting. She had Nathaniel, and that was all she needed. Her father's respect and trust didn't matter anymore. She was leaving; her life wouldn't be lived in England.

Nathaniel traced her lips with the tip of his tongue, languidly playing with her as if they had all the time in the world. Charlotte could feel herself responding hungrily to him, and she placed her hands greedily on his hips, pulling his shirttails out of his waistband. There was time for this. There was always time for this.

"No," she heard Nathaniel say through the sultry fog of her mind. She ignored him, pulling his shirt more until he grabbed her hands and placed them in between them.

"No?" she asked, the words tumbling out of her mouth in a rush of frustration. Charlotte had so many feelings swirling inside her, so much energy bottled up and ready to use. What better way than to ravish her husband?

Unfortunately, Nathaniel still was of a mind to talk. When would husbands learn that there were better uses for their mouths?

"You have to pack."

Charlotte stood up on her tiptoes, capturing his mouth in a kiss that left very little to the imagination. "I can pack later."

"No," he repeated. His nostrils flared with frustration. Charlotte could feel him grow hard against her. He wasn't as impervious as he wanted her to believe. "We are sticking to the plan and leaving in the morning."

"The morning? I don't understand. Is there a boat leaving?"

Nathaniel pinned her with a hard stare. "We aren't going to America yet."

"Then where are we …?"

She watched as Nathaniel bent to the side to pick up the ermine cloak her tailor had made for her to wear to the tournament. It was heavy and grandiose, the kind of clothing that made a statement. Clothing fit for a duchess.

"No," Charlotte whispered. "No," she said once more when Nathaniel continued to hold the garment. "I don't want to go anymore. I just want to leave and start our life together. We were naïve to think those people would ever accept you, and now we don't need them to. Let's just forget about the tournament. I already have, actually."

Nathaniel's mouth screwed up to one side. "I don't believe that for a second. You've been planning to go to this tournament for months, and I won't take it away from you now. There's plenty of time to leave after. Besides," he continued with an amused glint in his eyes, "it isn't every day I get to kiss a lady-in-waiting."

"We're not that special," Charlotte groused.

"Maybe the others aren't, but you are," he returned easily. "I want to see you take your place next to the Queen of Beauty. I want to watch as everyone stares at you and dreams that you could be theirs. And," he added, tossing the cloak back to the bed, "I want you to talk to those men you told me about. You had plans to offer for a few more alpacas, and I won't have things change just because of your father."

Charlotte's stomach flopped. The alpacas. What would she do with them now that she'd insisted on leaving? Did her little farm even matter anymore?

Yes.

"How will we get them to America?" she asked.

Nathaniel answered without missing a beat. "I've already

thought of it. I have some contacts that could bring them over. It's not easy with animals—many die in the process—but I trust these men to do the job right. Don't worry, my love. I'll bring your little babies to you."

"My babies?"

Nathaniel lifted a rakish eyebrow. "Aren't they? When I first met you, you didn't even know the difference between alpacas and llamas—"

"No one does!"

"—and now they run to you every time they see you. You've come a long way, Mrs. Lawrence."

Mrs. Lawrence. It sounded lovely to her ears.

"Call me that again," she said. She ran her arms around his neck, tugging on the bottom of his hair.

Nathaniel smiled against her lips. "Mrs. Lawrence," he said before kissing her to within an inch of her life. "We don't have time."

Charlotte giggled, falling back on the bed, pulling him toward her. "Let me worry about the packing. You just worry about pleasing your wife."

Nathaniel still appeared to be worrying over something. Charlotte reached out and placed a finger in between his eyes, smoothing out a wrinkle. She wondered if she was magic, because it worked instantly, and Nathaniel grinned wickedly. "I can do that, Mrs. Lawrence. I can do that, indeed."

CHAPTER TWENTY-ONE

Eglinton Castle, Scotland August 28, 1839
The Eglinton Tournament

NATHANIEL HELD BOTH hands above his eyes as the rain plummeted on the fields. Despite the earlier sun—which had been nothing short of brilliant—the Eglinton Tournament had been marred by a torrential downpour and a late start that he couldn't even begin to understand.

He'd stood among the frustrated many in the grandstand waiting for the event to finally begin. Three hours past start time, the procession made its way down from the castle, and it was only now that the knights were beginning the jousts. For the most part, Nathaniel had no interest whatsoever in the decadent fools galloping inside the arena with their ridiculously unyielding costumes and drenched feathers drooping from their helmets. As usual, his eyes stayed on Charlotte. The only reason he wasn't shivering along with everyone else was because she looked so miserable, and he couldn't do anything about it. He was too incensed to be cold, so hot he could practically see steam rising off his overcoat.

"I'm sorry, what were you saying, Lord Broadripple?" Nathaniel asked, flickering his gaze between the gentleman at his side and Charlotte, who was seated further down the rows in the center of the pavilion, right next to the Queen of Beauty, Jane Seymour. Lady Jane's brother was doing the honorable thing and holding an umbrella over his sister, but it had a paltry effect. No one was saved from the elements today, not even quasi-royalty.

Lord Broadripple blew hot air against his gloved hands and rubbed them together. He crossed his arms and crammed his hands into his armpits. Like so many others, the lord had dressed in period garb and looked like he'd jumped straight from the pages of a King Arthur tale. The poor man needed an overcoat. His meager tunic and ridiculous red hose didn't appear remotely warm enough for this blustery Scottish weather.

"Ah, yes." He shivered. "The alpacas. Yes. I had two, you see, but one died just last month. I just can't seem to keep the things alive. I don't know what's wrong with them. They're more trouble than they're worth."

That was what Nathaniel had been waiting to hear. Lord Broadripple was the third man he'd spoken to about alpacas since arriving in Scotland with Charlotte two days before. And they'd all ended up saying the same thing. So many of the peerage loved collecting animals from far-off locales, but never took the time to learn how to treat them.

And it wasn't just alpacas. While in London, Nathaniel had seen bears, lions, and even alligators traipsing down the muddy cosmopolitan streets with nothing more than a collar and a pathetic excuse for a leash. No one was safe—not the animals, and certainly not the people.

"I agree," he said, watching two new knights come out onto the field. Since a herald couldn't be heard above the rain, no announcement was made regarding the competitors. However, some of the crowd must have had an inkling, because this was the loudest he'd heard the cheers since they entered the dismal lists. He raised his voice. "That's why I wanted to speak with you, Lord Broadripple. You see, my partner and I are starting an alpaca farm, and—"

Nathaniel's words fell off, and he blinked. He couldn't believe his eyes. "What the hell does that bastard think he's doing?"

Lord Broadripple blanched, knocking his soaked Tudor bonnet off his head. "I say, sir, contain yourself. Lord Somerset is only approaching the ladies for a favor. And good for him. This has turned into a farce. At least he is trying to warm some blood." The lord elbowed Nathaniel in the ribcage and gave him a knowing look. "And what sweet blood it is, too."

Nathaniel's hands clenched, but he kept them at his sides. Punching Lord Broadripple in the face wouldn't make him feel better.

Punching Lord Somerset would, though. How dare this Knight of the Sun gallop up to his wife in the stands, lower his lance for all to see and admire, and ask for her favor? And why the hell did she have one to give? But there it was—the pink ribbon had been at the ready for Charlotte to tie to the end of Somerset's lance. Christ, the imagery was obvious enough. A man dipping his lance like that toward a woman. Nathaniel was sick just thinking about the innuendo.

His impotence only intensified. Because all he could do was sit and glare at the pretty scene as his wife smiled adorably through her shivers and the entire crowd clapped with stars in its eyes for the beautiful pair. *Fuck!* Nathaniel hated hating people, but he fucking *loathed* the Earl of Somerset. *Fucking golden peacock!*

"You are suggesting you take the animals off my hands, then?"

Nathaniel heard Broadripple speaking again, but he couldn't focus. Not when Charlotte was there, away from his side. Not when she was in the center of her world ... as she always should be. And Nathaniel was on the outskirts, talking business, as he always should be.

Was he fooling himself? Would she be content with him in Boston? She loved him; that was plain. But love faded. These people, this establishment, these connections, never did. Was it fair to take her away when she was so obviously at home in this place?

Lord Broadripple blocked Nathaniel's line of sight. The lord's spider-vein-filled nose filled his vision. "Did you hear me? I asked how much you would give me for them. I won't drive a hard bargain; however, I want my money back, if you understand my meaning. Though I can't help but warn you. You've got a losing battle on your hands. Those alpacas aren't from here, and no matter how long they stay, they don't belong here. Perhaps the most humane thing we can do is just send them back home and forget all about them."

Nathaniel stretched around Lord Broadripple and found Charlotte, who was giggling at something Lady Jane said in her ear. As if feeling his attention on her, she turned her graceful neck and found him. Immediately, a smile covered her face—her real smile, not the one she used for everyone else. She brought her fingers to her mouth and rubbed them softly, seductively, over her plump bottom lip.

Nathaniel was silently hoping she might stick them in her mouth when a loud *crash!* came from the field.

A knight was on the ground. *Finally*, someone had been knocked off his horse. And it was none other than the Knight of the Sun—England's magnificent son, Lord Charles, Earl of Somerset—who had taken the glorious fall! It shamed him, but Nathaniel was giddy as all hell.

"Well, I say," Lord Broadripple said, fixated on the scene with a flabbergasted pout. By his woeful tone, it sounded like *he* had been thrown off his horse. "Lord Royce brought him down. I didn't know he had it in him. I suppose that's why they say anything can happen in a joust. Any knight can earn his spurs."

The odd expression pricked Nathaniel's ears. "I'm sorry. What was that?"

The lord chuckled. "I forgot you are American. It's an old saying. It means any man can be a knight and earn his fortune. I suppose that's what makes these contests so stimulating. Men throughout history—like William Marshal, for example—have been able to rise above their stations and lowly births and prove their worth in these tournaments. It's what makes them so exciting. Reputations could be made in an instant on the lists. A man can be a knight. Any young woman can be a queen."

Nathaniel regarded the man curiously. "I didn't know you were such a romantic, Lord Broadripple."

"Nor did I, Mr. Lawrence," the lord returned a little gruffly, shifting in his seat. "I don't know what came over me. I hope I haven't turned you off with this maudlin talk."

"Not at all. On the contrary. You've given me much to think about."

Lord Broadripple preened with satisfaction. "Now, back to the alpaca—"

Nathaniel slapped him on the back, spraying them both with more rain. "Don't worry about the alpaca. You'll get your money back. Nothing is going to harm that animal while it's in my care."

The lord nodded and returned his interest to the action. The Earl of Somerset was being helped off the field. The poor bastard was limping something fierce and appeared to be in a lot of pain.

Not Nathaniel.

He felt right as rain. And a little romantic.

LATER THAT NIGHT, Nathaniel entered his room at the castle and stopped dead in his tracks. His wife, whom he had seen so little of since they'd arrived in Scotland, was waiting for him in his bed. Naked or close enough to it.

Sitting up against the headboard, Charlotte pulled the bedclothes high to her chest, showcasing the lovely slope of her shoulders. "I've been waiting for a mighty long time, Mr. Lawrence," she said, feigning irritation.

In keeping with their ruse, the couple had been forced to sleep in two different rooms at Lord Eglinton's castle, and this was the first time Charlotte had surprised Nathaniel in his. Her schedule had been too packed the previous nights with preparations for the event.

"I'm terribly sorry, my dear," he said, sauntering into the room. He tore at his necktie, leaving it and most of his clothes on the floor in seconds. He toed off his shoes just as he neared the bed. His wife's breathing grew shallow as she stared at his chest. "I had some business I had to attend to."

"Business?"

Leaning one hand on the bed, Nathaniel slipped off his stockings with the other. "Alpaca business. I think I got you three more today."

Charlotte clapped her hands, allowing the bedclothes to fall lower to the precipice of her nipples. "Wonderful," she replied. "I am surprised. I didn't believe many men would be in the mood to speak tonight after everything that happened."

Everything, indeed. Soon after Lord Charles took his dramatic fall in the joust, Lord Eglinton called the whole thing off, blaming the rain. It never should have begun in the first place, though Nathaniel could understand the earl's desire to play for the crowd. Over one hundred thousand people had shown up that morning hoping to catch a glimpse of the empire's long-lost chivalric tradition, and the majority had left the fields soaked and disappointed.

Nathaniel couldn't decide if Lord Eglinton had planned poorly, or if he had simply been misguided. Even if it hadn't rained, the event, most likely, would have come off as shoddy at best. Sure, the field had looked spectacular at first glance with its colorful tents, heraldic banners, and newly constructed lists and grandstand, but one only needed to peer behind the curtain to see that nothing was organized well.

A better-crafted grandstand and center pavilion should have been able to withstand the wind gusts and rain shower, and yet it had been torn apart quicker than a house made of straw. And no forethought had gone into providing the crowd with places to stay. A warm room and a dry bed would have been a swift consolation after the joust was called off, but the nearby town was not equipped to deal with the rush of people. Nathaniel heard whispers that most had to make do with bedding down in makeshift shanties and barns—and those were the fortunate ones.

One could have the best ideas and intentions in the world, but if it wasn't properly planned, then it was merely a dream. Eglinton's dream had ended in a catastrophe that day.

Nathaniel unbuttoned his trousers but left them on for the time being. Charlotte must have something on her mind if she came to him like this, and he knew that once he was completely naked, he wouldn't be in the correct mindset to listen.

He could hardly be blamed. His wife was the epitome of temptation as she sat there angelically in the bed. She'd let her hair down, and it poured over her shoulders like a glorious shower. Her face was scrubbed pink, with her little, pouty lips puckered in thought. Nathaniel couldn't wait to kiss those thoughts right out of her head.

What had she asked him about? *Oh, her alpacas.*

"You're right," he said. "They weren't in the mood to talk, but many were in the mood to drink, which eventually led to a lot of talking."

"What did you drink?" she asked.

He shrugged. "Tea. Too much tea. I have a feeling I won't be able to fall asleep for hours."

Charlotte tapped her fingers lightly on her lap. "I wonder what we could do to pass the time."

Nathaniel flashed a grin. "I wonder …"

With a burst of speed, he whipped the covers off the mattress and latched on to Charlotte's feet. She yelped as he dragged her to meet him at the edge of the bed, spreading her legs around him.

"I'm so cold." She trembled, crossing her arms over her chest.

"I'll warm you up," Nathaniel answered, rubbing his hand over her forearms and down her belly.

"Today when I was standing in all that rain, I didn't think I'd ever be warm again."

"And then you remembered your husband, and you knew that was a ridiculous thing to think."

Charlotte rolled her eyes. "You've come a long way in your confidence, husband. It wasn't so long ago that you were afraid to even touch me."

Nathaniel shook his head. "No, wife. Never afraid. Intimidated, maybe. Overwhelmed, most definitely."

"Overwhelmed?" she squeaked. "By what?"

Nathaniel succeeded in uncrossing her arms and placing them at her side. He took his time caressing her breasts, massaging the heat back into her harassed skin.

"Oh," he drawled with a lopsided smile. "You're asking for compliments now."

"I'm not!"

Nathaniel leaned over and placed a light kiss under the swell of each breast. "You, of course. Everything about you is overwhelming, from your translucent hair to the ever-changing blue in your eyes …"

Charlotte let out a lengthy sigh, as if she'd heard this all before. Nathaniel was certain she had.

He kissed her stomach, nipping at her skin with his teeth. "Don't be impatient with me. I'm not done. Then there's the way that you speak, all commanding and assertive. That's awfully overwhelming. And there's your business acumen. It took me years to learn to negotiate, and you picked it up in no time."

"And?" she said, placing her hands behind her head. "Keep going."

"And," Nathaniel said, coming down to his knees, "the way you unpeeled your robe and dropped it on the floor the night of our wedding. *Fuck*." He closed his eyes, as the vision still gave him heart palpitations. "I still can't believe you did that. So fucking brave."

"I didn't feel brave." Charlotte's whisper was so light, it was as if she was issuing a confession.

He met her gaze over the expanse of her naked body. "It was the bravest thing I'd ever seen. You wanted something, and you were going to get it. That heir."

"No," Charlotte said, edging up on her elbows. "I wanted you."

Overcome with her admission, Nathaniel lowered his head into the crevice of her thighs and took a deep breath. Her scent flooded him with memories of their passion. He loved eating from her, craved the way her legs braced against him like she was wringing from him all the pleasure he could give her. More, more, and always more. That was what he could give.

Charlotte's body tremored the moment he licked her, telling him that this wouldn't be long. It couldn't be helped; they hadn't been together in two days, which was two days too long.

But as Nathaniel tried to lose himself in the beautiful act, laving her with her tongue, his hands stretched wide over her pelvic bones as she writhed beneath him, he continued to torture himself with more ways he was overwhelmed.

It wasn't just who Charlotte was—it was *what* she was and all she was giving up being with him.

He found her little hidden nub and worked it with his tongue, flicking it back and forth in time with Charlotte's breath. Her hips were pumping into him now, rising and falling. Nathaniel could barely contain himself. Seeing her move like that, watching her body as it rolled like a wave, so fluid, so liquid, made him want to forget everything and plunge into her.

Her inner thighs squeezed him, and Nathaniel knew she was close to her peak. But the bastard in him wouldn't let her have it yet. He backed away just as she raised her hips in the air, waiting for him to continue.

"Nathaniel?" Charlotte whined, her tone as breathless as he felt.

"Don't worry, my love," he said, sliding his hands over her mound. He reached for his shaft and fit himself at her slick entrance. "Don't you know that I will always take care of you?"

With a solid thrust, he claimed her. Charlotte gasped as she took all of his length, her eyes widening as she stared at the ceiling.

"Answer me," Nathaniel urged, pumping into her again.

Charlotte's eyes found his. "I know that. I know you will always take care of me."

He thrust again. "And love you."

"And love me."

Nathaniel paused for a few heartbeats, letting his cock rest against her inner walls, content but restless. He bent over Charlotte, placing his elbows on the sides of her head. She watched him—hungrily and warily—as she waited to hear what he would say next.

"I will give you everything you had here and more," he said, his voice breaking with the urge to move. He needed to release into her, but he needed her to understand him more. "You are not giving up anything by being with me. Please know this."

Tears began to run down her cheeks. Nathaniel muttered a curse and wiped them away with his thumb. His damn hips started moving again, pushing him into her with sweeping pulses that made it difficult to form words. She just felt so good. Perfect. For him. And only him.

"I know that," she cried, throwing her arms around his neck. She brought him down for a long, drugging kiss that neither wanted to stop. Even when Charlotte released her hold, it wasn't by much, and Nathaniel's lips grazed over hers when he spoke.

"I will build you a castle to rival this," he said, picking up speed as he entered her again. He was making a vow to her mind as well as her body. "You will drip with jewels and feathers and furs. You will—"

"Nathaniel, please." Her finger was pressed against his lips. "Just love me."

"I do, my love."

Charlotte tilted her pelvis to take more of him inside. She arched up, and he took a breast in his mouth, sucking her nipple until she screamed. "Just love me," she said again. "That's all I need."

But I can do so much more, was on the tip of his tongue, but Nathaniel couldn't get it out. His release was upon him. Charlotte screamed again, and as she tightened around his shaft, Nathaniel pumped one more time before he followed her into oblivion.

He fell asleep with her hands in his hair, remembering that something was on the tip of his tongue.

But he only tasted her.

CHAPTER TWENTY-TWO

CHARLOTTE FELT THE bed dip next to her. She was too exhausted to stay silent anymore. "Please stop moving," she said, throwing an arm over her face. "It's nowhere near dawn."

She heard Nathaniel sigh before he leaned over and kissed her on her shoulder. "I'm sorry, my love," he said.

"You really did have too much tea," she remarked with a yawn.

Nathaniel chuckled, and Charlotte cracked an eye open at the window. The sky was still pitch black. The rain wasn't as loud as it had been earlier, though she could still hear a faint sprinkle against the window. She couldn't have been asleep for long, and she doubted Nathaniel had been at all.

Something was bothering him, and Charlotte wasn't sure how to remedy it.

She placed her hand on his cheek, stroking him gently. "Tell me what's wrong."

Nathaniel groaned, kissing the inside of her palm. "Oh, I'm just thinking about nothing and everything."

"Tell me."

He hesitated, seemingly weighing his words. Eventually, he let loose what was inside. "Why don't we tell everyone we're married today? Before we leave, we can let them know. Surely you'd want to announce it before we are in America."

Charlotte slid up higher on the bed. Nathaniel looked so hopeful that it threw her. "We talked about this," she began slowly. "It's best if we wait until everything has ended; that way we don't have to suffer through all the questions and comments. We agreed, remember?"

Nathaniel ducked his head. "Of course, yes. I just …" He shrugged. "I thought since the tournament is over, it wouldn't matter anymore."

"But we don't know if it's over. I heard some talk that the knights were going try again after the lists dried. Lord Eglington still wants to host the ball and dinner as well, so we're stuck here a few days longer."

"I know. I know," he said curtly, betraying his impatience. He held her hand in his, caressing each of her fingers one at a time. "I just … I want them to know you're mine."

Charlotte narrowed her eyes. Now she was beginning to understand. "Is this about what Charles did yesterday? The favor?"

Nathaniel scoffed. "This has nothing to do with the bastard—"

"I had to do it, you know. I had no choice. It would have been rude not to tie my ribbon—"

"On his lance."

Charlotte laughed. It sounded so ridiculous when one said it out loud. "Yes, on his lance."

Nathaniel looked up from her fingers, a small smile pulling on his lips. "It really has nothing to do with him. I just don't want you to be afraid of what they think. I want you to be proud that you're married to me."

"I am!" she said, holding his head in his hands. "I am so proud of us."

Nathaniel stared into her eyes as if he was searching for the truth. "Then why won't you tell them?"

Charlotte's hands fell to the bed. A flash of irritation coursed through her. Why was he asking this of her? Didn't he know she was doing it for his benefit? "We've discussed this," she said.

"These people might speak of chivalry and gallantry, but they won't be kind to you … to us. They will smile in our faces and stab us the moment we turn. I don't want you to have to endure that before we leave."

"Are you worried about me or you?"

Charlotte let out an acerbic laugh. "You are not serious."

"I am," Nathaniel said stoically. "I can handle these people. I'm not your father. You don't have to worry about them hurting me." He paused. "Are you embarrassed to tell them about me, Charlotte? Don't be afraid to tell me the truth. I need to know this."

Charlotte could feel tears beginning to build. Her whole chest stung from Nathaniel's words. Did he have so little faith in her?

"Please, my love, don't do this." She unwound herself from the sheets and crawled over to him. She forced him to sit up so she could straddle him. Charlotte needed to look him straight in the eyes. "I could never be embarrassed of us. Is this why you said those things last night? I don't care if I live in a castle like this. They're freezing most of the time anyway. And I don't want jewels, because they are so heavy and cumbersome. I don't mind feathers, but furs can be so scratchy." She placed her hand over his heart, feeling the beat immediately quicken. "I want a beautiful life, and I know you will give me that. That is why I chose you."

Nathaniel sighed. He copied Charlotte's position and placed his hand over her heart. "I just can't help but think I don't deserve you."

Canting her head, Charlotte placed a kiss on his neck. "You showed me what real love was. You showed me you believed in me. I can never thank you enough for that." When he opened his mouth to speak, she cut him off with a swift kiss. "I know you have thoughts about earning everything you have. And I have no doubt you will earn your next fortune just as your father taught you to. But you don't have to earn me. Our love is a gift, and one doesn't need to earn a gift. One should only be grateful and say thank you. Can you do that, my love?"

"Thank you," he said softly. Nathaniel snaked his hand behind her head, pulling him toward her. "Thank you," he whispered again before another kiss. And then he proceeded to show her how grateful he was.

⫸⫷

"I HAVE IT, my lady," Charlotte's maid said, coming into her room, holding a gown. What a difference a day made! Just twenty-four hours ago, the dark green dress had been soaked and muddied from the storm, and now it looked good as new. The young maid looked proud and not a little bit relieved. "It took me a while, but I think it will suit you well today."

Charlotte twisted in her chair in front of the vanity mirror. "Anna, you are a wonder," she said. "I can't believe it's the same dress."

The maid placed it on the bed and went over to the vanity. Charlotte's hair was finished, and they just needed to add a few finishing touches before she would join the others in the procession.

After ascertaining the damage from the storm yesterday, Lord Eglinton had decided that the party could try again. Along with the earl's men on the estate, the knights had worked tirelessly to make sure the grandstand was fixed and the lists were safe enough to use. Unlike before, it would be a subdued affair. Charlotte wasn't sure how many would be in attendance; however, the knights felt like they had unfinished business, which meant that she still had a part to play. The Queen of Beauty couldn't be there unless her ladies accompanied her.

She and Nathaniel had one more day. After the joust and the subsequent dinner and ball, they would be able to finally leave and never look back. Charlotte couldn't wait.

"Are you ready, my lady?" Anna picked up the diadem on the

vanity and held it over Charlotte's head, almost as if she was taking a moment before crowning the new sovereign.

The thin golden band wasn't nearly that grand. It had belonged to Charlotte's grandmother and was brought out so infrequently that she had forgotten it existed until her father gave it to her. As lady-in-waiting, Charlotte had been nervous to bring it, thinking it too fancy for her role. Luckily, Lady Jane had brought an actual crown with her, making Charlotte's diadem seem like a childish trinket.

Anna placed it on her head, balancing and pinning it in place, close and tight to Charlotte's forehead. As beautiful as it was, Charlotte wouldn't miss situations like this. In her heart, she knew Nathaniel was still nervous about bringing her to Boston to become a businessman's wife. He couldn't understand that the jewels that she wore came a paltry second place to him. Yes, they were lovely and awe-inspiring, but they were also cold. And Charlotte was tired of being cold. She wanted Nathaniel's warmth, now and forever.

"Have you seen my—Mr. Lawrence?" Charlotte asked, stopping herself at the last second from saying "my husband."

Anna offered a shy smile in the mirror. The girl knew about the marriage but had vowed secrecy along with the rest of the duke's household. Charlotte didn't know why she stopped herself. It just still seemed like the safe thing to do.

"I haven't, my lady," Anna said, returning her attention to Charlotte's hair. She held her tongue tensely between her teeth while she stuck in more pins. "Many people woke early this morning to get a jump on the day. I know I'm glad I did. I can't believe all that's happened already."

"What's happened?"

Anna stared at her wide-eyed in the mirror. "You don't know?"

Charlotte shook her head. "You know I haven't left my room."

"I'm sorry, my lady. The gossip is so good and loud that I

must have thought it traveled through all the walls of the castle."

"Tell me!"

Anna's face turned pink with excitement, and she ducked her head, speaking in hushed tones even though they were the only two in the room. "It's about Lord Charles. He ran off late last night, or early this morning."

"Charles? Why would he leave? Is he coming back?"

Anna shrugged. "I don't know."

Charlotte played with the diadem in her hair, checking to make sure it didn't wobble. "Well, of course he's coming back. He wouldn't miss this; he's been waiting all year for this event. He's the Knight of the Sun!"

"I don't know," Anna repeated warily. "It's true he left all his things behind, as well as his valet, but it's awfully curious."

Charlotte dropped her hand to her lap. "What is?"

"He's not the only one missing."

She waited for Anna to say more until she couldn't help herself. "Who else is missing, Anna?" she blurted.

The maid's eyes went back and forth furtively. *Honestly, the drama!* "Lady Louise."

Charlotte leaned back in her chair. "Lady Louise? The Marquis of Marlborough's sister?"

"Some say they saw her leaving with a man in the middle of the night."

"No, no," Charlotte said, back to shaking her head. "It can't be Charles. He wouldn't do something so … reckless. I've never even seen them talk. I don't think I've ever seen Lady Louise talk to anyone, for that matter."

Anna threw up her hands, going back to Charlotte's hair. "That's all I heard. I suppose we'll have to wait and see. Lord Eglinton is furious because now he's down a knight—two knights, actually, though I don't know who the other one is that's missing. Another maid told me that he'd been running around the castle, trying to see if anyone could fill the position."

Charlotte laughed. That was even more ridiculous than the

gossip about Charles. Lord Eglinton knew how dangerous it was to joust, and he'd been training for months. He wouldn't just pull someone up to join in the event, unless … he felt so upset about the previous day's failure. Maybe he felt the need to make it up to the spectators?

And who would be foolish enough to take him up on the offer? All the men who'd wanted to prove their prowess and worth were already involved.

An uncomfortable ache twisted Charlotte's stomach.

"I'm sorry," Anna said, thinking Charlotte had become anxious for her to be done. "I'm almost finished. Just a few more pins. Are you all right, my lady? You look as pale as a ghost."

"I'm fine. I'm fine," Charlotte whispered, placing a hand on her temple. The side of her head was beginning to throb, and it had nothing to do with all the bloody pins.

Anna nodded, though she kept her eye on her mistress a second longer. "I wouldn't worry too much about Lord Charles," she went on. "I know he's your friend, but you're right—he would never do something so reckless." Her mouth puckered up on one side. "Though … he is a knight, isn't he? He might do something that romantic."

CHAPTER TWENTY-THREE

"**I** CAN'T BELIEVE it," Lord Eglinton said, perusing Nathaniel as he stood in the center of the room. "It fits."

Nathaniel could barely believe it himself. When the earl had taken him to Lord Charles's room and shown him the man's armor, Nathaniel didn't think there was a chance in hell that he would fit. Even though he and Charles were similar sizes, the odds had seemed against him. Armor was made to fit the specific man.

But as Lord Eglinton had explained, this set of armor belonged to the Earl of Somerset's family. It had been passed on from generation to generation. Not wanting to alter its history, Charles hadn't had it tailored exactly to his form, which was advantageous for Nathaniel, who was bulkier in the chest and arms, not to mention a few inches taller. It wasn't perfect, by any means. The breastplate cut a little too sharply into his sides, and the sabatons pinched his toes something awful, but it would do for the day. And only this day, because Nathaniel wasn't going through this nonsense ever again.

He strutted from corner to corner, putting an abnormal amount of focus on the simple task. The effort made the journey slow and cumbersome. It felt like he was marching over dry, crumbly sand. Every time he lifted his arms or bent his legs, he squeaked. Knights were definitely not covert. But that was the point, wasn't it? When men dressed up in this much steel, they wanted others to see it.

Nathaniel was no different. He wanted all eyes on him today. One set in particular.

Heaving a giant sigh, he placed the helmet on his head. "Do you know why Lord Charles ran off?" he asked. He heard a pewter cup fall to the floor and suspected that he was the one who'd awkwardly knocked it over—though he couldn't actually see the damned thing from his narrow view.

Lord Eglinton made an angry noise in his throat and ran a hand over his bushy sideburns. Nathaniel wanted to tell him to try a full beard instead. The earl's round baby face would benefit from it; however, Nathaniel understood that he was just partial to beards and missed his own greatly. "No idea," the earl replied. "Nor do I know the reason behind Lord Royce's disappearance. All I know is that his carriage is gone, along with Charles's horse. Selfish bastards. They know how important this is to me. Knowing Charles, it must have something to do with a woman. It's the only explanation for his doing something so stupid. But don't ask me which woman, because I am too much of a gentleman to gossip." He paused, scratching his head. "Although, I have to say … I thought it would be a different woman."

Nathaniel's anger rose high and fast, making the armor even less comfortable. He didn't have to ask the earl *which* woman he'd assumed Lord Charles would behave so stupidly for. As Nathaniel ambled through the castle this morning, it was obvious that everyone had assumed something similar. When anyone remarked that Lord Charles had vanished in the middle of the night, the next question was always the same: *With Lady Charlotte?*

Maybe that was the main reason Nathaniel had jumped on Eglinton's offer to join the tournament. He'd be lying if he said it didn't play at least a small role.

Eglinton slapped him on the back, almost tipping Nathaniel over like an ungainly teakettle. "You are a big bastard, aren't you?" He laughed. "I did hear they grew them big over in America, but it's quite another thing to see it face to face. You'll look great out there. And don't be afraid. Everyone has been taught to aim for the chest. Just try to do the same. I assume you know how to ride, don't you?"

Nathaniel scowled back in answer, but the effect was muted underneath the helmet.

"I do apologize; I had to ask," Eglinton said with a shrug. "One never knows with Americans."

"I can ride," Nathaniel growled.

Lord Eglinton smiled. "Very good. Then I'll see you there. You won't have to suffer through a procession this time. Best to just get out and give the people some action." The earl's excitement was palpable, and he practically skipped to the door before he stopped with his hand on the knob. "Wait," he said, turning back. "You never did tell me why you volunteered for this. To be honest, I didn't expect you or anyone else to. You were the only one. Why?"

Nathaniel let out a noiseless laugh, raising his hands at his sides in a helpless gesture. "I guess you could say I'm just as stupid as Lord Charles."

Eglinton snorted and lowered his head with a shake. "A woman. Yes. Of course. It's a good reason," he said, opening the door to leave. "The best one, actually. You might just make a good knight, Yank."

»»»«««

"Are you looking for anyone in particular? I daresay you're facing the wrong direction. All the important men are on the field."

Charlotte blinked, finally noticing that someone was addressing her. Not just someone—the Queen of Beauty. She closed her eyes, remembering and straining for her manners. "No, ah … not really," she stammered, feeling ridiculous and horribly inarticulate.

Lady Jane regarded her shrewdly, narrowing her eyes down her lovely nose. Almost everything about Jane Seymour was lovely, from her raven hair to her translucent skin and rosy cheeks. She was the epitome of style and grace, known to be nothing less than witty and charming. At twenty-nine, she was also married to the heir of a duke.

To Charlotte—and many unmarried women in the *ton*—Lady Jane had been a source of inspiration and emulation. In fact, as a young girl, Charlotte had idolized the woman, thinking that Lady Jane had the life that she would one day have. The woman never put a foot wrong, and everyone loved her for it.

And now, the grand lady was studying her with such interest that Charlotte felt the young, untested girl whose voice croaked each time she was asked to speak in public.

"No?" Lady Jane said. "Or not really? Which is it?"

Sweat began to run down Charlotte's back. This day couldn't be more different to the previous two. The sun was splendid and truly welcomed; however, its unwavering intensity made wearing such finery a bit of a challenge. Charlotte wasn't sure how Lady Jane did it. As Queen of Beauty, she wore a glorious violet velvet skirt as well as a voluminous crimson velvet mantle, and Charlotte could not detect one bead of sweat on her imperial brow. *Some women have all the grace and luck …*

She attempted to relax her face and appear nonchalant. "A friend of mine—a friend of my father's—Mr. Nathaniel Lawrence. I haven't seen him all day. It's … odd."

Lady Jane's forehead furrowed under her pearl-encrusted crown. "The large American?"

"Yes."

"Are you worried he went the way of Lord Charles? Skipping out before the tournament is over?"

Quite the opposite, really. Charlotte's laughter was unconvincing to her own ear. "I doubt he would do that."

Sitting on her throne, Lady Jane straightened herself, peering out onto the field with obvious intent. The knights were practicing and warming up their muscles and horses before the joust was to start. There was no fanfare, no grand announcements, and very few trumpets to signal the day. But the crowd—what little remained—was content and undisturbed. It was amazing what a lack of rain and sunshine could do to a collective temperament.

"I heard Lord Charles ran off with Lady Louise," the queen said out of the corner of her mouth. "Her mother told everyone that she went back to London because she wasn't feeling well, but it all seems too damning to me."

Charlotte stared back at the woman open-mouthed. She'd never heard that Lady Jane was a gossip.

"Such an odd creature, Lady Louise," the Queen of Beauty went on. "We were forced to spend so much time together this summer, and I can't even tell you what her voice sounded like. It's almost like she didn't *want* to be in my good favor."

Charlotte nodded noncommittally. To someone like Lady Jane, not wanting to be her friend or acquaintance must have been a grave offense.

"She is a very strange bird," Lady Diana said, jumping into the conversation. She sat on Charlotte's other side and practically draped herself over her torso to enter the conversation with the queen. "She and her mother have been staying at our townhouse, so I am intimate with the subject. I have no idea what Charles would ever see in someone like her. She's always so secretive and quiet."

"She's very beautiful," Charlotte remarked, thinking the poor girl needed at least one person to stand up for her. "Her red hair is rather pretty, and she has a lovely laugh."

"She's tolerable at best," the queen said. "But I think Lady Delilah is right. A woman who holds secrets is a woman looking for trouble. You can't trust a woman like that."

"I quite agree," Lady Diana said excitedly, not seeming to

care that the queen had butchered her name so badly. "It's no wonder she has no real friends."

Charlotte sat quietly, fuming as the pair continued their henpecking. By their own admission, they didn't even know Lady Louise, and here they were maligning her character. And Charles's, for that matter, though even Charlotte could admit that men rarely were held to the same unforgiving standards as women when it came to scandals.

She wondered what these women would say about her once her own perfidy was found out. Charlotte would be long gone to America, but she was certain her story would make the rounds, even become a cautionary tale for young women coming out. To these people, there was very little worse than marrying beneath oneself. A daughter of a duke marrying a textile manufacturer—even a rich one—was not something to be celebrated. Even if they learned of her lack of dowry and her father's financial problems, the *ton* would never look at her the same way again. Such was its prejudice.

And its loss. Because Nathaniel was worth ten of the men out on the field. Just because they didn't know it—or refused to acknowledge it—that didn't make it untrue.

"Why are you smiling, Lady Charlotte? Something has finally pulled you out of your fog. Whom do you see out there?" the Queen of Beauty asked, placing her hand over her eyes as she scanned the field. Suddenly, she shot up from her chair. "Wait, is that …? Did he come back after all?"

Charlotte followed the queen to her feet as a collective murmur ran through the crowd. The lists had emptied, readying for the first riders of the day. Only two men had emerged from their tents: the Knight of the Griffin and … the Knight of the Sun.

"Lord Charles," Lady Diana breathed dramatically as the knights approached the grandstand on the horses. "He came back for us."

Charlotte rolled her eyes at the woman's infatuation. However, the more she regarded the knight, the more she doubted the girl's certainty. The knight was indeed wearing Charles's armor, emblazoned with the sun on the breastplate. And his helmet was definitely Charles's, with its striking red plumes, but the picture felt off. The rider was adept with the horse and holding his own, but the lazy confidence that Charles exhibited was missing. With his straight back and high head, this knight betrayed an earnestness that Charles lacked. And it was that earnestness—not to mention his attention pinned on her—that made Charlotte's stomach lurch to the floor.

"Get your favors ready, ladies," the queen instructed them, pulling a handkerchief out from underneath her miniver-lined jacket.

Lady Jane needn't have bothered with the order, since most of the ladies sitting in their row already had their favors in their expectant hands. Except for Charlotte. She'd already given hers away—to this same knight, only on a different day. But he was different now. These were different eyes peeking out of the slit in the helmet. As blue as the blood of the peers Charlotte was sitting alongside.

Nathaniel was the Knight of the Sun. And no one knew it except her.

"My lady," the knight said in his rich timbre. "I come asking for a favor from the loveliest woman I've ever seen. A true English rose."

The crowd rumbled with a few sighs and giggles.

Charlotte showed her empty hands. "I have nothing for you, Sir Knight. I have already given my favor to the Knight of the Sun. Are you not he? Have you lost it? I don't know what to think about that."

"For goodness' sake," the queen hissed. "Here's mine."

Lady Jane shoved the lacy square into her hands, but Charlotte wouldn't take it.

The knight was not dissuaded. "I lost nothing. So much has changed in those mere days. It's true, I am the Knight of the Sun, but I am a new man."

"A new man? So, you're saying I gave my favor to another?"

"You did," the knight answered. "But not your heart?"

Charlotte shook her head. "Never my heart."

"Perhaps if you declare your heart to me in front of all these people, then that will suffice."

Lady Diana gasped and flopped a hand on her chest. Charlotte was surprised she didn't faint then and there.

She could only see Nathaniel's eyes in the slits of his helmet. Hard and demanding, bluer than the fair sky above. Full of love … but also a little fear. Charlotte wanted to take him into her arms and kiss that uncertainty out of him. But she already knew that wouldn't work. She'd done that before, and still, it had taken root inside him like a weed. She would have to do something better. Something chivalrous and gallant, something poetic, a sign of utter devotion and love.

It came to her at once. Its simplicity disarmed her, and yet she had never felt so invincible.

"I will do as you ask, Sir Knight, if you do something for me first," she announced.

"And what is this thing you ask of me?"

"Remove your helmet, so that all will know whom I've pledged my heart to. So that all will know the true knight behind the mask, this new man who has the courage and strength and virtue of ten men."

The knight paused. "Are you certain, my lady? There's no reason—"

"There's every reason, Sir Knight."

The knight moved his hands slowly, with great intent. When he lifted his helmet, a resounding gasp came over the crowd.

Lady Diana fanned herself with disappointed vigor. "Well, that's not Lord Charles!"

"No," Charlotte said, a small smile creeping on her face. "No, it's not."

"Well, who in the world is it?" Lady Diana lamented.

"That's the Knight of the Sun, obviously. My husband."

CHAPTER TWENTY-FOUR

WITH HIS WIFE'S love and acknowledgement, Nathaniel felt like he had the strength, courage, and virtue of ten other knights.

Unfortunately, he didn't have their experience or months of practice. The first time Nathaniel was struck by the Knight of the Griffin, the lance landed so hard that his teeth rattled in his mouth. The other knight had hit him right in the center of his shield, and somehow Nathaniel had managed to stay on his horse.

The other two passes were less bone-shaking, though he was still whacked both times. He considered it a triumph that he was able to hold his lance straight for more than a few seconds without dropping it to the ground.

Nathaniel faced two more men that afternoon—the Knights of the Ram and the Black Lion. They were both routs. Nathaniel never stood a chance.

However, a couple of points kept him in good standing with his fellow knights. Nathaniel always kept his seat … *and* he didn't accidentally kill anyone. Apparently, that was enough to gain their respect for the day. Nathaniel's ass hurt like the devil, the stupid armor was chafing his skin to high heaven, and his feet smarted so bad inside his sabatons that he was certain he'd be hobbling around for a month.

But he wasn't alone in that torture. All the knights felt the exact same way, and that solidarity provided a fraternity for those that lived through the minor miseries. As they rode back to the castle later that night, hungry and bedraggled, the men gave each other knowing looks and proud smiles. They'd finally accomplished what they'd said they would. They'd become knights, participated in a medieval tournament, and lived to tell the tale.

And thank God it was over.

It was time to drink and dance. And for Nathaniel to find his wife.

"So …" Lord Eglinton began, riding up alongside him. Dirt smeared his handsome face and his short hair fell limp on his head from his wearing the helmet all day. But the man who'd started this all was undeniably happy and content. "Lady Charlotte is your … wife?"

"She is," Nathaniel stated firmly. As if by magic, his ailments disappeared—or close enough.

Eglinton nodded through a frown, as if trying to make himself believe the unlikely news. "Is this a … new thing?"

"About a month now."

"Ah."

The Knight of the Griffin cantered up on Eglinton's other side. Seeing him, Nathaniel was overburdened with embarrassment. The man was old and rather portly, and he'd handily defeated Nathaniel at every turn. "So, you've been hiding away for the past month?" he said. "I can't say I blame you. If I was your age and had a wife like Lady Charlotte, I wouldn't leave the bedroom either."

Nathaniel clenched his jaw at the man's rude familiarity. "We weren't hiding. We were waiting … enjoying … married life," he replied curtly.

The Knight of the Griffin *humphed*. "Oh, to be young again."

As the knight rode off, Nathaniel could feel Eglinton grow pensive as they found themselves alone again. "I suppose you'll be taking her back to America, then?" the earl asked.

The force of the decision hit Nathaniel in the chest. He almost couldn't believe it. Would he miss this place? "Yes," he answered. "Very soon."

"Ahh," Eglinton drawled. "That's too bad. I think you would have done well here, Yank. Sorry to see you go. But you naturally have family there. Friends."

Nathaniel wasn't sure how to answer that. Lawrence Textiles was based in America, and he'd always considered that family. It had been everything. *Work* had been everything, and it had been a lonely existence. And was set to be again. How would he navigate that with Charlotte in his life? It would be an adjustment, that was for sure.

"I'm certain we'll be back from time to time," he said.

"Well, then I'll look forward to those times." Eglinton held out his hand. "You served well today. Once a knight, always a knight. I'm glad you answered my call."

Nathaniel shook the man's hand warmly. "As am I."

CHARLOTTE CAME UPON Nathaniel in his room just as Lord Charles's valet was leaving, a stack of armor cumbersomely piled in his arms.

She held the door open for the valet, waiting for him to exit completely before facing her husband. It was a monumental task, since Nathaniel's gaze was on her the second she entered.

"Are you ready to explain yourself?" She leaned against the wood, her hands tucked behind her back.

Nathaniel slumped in his chair, his knees out wide. "Do I need to?" he asked, hanging his head.

Charlotte's lips twisted to one side. The poor man. He looked like he'd been run over by a four-in-hand, which was somewhat close to the truth. The day hadn't been easy. The other knights hadn't been easy on him. But he sat in front of her with his beard shadowing his skin, his eyes limpid and achingly fulfilled, and his dark hair plastered against his forehead. He needed a bath. He needed a good, long sleep. He needed—

"I need you," Nathaniel said as if he'd broken into her mind and stolen her thoughts away. He stretched out his arms, and Charlotte didn't waste the moment. She hurried to him, hugging his sweaty head to her belly, holding him so tightly that (hopefully) no silly ideas would ever be able to get inside his thick skull again.

Charlotte's resolve and her voice broke. "What were you thinking?" she chided, caressing his locks off his forehead. Nathaniel purred against her like a well-fed kitten. "You could have been hurt."

"I wasn't," he groaned.

She yanked his hair. "But you could have been."

"But I wasn't."

Charlotte sighed. Maybe his brain had been addled today by all the beatings. The man couldn't see reason. She would have to coax it out of him.

Gently, she placed her hands around his head and tilted him up to look at her. This close she could make out light blue and purple bruises to the side of his jaw, the pale red lines streaking out from his iris into the whites of his right eye. She bent over to place a firm kiss on his cheek. Nathaniel must have closed his eyes, because they were still shut when she straightened.

"Why?" Charlotte asked.

Nathaniel opened his eyes. His expression was so very sharp, it almost wounded her.

"I had to earn you."

"No," she said, shaking her head. "You already did, just by being you."

He squeezed her hips. "I know I have you. I know you love me as I love you, but that doesn't mean that I've earned you. At first, when you and your father told me about this tournament, I thought it was ridiculous." His laugh was brittle. "Grown men playing at being knights. However, the more I thought about it, the more it all began to make sense. These people—your people—were never going to accept me whether I was a duke or not. It didn't matter how rich I was. But then I remembered the stories your father told me about the knights in your family, the men who came from nothing."

"Those were just his stories." Charlotte sighed. "You shouldn't listen to them; they're probably not true."

"It doesn't matter. The lists were an even playing field. Your name, your background, the gold in your pocket ... It was all worthless. All one needed was the strength in one's heart. A man like that could be worthy of a woman like you."

Tears clouded her eyes, but Charlotte refused to take her hands off Nathaniel to wipe them away. "Did you ever stop to think that it was I who was not worthy of you?"

Nathaniel shook his head slowly, never taking his gaze from her. "Never. Not once. Because it isn't true."

"Your mind is bruised."

"My body is bruised, not my mind. I've never been so clear in my life," Nathaniel said. "England has its faults. You have too many crazy aristocrats hiding away in your castles, your food is bland at best, and the Thames at low tide is the worst smell in the history of smells. But it got one thing right. You, Lady Charlotte, are a perfect rose. And I needed to prove to everyone—I needed to prove to myself—that I am the man for you."

He brushed the tears off her face. The muscles constricted in her chest as a slow-blooming sense of unease filled her. "Did you do that today?"

"Hell no, I didn't." Nathaniel laughed, squeezing her again for extra measure. "I got beat today. My ass will be black and blue for a month." He stood up and cupped Charlotte's face before she could offer anything in return. "But I didn't quit. I went back out on that field. Again and again. And faced those smug bastards. I failed, but I learned. I'll never quit, Charlotte. Not on you. Not on us. Whatever you want in life, I will get for you. Wherever you want to be, that's where we'll be. I only need you."

Charlotte couldn't take it anymore. Nathaniel was much too close, and he was saying too many sweet things. She threw herself at him, capturing his lips in a demanding kiss that was full of all the fear and pride and pure love she'd encountered throughout the day. Nathaniel caught on quickly and plunged his tongue into her mouth like a man starved. He tasted like tea and honey, sugary and bitter and earthy—homey and rich and just a little bit spicy. He made her hungry. Hungry for so many things.

When Charlotte eventually tugged away, she was grateful to see he was just as flushed as she felt. "I only need you. Only you. So, you need to take care of yourself, you impossible man. No more playing at knights."

"We shall have no argument over that," he agreed readily. "After tonight, I will hang up my armor for good."

Charlotte frowned. "After tonight?"

"The banquet and the ball."

Ugh. She'd forgotten about the ball. She couldn't believe it. The Charlotte of six months ago would have been disgusted. *That* Charlotte was a completely different woman. "My love," she said, toying with the strings of his tunic, "we don't have to attend the ball. After what you put me through today, I feel like I've aged a decade. Let's just go to sleep and leave first thing in the morning."

"Nonsense," Nathaniel said, dragging her over to the tub. She'd been so fixated on telling him off that she hadn't realized that one was in the room and filled to the brim with steaming water. "I will give you a bath, and then you will feel as right as rain."

Charlotte gazed at the water. It did sound lovely, and it reminded her of their first romantic tryst. Suddenly, her cheeks blazed.

Nathaniel's smile was rakish. "I'm thinking the same thing. But you sound tired. I wouldn't want to deplete all of your energy before the ball."

He unhooked her mantle and dropped it to the floor then started on the buttons of her gown. Charlotte bit into her lower lip, watching his hands move, how sure and confident they were. She would always be safe with them around her. "I'm sure you couldn't deplete *all* of my energy."

Nathaniel's fingers stopped, and he bent over so they were face to face. "That isn't a challenge, is it?"

Charlotte lifted one eyebrow and backed away. Slowly, she peeled off one long glove and let it drift to the floor.

"Is that what I think it is?" he asked.

"It is."

Nathaniel passed a hand over his face before planting both on his hips. "You literally threw down your gauntlet."

Charlotte smiled. "Do you accept?"

"This is a very big decision."

She stepped closer to him. "Do you accept?"

"I don't know. All of a sudden, I'm feeling quite on the spot."

Charlotte's chest was against his now. She could feel him harden. "Do you accept?" she repeated softly.

Nathaniel wrapped his arms around her middle and picked her up off the floor. "Always, my lady. Always."

CHAPTER TWENTY-FIVE

London, England
September 13, 1839

"**D**ID YOU HAVE to bring the pig?"

Charlotte twirled around to face her husband, aghast at the annoyance she detected in his voice.

"You expected me to leave Jolly behind? Never!" She hugged the pug closer against her chest as she stood on the deck of the *Titon*. "He'd be lost without me, and besides, I think you'd miss him more than I would. I've seen plenty of kisses exchanged between the two of you when you think I'm not looking."

Her husband rolled his eyes, clearly pretending not to notice the way Jolly strained against Charlotte's arms, wanting to jump onto Nathaniel's chest. "I can't help it if the ridiculous animal has no manners," he grumbled. "You've trained him to pounce on me whenever he can. He licks me with that incorrigible tongue every chance he gets."

Charlotte kissed the top of Jolly's head. "You like it," she returned smugly.

When her husband refused to play along, she turned back to the pier and let out a sigh. Her husband's mood was not to be helped. And she knew exactly whom to blame.

"You can stop looking for him. He's not coming."

Nathaniel ignored his wife's pessimistic view and continued to scan the docks, searching through the horde of people coming and going along the cluttered piers. "He's late," Nathaniel stated firmly. "He said he would come. He's coming."

Charlotte's mouth pinched; however, she kept her feelings to herself. If her husband was determined to be disappointed, then she couldn't help it. She'd told him that her father wouldn't see them off. Though the duke had said he understood their decision to move to Boston, he hadn't pretended to be ecstatic over the fact.

After returning from the Eglington Tournament, Charlotte and Nathaniel had spent two weeks at Wembley House, preparing for their journey, and the duke had kept away most of that time. In an estate such as his, it wasn't difficult to stay hidden, but the lengths her father had gone to surprised even Charlotte.

She may have been hurt by his aloofness at first, but she quickly got over it. Anger was still too close to the surface, and easily engulfed any feelings of abandonment.

Nathaniel, on the other hand, did not take it as well. At the time, Charlotte had assumed her husband was aggrieved for her sake; however, she soon realized that Nathaniel was mourning the loss of another father. There were times during those last two weeks when she'd wanted to remind him of all the treachery and duplicity her father had been involved in regarding their lives so that her husband would stop acting so disjointed. But the words failed to come to her. The duke and Nathaniel had fashioned a relationship quite independent of her, and she was hesitant to interfere. For all his faults, her father had touched Nathaniel's life in ways she couldn't understand. Who was she to alter the memory? In the end, they would both have to grieve in their different ways.

Unfortunately, Charlotte's grieving was still running on the hot side.

"You have to prepare yourself," she said gently, placing a

hand on Nathaniel's arm. "My father doesn't take loss very well. He's never understood how to deal with things not going his way. He doesn't have it in him to face you or me. You mustn't judge him too harshly for it. It's just the way he is."

Nathaniel's smile was kind as he turned to her, taking her hand and kissing the inside of her palm. The wind was harsh on the water and whipped against Charlotte's face. However, it only took one small look from her husband to make all of that fade into harmless nothings.

"You don't have to worry about me, Charlotte. I may not understand your father's mind entirely, but I can have empathy for him." Swiftly, he ducked down and kissed her firmly, causing a few whistles from the passing sailors. "I just don't want to leave without you speaking to him. I thought …" He wrestled with the words, and his shoulders sank. "I thought he would try to make things right."

"There was nothing to make right," Charlotte said, tempering her voice. She could feel her insides clenching again, and she righted herself with a breath. She didn't want to leave England all flustered and angry. Doing that felt like a disservice to her new life. "He told us the truth, and that's it. As he said, there's nothing more to be done. He will live out his life as the duke, and our lives will take a separate path. Besides," she added, rather icily, "it's not like we'll never see him again."

Nathaniel gave her a stern look. "Don't be angry with me. It was the best decision."

"I'm not angry, even though it was you who said my babies were coming with us."

"And it was *you* who negotiated a sale from the Spanish count for fifty more alpacas."

Charlotte couldn't hide her smile. It had been the one saving grace of attending the Eglinton Ball. She'd been lucky enough to be sitting next to Count de Olaso, who had a healthy shipping empire that ran back and forth from South America. He'd been lamenting a sale gone wrong that involved a large shipment of alpacas that were supposed to be llamas. Needless to say, by the end of the night, both Charlotte and the count had reached an agreement that satisfied both parties.

Nathaniel continued, staring at Charlotte's smile. "Purely from a business point of view, it makes sense to keep them on your father's land. We can trust Peter to look after them, and the factory will be close by to process all the fur. You can start another farm in America."

"I will," Charlotte stated firmly. "I'll need something to do with my time."

Nathaniel grinned. "You don't think running Boston society, along with running me, will keep you busy?"

He wrapped an arm around her shoulder and caressed the back of her neck with his fingers. Charlotte had no idea how she'd spent her life not being touched by Nathaniel. At this point, it was just as important as breathing.

She grinned up at him, loving the way the salt air marked his cheekbones and ears, giving them an adorable pink luster. She reached up and skimmed her fingers over his chin, where a healthy beard was beginning to regrow. "Oh, I don't think you'll be so bad," she said wistfully. "And as for the ladies of Boston—"

"Lady Charlotte!" a deep voice interrupted her, ringing clear from outside the boat. "Lady Charlotte of Wembley! I need you!"

A flurry of people clanged and bumped into each other as a colorful madman hurried down the docks, skidding his heeled shoes toward the pier.

It can't be.

But it was. The Duke of Wembley was difficult to miss even on the days when he wasn't so ostentatiously dressed. And today was not one of those days. Vivacious in a deep purple coat and bright fuchsia cravat, he dodged between the sailors and porters in an effort to reach the *Titon*. Charlotte could make out no fewer than five rings on his fingers as he held his hands around his mouth and called out, "Lady Charlotte of Wembley! I need you, dear girl!"

Since Charlotte was located toward the stern of the ship, her father couldn't see her. But she could see him. The poor man looked sweaty and panicked, not ducal in the least.

Nathaniel nudged her in the back. "Go to him," he said.

Charlotte didn't move. "It's too late."

"I know what too late is, my love. Trust me when I tell you that it's not too late for you."

The hitch in his voice pulled her focus from the pier. She turned to her husband and stood up on her tiptoes, placing a chaste kiss on his lips. "Thank you for loving me," she said. "Thank you for knowing me."

Nathaniel's expression was overwhelmingly gentle. "Go," he repeated.

Charlotte nodded and proceeded to the gangplank. Mercifully, it was still straddled between the ship and the pier, and her feet picked up speed the closer she came. "Father!" she yelled, throwing out her arms so that he could see her through the people.

Her father's relief was palpable when he spotted her, and he made haste to meet her. "My lovely girl, give me your hand," he said, reaching out to grab her the moment she stepped off the plank. Charlotte wasn't ready for his exuberance. The moment she touched him, he hauled her into his chest with a force she didn't know he possessed. Her hat nearly came off her head while he hugged her, cramming her cheek against his luxurious coat. His smell enveloped her and instantly brought tears to her eyes, because it wasn't the acrid aroma of alcohol and sweat that she'd learned to associate with her father. Instead, it flooded her senses with scenes of long ago, when her father would sit outside with her in the fields for hours, watching his animals roam his fields, telling his only daughter stories of the moment he first fell in love with his beloved wife. It was a lovely and tantalizing mixture of sadness and sweet grass, minty herbs and black dirt.

"I'm sorry I didn't come sooner," the duke said, squeezing her tight. His voice choked as he repeated the words again and again:

I'm sorry. I'm sorry.

"You're here now. That's enough," Charlotte replied. It amazed her how quickly forgiveness came and how overwhelming it felt to allow it.

"No," the duke said, jerking her away to arm's length. "It's not enough. It will never be enough. But I will keep trying. I'll take care of the farm. I'll make sure it's the success you want it to be."

"Father, I know—"

His face was racked with agony. Charlotte held his arms tighter, thinking he was going to faint.

"No, don't say anything. I need to get this out before you leave."

"Father, it's fine. We'll come back to visit next year. We have time—"

"No!" he said more emphatically. "Now." He gulped, and time seemed to slow for Charlotte. The people milling around moved at half-speed, even the wind came to a halt as her father studied her face. In his silence, as his eyes flitted about while he thought of all the things he could and should say, Charlotte heard everything. Her father apologized for not seeing her before, for not encouraging her to be more than a pretty face. He apologized for his lies and his ambivalence, for his years living a half-life between the past and the present, and for never planning for the future until it was too late. He apologized for not loving himself enough, which left him incapable of showing others the love that they so desperately deserved.

Charlotte heard it all and more, and kissed her father on the cheek.

When she pulled away, the duke's expression was clear and peaceful. He took her hands in his. "You will make a wonderful duke."

"I know." She laughed through her tears. "I've always known."

"You may call yourself Mrs. Lawrence, but you will always be

Lady Charlotte of Wembley—a duke's daughter. Remember that."

"I will," she sobbed.

Calls came out from the ship, telling everyone that it was ready to depart. Father and daughter hugged again, and the duke finally relinquished her. Before she stepped back on the plank, he caught her hand and placed a crisp white envelope inside.

"Read this on your journey," he said. "It will help pass the time, I think."

Charlotte nodded, wondering at his odd smile.

Nathaniel found her instantly after she boarded and placed a comforting arm around her waist. Together they faced the pier and the duke who hadn't budged. "Take care of her," the duke yelled out above the clamor.

"I will," Nathaniel promised. "Always."

EPILOGUE

Boston, Massachusetts
December 1, 1839

CHARLOTTE HAD EVERY intention of reading her father's letter. However, she swiftly learned that some people were born to be sailors and some—such as her—were not. The moment the *Titon* set sail, her stomach was bombarded with the sort of violent uprisings that wouldn't soon be forgotten. She spent those two weeks traversing the Atlantic with her head down in a bucket or over the side of the ship. Making conversation with her husband was difficult enough; reading her father's untidy scrawl as the *Titon* ambled across the ocean was next to impossible.

Despite Charlotte's hopes, planting her feet back on land didn't help matters. Boston proved just as unsettling. While Nathaniel morphed into a whirlwind of energy, settling them in his modest home in the north end of the city and reacquainting himself with his old life, Charlotte spent her first month in America putting little touches on her new home whenever her tumultuous stomach allowed—which wasn't often.

It wasn't until the vibrant, jewel-colored leaves had completely fallen off the trees that Charlotte was confident enough to leave the house for an extended period of time. She even managed to attend a few dinners with Nathaniel that his close business associates held in their honor, though forcing herself to eat the traditional fare still remained a challenge, especially since Boston's idea of baked beans were a sugary enigma to her.

Needless to say, the duke's letter had been lost in the shuffle of life. Charlotte had almost forgotten it existed when she stumbled upon it one night while readying herself for bed.

It was a rare night when Nathaniel had stayed late at his office, and Charlotte had eaten dinner (or tried to) by herself. In an effort to stay awake until her husband came home, she decided that she would try to read the book by Ralph Waldo Emerson that Nathaniel kept recommending. He couldn't stop harping on about *Nature*, and insisted she give it a chance; however, Charlotte had a sneaking suspicion that Nathaniel only liked the author so much because Emerson was also a Boston man who'd gone to Harvard.

As she was sifting through the books on top of Nathaniel's bureau, Charlotte came upon her father's letter, no longer crisp, but nevertheless intact. She was immediately infused with guilt at having neglected it so long, but that shame lifted the moment she began to read.

So engrossed was she in her father's tale that Charlotte didn't hear Nathaniel enter the house that night, and she certainly didn't take note of his footsteps as he hurried up the stairs. His shadow was looming over the page before she lifted her gaze and registered his presence, and by that time her eyes were too bleary with tears to take him in clearly.

"What is it?" he asked, dropping to his knees. "Darling? Is it bad news?"

Charlotte's hands fell to her lap, the letter still held tightly in her fingers. She shook her head, in a daze. "I honestly don't know," she said. "I have no idea."

"What did he say? Tell me."

"I remember he said something odd on the pier. He said I will make a wonderful duke. I thought it was just a slip of the tongue …"

Charlotte handed him the letter. Nathaniel stood up, pacing the room while he read. Charlotte thought that would be for the best. A letter like this needed to be read to be believed. One needed to experience it for oneself ...

August 28, 1839
London, England
Buckingham Palace

THE WHITE DRAWING Room wasn't what Thomas Cordry had expected. When he asked for an audience with the queen, he'd anticipated that she would meet him in the Throne Room. That was where he would have done it, if situations had been reversed. The Throne Room, with its opulent red fabrics and awe-inspiring chandeliers, held the right amount of gravitas, sent the right kind of message, when dealing with one such as the Duke of Wembley. Clear as day, it said: *You might boast of one of the oldest lines in this country, but it is my country. I am queen.*

However, when Thomas Cordry, Duke of Wembley, followed the stiff-lipped, starched servant into the White Room, into Her Majesty's presence, that notion flew quickly from his head. Because the gravitas was still present, leading him to believe that maybe it had less to do with fabrics and fancy chairs and more to do with the person sitting in them.

He'd met the queen many times before, but the majority of them had been before she'd gained the crown. As Cordry bowed elegantly and smiled gallantly, just as his father and grandfather had taught him, he was struck by how changed the monarch was. Yes, she was still a petite, severe-looking thing, making even the duke seem tall, and she was still rather plain, despite how the courtiers tried to spin her beauty, but there was a confidence there that he hadn't noticed before. Or perhaps he'd never really wanted to.

And for the first time, in a *rather* long time, the Duke of Wembley found it difficult to find the right words.

"You asked to see me, Duke," Her Majesty stated firmly. Even with her high, feminine voice, it still hit Cordry as stately.

"Ah … yes … ah … yes, Your Majesty …" he began in a gauche manner that made his olive-green coat feel remarkably tight. Then—fortuitously—he noticed a rustling at her skirts and saw her faithful dog sitting at her feet. *Dash*, he remembered was its name. A Cavalier King Charles Spaniel.

"May I?" the duke asked, bending over to call to the dog. It came at once, with the queen's hesitant nod coming soon after. The duke ruffled the beautiful dog's ears. "My daughter has a dog named Jolly. He's a good dog, loves her so much. He follows her everywhere. Is more of a shadow than a dog." Content with the duke's attentions, Dash returned to his master, and Cordry stood up again. "I have a feeling she's going to take him when she goes," he added with a frown, the idea just dawning on him.

"Go?" the queen said, her tone softening. "Is your lovely daughter going somewhere?"

The duke smiled through a wince. "America. That's where her husband is from. I expect them to leave soon."

The queen frowned. "I didn't know Lady Charlotte had married."

"Yes, Your Majesty, to Mr. Nathaniel Lawrence from Boston."

"Boston?" She scrunched her pert nose. "I hear it gets cold there."

"It does."

"And she still wants to go?"

The duke chuckled. "She loves him, Your Majesty. The heart makes us all do unusual things."

She laughed in a curious manner. "Like marry someone below our station." When her laughter died down, her beady eyes turned to slits. "Is that why you asked to speak with me, Duke? I've noticed before that neither me nor my father have ever been great favorites of yours. In fact, you like to go out of your way to point out your vast lineage. *Is more English than the queen,* is what I think you've said when you don't think I'm listening. Don't talk now. I'm speaking," she said, holding up a hand. The duke's mouth snapped closed. "Oh, I know what you think of me. I know what they all think. My uncle also knew it, which was why he wanted me to marry my cousin, Prince George." Her voice turned steely, creating even more of a chill in the drafty room. "But I will not be marrying Prince George."

The duke shifted his stance, finding his courage flailing. He'd known this wouldn't be easy—pushing one's pride aside rarely was—but he hadn't counted on the queen deliberately calling him out. He was so used to people whispering nasty things behind his back, and hearing it face to face cut deeper.

He cleared his throat and started again. "My daughter is a lot like you, Your Highness, which is why I'm here. As I'm sure you're aware, I have no heir. I thought I could make one, create one, even buy one, but it all amounted to nothing in the end."

"Yes, I've heard of such things. The hubris of men to think they can create heirs at their whims. My uncles know a lot about that, I'm sure. I've heard the Lord laughs when we make plans. I'm sure you agree?"

The duke *humphed.* "As you say. But that doesn't change the fact that my line dies with me."

"And you want my help when all you've ever done was look down your nose at my father. He died when I was young, but I've heard there was no love between you."

Because her father, Prince Edward, was a mean, nasty bastard. The duke much preferred George IV ... Now, *he* knew how to enjoy himself.

Cordry cleared his throat awkwardly. "Yes ... I've come to be ashamed of many of my past actions. But I've learned. Standing here before you, I can honestly say that I don't care about my title. Not one bit. I've made my peace with it."

The queen arched a thin eyebrow. "And?"

"And," the duke said, blowing out a long exhale, "I know now that I can't be at peace with it, not when it affects others besides me. I owe it to my daughter to ask you to help me amend the title. Not because I need an heir, but because the House of Wembley finally deserves the right one. My father and I were wastrels. I'd like to think our hearts were in the right place, but I don't know if that was true."

A quietness pervaded the room. "What does heart have to do with titles?"

"Everything," the duke replied. "You are young, and I am old, so let me tell you that if I've learned one thing in life, it's that. My daughter has it. She may not be a man, but she will wear the Wembley title better than any man before her. She is one of England's best. She is its rose."

"And yet she is across the Atlantic pretending to be American."

"That's my fault," the duke replied.

The queen responded with a wan smile. "You may think you know more because you are old and I am young, but let me tell you something. You ask for too much. You are a desperate man. A title—a crown—is no easy thing for a woman to wear."

"I understand that—"

"You understand nothing," she snapped. "You couldn't possibly." She paused for a moment, taking the time to pet Dash, as if the motion helped her to think. "Lady Charlotte, on the other hand, is not you. I've met your daughter and liked her very much. A pretty girl—beautiful, in fact—but there was more to her than meets the eye …"

The duke didn't realize he was holding his breath until it shot out of him in an embarrassing rush. Still … he held his tongue. He'd lived with women long enough to know whether one wished him to talk or not.

The queen cocked her head, looking up at the marvelously sculpted reliefs on the ceiling. "People say I like being the lone woman among all these men. They say I crave the attention, but nothing could be farther from the truth. It can be a lonely existence. So very lonely."

"I would be forever grateful, Your Majesty."

"Oh, you would?" She peered at him curiously. "I care nothing for your gratefulness. What else would you do for me?"

"My queen?"

She made a point of looking down at her voluminous skirts, patting away dust that the duke could not see. "I have two alpacas. A black one and a white one. Did you know that?"

Of course he did. Although the duke had initially thought they were llamas, which was why he'd purchased two llamas that were, in fact, alpacas. "I can't say that I did, my queen."

Her lips twisted wryly. "I was gifted a pair previously, but they died. I hope these do not share their fate. They make a beautiful fabric, is that right? Even more luxurious than silk or even cashmere?"

"That's very true," the duke said. "My son-in-law is in the process of starting a factory to process the alpaca wool from our farm. It was my daughter's idea," he added with pride.

"I know. Many people tell me many things," the queen replied. "So, if I were to give you these alpacas, as a gift, would you be able to make something new for me ... a gown or shawl, perhaps?"

"Are we assuming that you will also speak to Parliament about having my title amended to make my daughter my heir?"

"Yes," she said slowly. "I think we can assume that should be no issue."

The duke grinned. He had no idea what Nathaniel could do in that factory of his—he only knew he wasn't about to say no to the queen. "Of course! Anything you like! It will be a true one-of-a-kind piece that will make you the envy of everyone."

Her eyes came up sharply. "I'm a queen. I'm already the envy of everyone. But ..." The color of her cheeks ripened into a bright pink. "I'm expecting visitors in a few months ... family ... a cousin, actually, from Saxe-Coburg-Gotha. I haven't seen him in a long while, and … it would be appropriate for me to have something special … for the event."

It was then the duke understood the gossip from the sycophantic courtiers. Victoria could be quite pretty when she wasn't treating him so horribly. With the right clothes and accessories, she wouldn't appear nearly so cabbage-like. Not to mention, the poor thing was obviously in love—or something close to it—and was lacking in confidence regarding the match. Well, Thomas Cordry knew a thing or two about confidence, and even more than that about love.

This. Finally, the duke's axis shifted. He was on firm ground. Playing with the lace of his cuffs, he grinned with a conspiratorial air. "You know, I am a bit of a slave to fashion myself."

"I am hardly a slave—"

He waved his hand in the air. "Not a slave, you're right. You're on the forefront, as any queen should be." Without thinking—or asking permission—the duke took a seat next to Her Majesty, who appeared too stunned by the turn of conversation to say anything. "I'm told alpaca fabric is perfect for mourning, but that doesn't pertain to you! Have you considered a soft white gown? One of our animals has the most luxurious alpaca fur. Fit for a queen. With your complexion, you'd look dashing in white. Or maybe a dark green or even black riding habit—military style!"

"W-Wembley," the Queen said shakily, scooting away from him on the seat. "Your ideas have run away from you. You go too far."

The duke casually crossed his legs and lounged back onto the couch. "Oh, I've been accused of that once or twice, but I assure you, not in this case. I have just what it takes to make you an absolute vision. I know men *and* ladies."

Something glistened in the queen's eyes. The duke almost forgot how young she was. Young and hopeful.

"I confess," she said shyly, "I don't have much experience with men and women of a certain age … my age."

Yes, the duke thought. *The Kensington System.*

"Sometimes I find it hard knowing what to say or do. Being queen can be limiting in that respect. My maid laughs at me when I tell her that even something as silly as just sitting around others makes me awkward sometimes, like I'm not doing it right." The queen flushed, turning away. "I feel foolish. *It's* just foolish."

The duke smiled warmly. "My dear girl. *It* is never just anything, and you are right to think about such matters. Everything a queen does is a show, a master class in how to be. It's an art form, really." He tapped her on the hand. "It is fortuitous that I've called on you today. I know I can be of service. People are interesting creatures, aren't they? And there's so much to learn about them." He paused, contemplating Her Majesty as she inhaled a deep, settling breath. "Let me tell you a little story about my first trip to Vienna. If you think the French are depraved …"

Boston, Massachusetts
December 1, 1839

NATHANIEL LIFTED HIS head from the letter "He did it. The bastard finally did it. I knew he could."

Charlotte's heart felt like it was going to pump out of her chest. "Did he tell you he was going to speak to the queen? Did you know this would happen?"

"No," he said. "I hoped, but I didn't know for sure."

Charlotte nodded. She still couldn't believe it. Her father had put his pride aside and fought for his title—he'd fought for *her.* And charmed the queen with his ridiculous stories. *Naturally.*

Nathaniel dropped the letter on the ground. "You're going to be a duchess after all. The Duchess of Wembley. It has a lovely ring to it, don't you think?"

"It does," Charlotte said, finding her first smile. It didn't last long. She jumped to her feet, wrapping her arms around her husband. "We don't have to leave if you don't want to. I told you I would stay with you here, and I meant it. I'm only the heir anyway. My father still has a long life ahead of him."

"Don't worry about that," Nathaniel said before placing a gentle kiss on her forehead. "We'll figure it out. Let's just focus on the good things right now. You can plan to your heart's content tomorrow."

Charlotte's heart was already content. All because of him. So even as her mind was being run ragged, she paid it no heed. It could wait. Tonight was about them and only them. When the time came to take up the reins of the dukedom, Charlotte would be ready.

However, there was one point that she kept getting stuck on. It nagged at her as Nathaniel undressed them and picked her up in his arms. And it nagged her still when he laid her on the bed and draped himself over her.

"Darling?" he asked, sensing that her mind was elsewhere.

Charlotte chewed on her bottom lip. "You know what this means, don't you?"

He shook his head.

Charlotte rolled her eyes. "My father bought my title for two alpacas."

Nathaniel grinned and kissed his wife. "Well, I'm sure they were two very nice alpacas."

About the Author

I'm a lifelong reader of romance novels. Some of my earliest memories are of sneaking into my mom's room at night and stealing any books I could find.

After moving around quite a bit, I've finally put down roots in New England with my two sons and husband. I've always been a writer, starting out in newspapers, but it wasn't until my sons began going to school full-time that I began working toward my dream of becoming a romance author.

I enjoy crocheting toys for my kids, hiking with my Saint Bernard, and watching Real Housewives on the couch with my very old and very fat pugs.